Dedication

*To John Wisdomkeeper who inspired this story
and whose spirit guided this journey of
Inuit cultural discovery.*

Acknowledgement

BWL Publishing acknowledges the Government of Canada and the Canada Book Fund for its financial support in creating the Canadian Historical Mysteries collection.

BWL Publishing acknowledges the Province of Alberta for their ongoing support through the Alberta Publisher's Cultural Industry Operating Grant.

History

On April 1, 1999, the Canadian government, with assent from the Queen of England, created Nunavut Territory from the eastern portion of Northwest Territories. Nunavut means "our land" in *Inuktitut,* the language of the Inuit. Nunavut comprises a major portion of Northern Canada including most of the Arctic Archipelago. The land area of Nunavut, roughly two million square kilometres, is the fifth-largest country subdivision in the world, as well as North America's second-largest (after Greenland). It is the only Canadian territory or province not connected with others by highway.

The first "Nunavut Day" was celebrated On April 1, 1999, with the unveiling of the Nunavut territorial flag and coat of arms, followed by speeches from Jean Chretien, the Canadian Prime Minister, and Paul Okalik, the newly elected Nunavut Premier. The event recognized the creation of the new territory, a homeland for the Inuit people who have resided there for all of recorded history. Iqaluit (formerly known as Frobisher Bay) is located on the east side of Baffin Island, was chosen as Nunavut's capital city in 1995.

Other Canadian indigenous entities are recognized as First Nations. The Inuit are recognized as First People.

Table of Contents

Prologue

A fierce wind blew the pellets of snow. Each snowflake tore his face like a tiny shard of broken glass. Wolverine Pokaik lowered his head and closed his eyes. Trudging ahead with the enormous weight of his pack, he struggled through the accumulating snow. Good sense said he should drop the pack and seek shelter, but his burden's weight symbolized his obligation to the community. Many would eat the caribou meat strapped to his back. The community depended on hunters like him for survival.

His leg muscles aching from the effort, he lifted one foot, then the other, struggling to move ahead. He'd walked this path a thousand times so knew he was nearing the outskirts of Iqaluit. With each footstep taking every bit of his strength, he moved in half steps for a few minutes, hoping to find the *inuksuk* stone cairn designating the outskirts of Iqaluit. Exhausted, he turned his back to the driving snow and drew a breath. The elders said freezing to death was much like falling asleep. All you needed to do was surrender to the cold; your mind would trick you into believing you were warm as your spirit drifted away.

Turning into the wind, Wolverine clenched his eyes shut and screamed in frustration, the sound lost in the raging squall.

A firm hand shook his shoulder and his eyes popped open. A man dressed in white smiled. "You're having a nightmare."

Wolverine straightened the sheets and blanket he'd thrown aside during the nightmare. "It's good you heard me. Otherwise, I probably would've frozen to death."

The night orderly smiled and pulled the sheets around Wolverine's shoulders. "I'll make sure the thermostat is still set to 22 °C."

Watching the aide disappear into the hallway, Wolverine shook his head. "I like Bill. He always jokes with us."

Hanta, in the bed on the other side of the room, pushed himself up on his elbow. "Dreams are omens of the future. What did you see?"

"I suppose you had another one of your visions while I was thrashing around in bed."

Hanta nodded, then lay down. "*Anguta*, the thief of spirits, will visit you soon and take you to *Qudlivun*, the cloud world."

Wolverine snorted as he rolled over. "*Anguta* only steals the souls of people who die violently. I'll die in my sleep. My spirit will descend to *Adlivun*, the underworld, for purification after I die in my sleep."

Hanta shrugged. "I only tell you what I see."

"What violent death will come to me here, in The Lodge? Will I choke on a piece of caribou?"

"My visions only foresee the imminent arrival of *Anguta*, coming down from the northern lights to collect your spirit. I don't know the manner of your death."

Wolverine closed his eyes and muttered, "Your visions are cloudy. Maybe *Anguta* is coming for you!"

"No, my friend, it's your time. My spirit is destined to linger here a bit longer."

Chapter 1

Wednesday, June 30, 1999

Boarding the Iqaluit flight in Toronto, Christopher Pokiak took his window seat overlooking the wing of the plane. Dozens of Inuit people shuffled past as he watched the baggage handlers load a conveyor carrying their luggage into the plane. He sensed a person stopping in the aisle and turned as Iris Ashoona struggled into the seat next to him. Coming from a town of 7,500 people meant he'd seen most everyone who lived there, including Iris and her family. Settling into her seat, Iris turned to Christopher, "I haven't seen you in several years. Are you moving back to Iqaluit?"

"I've got another year left at the University. My grandfather asked me to fly back for Canada Day."

Satisfied with the answer, Iris opened her spacious purse and retrieved a dog-eared book. She set her purse on the floor and slid it under the seat in front of her. As the last people took their seats, Christopher studied the woman's lined face. Like many of the older Inuit people, Iris had lived much of her life outside, leaving her skin dark and deeply lined.

After listening to the flight attendant's safety briefing, Christopher leaned his head back and closed his eyes as the plane taxied to the runway. Stopping briefly, the plane's engines revved and they gained speed before lifting off. Christopher heard the landing gear being raised before he fell asleep.

A sudden drop and Iris' grip on his forearm jarred Christopher awake. Several people gasped as the plane dropped. Paper coffee cups and soda cans flew into the air and bounced off chairs, heads and shoulders. The flight attendant was in the aisle ahead of them. Grabbing a seat, she was able to prevent being thrown against the ceiling. The plane stabilized and the pilot apologized for hitting the unexpected air pocket that caused their sudden descent.

The flight attendants rushed down the aisle, one handing out paper napkins and the other retrieving debris from the floor. Iris released her grip on Christopher's arm. Still holding her book, she let out a breath. "If there was another way to reach Iqaluit, I wouldn't fly."

Having never thought about any travel option but flying between Toronto and Nunavut, Christopher was surprised by the comment. "You're right, there aren't any roads that connect Iqaluit with anywhere else in Canada, so driving isn't an option. Without the freighters and barges delivering goods from lower Canada in the summer, and air deliveries in the winter, our lives would be bleak."

Iris shrugged. "We got by without the government handouts." She inserted the bookmark into her novel and studied Christopher's face. "Did you graduate from high school with any of my children?"

"I'm younger than them. I graduated in 1996."

"And then you went away to college. Have you stayed in touch with any of your classmates?"

"No, I've been in Toronto, and we've lost touch. I might see some of them at the Canada Day celebration."

"This is the first Canada Day since Nunavut became its own territory separate from Northwest Territories. Iqaluit is planning quite a celebration. It should bring in a lot of people." Iris paused. "Is there someone special you hope to see?"

Christopher shook his head. "Mostly, I came back because my grandfather asked me to return. If I see anyone from school, it'll just be by chance."

As he nodded off, Christopher thought briefly about school friends who'd played lacrosse, and about a girl he'd dated. *Yes, it would be nice to see Rob and Tommy. I wonder if Connie is married, or if she ever got a job in television?*

He awoke when the flight attendant announced their final approach into Iqaluit

Airport. The Boeing 737 shuddered as the pilots deployed the flaps. The flight attendants walked the aisle, making sure all seats were in their full upright position. The whine of the hydraulics signalled the lowering of the wheels as they neared the runway. To the untrained eye, the tundra below looked like a barren wasteland. To Christopher, who'd been raised by his grandfather, Iqaluit was a lush landscape visible only for a few months of Nunavut summer.

The afternoon sun blazed through the windows as the aircraft swung around, making its final approach to the runway. In the distance, caribou grazed, curious, but unalarmed by the plane's descent. The sun would set in six hours. But during the Arctic summer, twilight lingered, leaving eerie half darkness between sunset and sunrise.

Iris leaned across Christopher to look out of the window. "I prefer when they fly over the city. I like seeing my house."

"I'm sure it's still there, Mrs. Ashoona," Christopher replied, amused by the woman's chatter. Living nearer downtown Iqaluit, the Ashoonas were acquaintances.

"I'm sure it is. But I still want to see it." The woman leaned back and studied Christopher's face. "You're coming home to see your grandfather for Canada Day?"

Having been questioned off and one by the woman during the five-hour flight from Toronto, Christopher bristled at yet another question. "As I said, my grandfather asked me to return."

"Your grandfather is Wolverine Pokiak?"

"Yes, my grandfather is Wolverine."

The woman with a deeply lined face nodded. "He was quite a force of nature in his day. It's hard to believe Wolverine is the same person he was when we went to school together. You know, he *earned* the name, Wolverine."

"Grandpa has slowed down in the last few years," Christopher replied.

The woman snorted. "All who are still alive at our age have slowed. Most are gone."

The woman grabbed Christopher's arm when the plane shuddered as its wheels touched down. The engines roared, slowing the plane. "Planes only crash when they hit the ground. It's the landings that are deadly," she said.

The comment caught Christopher off guard, causing him to flash back to the day he moved in with his grandfather. A Mountie had knocked on his parents' door, Iqaluit's social worker standing behind him. Their words were lost following their announcement that his parents had died in a plane crash. Their float plane had been carrying supplies to a fly-fishing camp when it flipped on landing. Christopher had a vague recollection of the Mountie saying, "If it's any consolation, they were knocked unconscious before they drowned."

Even now, the Mountie's comments seemed like a stupid thing to say to an eight-year-old boy. But over the years, Christopher came to understand that the Mountie had been trying to comfort him. He didn't know what else to say to a child who was now an orphan. The social worker had helped him pack a paper bag with clothing. She and the Mountie had driven him a few blocks to his grandfather's house. Christopher remembered that as the first day his grandfather seemed old. Wolverine had looked up from his coffee cup and nodded to Christopher when the Mountie opened the door, as if he already knew the bad news.

Wolverine looked up from his spot at the kitchen table when the social worker escorted Christopher into the house. "Set your bag next to the door. You'll sleep on the couch until I sort out something else."

Christopher was brought back to the moment by a question from the woman. "How are you getting to The Lodge?"

"Why would I go to The Lodge? I'm going to Grandfather's house."

"You don't know that Wolverine moved to the old people's Lodge?" Seeing the answer in Christopher's eyes, the woman nodded. "My husband is picking me up. We can drop you at The Lodge on our way home."

Not having a plan for transportation, but not wanting to impose, Christopher said, "I don't want to be a bother."

The old woman sighed. "It's no bother. We'll give you a ride."

Mr. Ashoona met them at the baggage claim. He was tall and thin. His graying hair was tied back in a ponytail, and he wore a ragged flannel shirt over jeans that were so thin in places that his skin was visible. "Gordon, do you remember Christopher Pokiak?"

The man's response was a dip of his head, acknowledging Christopher.

"We're giving him a ride to The Lodge."

Considering the woman's words, the man frowned. "The dog's sitting in the front of the pickup with us. Christopher will have to sit in the back, on the spare tire."

"I appreciate the ride," Christopher said, as he set his backpack in the pickup bed and climbed over the tailgate."

The dog, sitting in the middle of the front seat, turned his head and looked at Christopher through the window. "I get it," he said. "You're family. I'm just someone getting a ride."

Chapter 2

Christopher hadn't seen his grandfather in years. The old man at the dining room table in the Iqaluit Senior Lodge was grayer and thinner than he remembered. His shoulders were stooped, and he looked tired. The sight of Christopher caused Wolverine to struggle out of his chair. Steadying himself with the table, he waved and called out his grandson's name from across the room. "Christopher!"

After a *kunik*, touching his nose to Christopher's forehead, Wolverine introduced his grandson to the other men sitting around the table. An aide brought a chair. A moment later, a plate of roasted caribou with potatoes and gravy appeared in front of him. "I used to come here for meals," Wolverine explained as Christopher took a bite of caribou, savoring the slightly gamey flavor. "Then they had an opening, and I decided it would be easier to live here than to walk down just to eat. Especially in the winter."

Christopher looked around at the dining room. "This must be expensive."

Wolverine snorted. "Nunavut takes care of the old people who don't have families. It's a nice place and they feed us well." He leaned close, "And I don't have to put up with a bossy daughter-in-law who resents my presence in her house. That's how most old widowers end up."

"I was surprised when you sent money to buy a plane ticket home for Canada Day," Christopher said as he mopped up gravy with the potatoes. "Iqaluit is a long trip from Toronto."

Wolverine drew a breath and looked at his tablemates. "I own a land grant near the Soper River. I want to give it to you as part of the Canada Day celebration."

Hanta, a friend Christopher remembered from the past, nodded. "Wolverine got one of the prime land grants. The fishing is good on that portion of the Soper River. Most of us got sections that are nothing but scrub. I'd die of old age before I walked to my grant."

Wolverine wrinkled his nose. "Hanta, it's a lot more land than you owned before."

Confused by the topic, Christopher frowned. "How did you two get land grants?"

"The government passed the Land Grant Act. Each Inuit can claim a section of land."

"A section? How big is a section?"

Hanta smiled. "It's big."

"How big?"

Hanta's eyes sparkled as a memory came to his clouded mind. "They're as big as my second wife. I had to rub her with seal blubber, so she fit into the igloo."

Wolverine shook his head. "Your second wife was the skinny one. You're thinking of your third wife."

Hanta frowned, trying to remember. Past details became difficult to recall as his dementia became more severe. "That's right. My third wife was the fat one with the tattooed chin."

Frustrated by the meandering conversation, Christopher interrupted. "How big are the land grants?"

"The elders were told that each section is a little over two and a half square kilometers," Wolverine replied. "My section is near Mount Joy and the Soper River."

"What will I do with a section of Nunavut land? I don't even live here anymore."

The happiness bled from the old man's face. "I hope you'll return to Iqaluit some day."

"Why? There's nothing here but tundra."

Wolverine reached out, wrapping his hand around Christopher's. "Nunavut is your home."

Studying his grandfather's hand for the first time, Christopher saw the protruding veins under the old man's paper-thin skin. He looked up and saw the watery brown eyes, the lenses clouded by cataracts. "I'm not sure what I'll do after I graduate from college. There aren't many jobs here."

Wolverine patted Christopher's hand. "You don't need many jobs. You only need one."

Hanta leaned close. "You should marry my granddaughter, Tanaraq. She has wide hips and would bear you many children."

Grimacing at the prospect of a grandfather suggesting that his granddaughter, who Christopher knew by her nickname, Tatty, would make a good wife because of her wide hips, Christopher paused. "I haven't seen Tatty since I was a child. She was several years ahead of me in school."

Hanta waved off Christopher's comments. "Age becomes irrelevant once you're married. You want a wife who cooks well and bears you children. Tanaraq will be perfect for you."

Christopher glanced at Wolverine, who was shaking his head. "Be careful of Hanta's matchmaking. He's been trying to marry Tanaraq off to any single man who walks through The Lodge. He was even trying to get the night orderly to divorce his wife so he could marry Tanaraq."

"Bill is already married?" Hanta asked.

Their discussion was interrupted when an aide arrived with a tray of pills in tiny white paper cups. She held out a cup and said, "Wolverine, I have your heart medicine."

"This is my grandson."

The aide smiled politely, then held the cup closer.

"He's going to university in Toronto."

Standing, Christopher said, "I should go to the house and unpack."

After taking the cup and swallowing the pill with a bit of water, Wolverine gestured for the boy to sit down. "I haven't seen you in nearly three years. Tell me about your school."

"I've been traveling all day and you're tired. We can talk tomorrow."

"You're staying at our house, right?"

Christopher nodded. "That was my plan before I knew you had moved to The Lodge."

"Then it's settled. Stay at the house. Sleep in the big bed. I froze a package of caribou tenderloins for a special treat. Thaw them and we'll eat them tomorrow night."

"I..."

"It's settled. The pickup keys are in the sugar bowl, and it has half a tank of gas unless Evelyn Purdy has been borrowing it. Go!"

* * *

After walking five blocks, Christopher was at his childhood home. The house he remembered from childhood now looked small, old, and tired. The pickup that had driven them around Iqaluit sat on four flat tires. The house paint was peeling, and the wooden steps creaked under his weight.

Upon opening the screen door, he stared at the doorknob, realizing he didn't have a key for the lock. To his surprise, the door wasn't locked, and the house was warm. Unlike Toronto where every door was locked and no one left keys in their car, Iqaluit was different. People often left their doors unlocked and keys were left in pickups in case a neighbor needed to use them.

A layer of dust covered the small kitchen table and counters. The refrigerator and its freezer doors had been propped open by whoever cleaned it out and unplugged it. "So much for having caribou tenderloins tomorrow."

Christopher dragged his finger through dust on the counter, then turned on a faucet to rinse off the dirt. Water sputtered for a few seconds before a rusty surge sprayed out, followed by a steady flow.

The late afternoon sun cast long shadows across the living room floor. Picking up the television remote, Christopher was amazed when the screen lit up, showing the CBC news. The living room, with one upholstered chair and a couch, seemed as tiny as his dormitory room at Trinity College. A small dresser next to the TV caught his attention. Inside the top drawer he found neatly folded underwear and t-shirts, just as he'd left them when he'd moved to Toronto. In the second drawer were jeans and white athletic socks, aligned by Wolverine in two neat rows. He unrolled the socks in the farthest corner and found the $43 dollars he'd left there. It was his personal rainy-day fund, earned by helping elderly neighbors.

Christopher was startled by a knock on the door and was spooked when the door opened before he reached it. "Christopher?" Evelyn Purdy, their neighbor, peeked around the edge of the door.

"Hello, Mrs. Purdy."

"I saw the lights were on." The woman's round Inuit face smiled, showing crow's feet at the corners of her eyes. "I'd hoped you'd come back for Nunavut Day, in April."

"Grandfather asked me to come back for Canada Day."

"You know he's not well."

"I just walked here from The Lodge. We had supper together and he seemed okay."

"He's been waiting for your visit. He..."

Christopher turned off the television and gestured toward the living room chair. "He's aged."

Mrs. Purdy dusted the seat with a tissue before sitting. She sighed while composing her thoughts. "A lot of older people focus on an upcoming event and rally. It gives them something to anticipate. Once the event has passed, they give up."

Christopher sat on the couch, leaning his elbows on his knees. "Do you think my grandfather is about to die?"

"I don't know that, but he's been perkier these past few weeks. Before that, he'd been in declining health. I think all his energy has been directed at your visit. Once you're gone, he may choose to depart to the spirit world."

"But..."

Mrs. Purdy frowned. "Inuit tradition allows people to let go of their physical being and move to the spirit world. It's not something we fear. It's just another phase of being."

"And you think my grandfather will let go soon?"

"I don't know that. But I suspect he will find peace that's been eluding him while you've been away."

"I'll talk to him."

Mrs. Purdy stood and put her hand on Christopher's shoulder. "Don't rob him of the dignity he'll find in his departure. There's nothing sad about dying. We just move to a different place and time. Perhaps he'll be the caribou on the hillside, or a ptarmigan. His spirit will go on even after it departs his body."

Footfalls on the wooden steps preceded the opening of the door. The young woman wearing an RCMP special constable's uniform and carrying shopping bags seemed surprised to see people in Wolverine's vacant house. "Mrs. Purdy. Christopher."

Mrs. Purdy frowned. "Tanaraq Etok, I didn't know the RCMP delivered groceries."

The officer smiled politely, "Please call me Tatty. Wolverine gave me a few dollars and asked me to fill the propane tank and turn up the heat before his grandson arrived. I was delayed by a call, or I would've stocked the refrigerator earlier."

Mrs. Purdy looked skeptical and stepped to the door. "Christopher, knock on my door if you need anything."

Smiling at Christopher, Tatty walked to the kitchen table and set down the shopping bags. "The regular Mounties don't deliver groceries, but you're getting extra service from the RCMP Special Constable. I knew you would need a few things when you arrived." Without invitation, Tatty removed the towels propping open the refrigerator doors and plugged the appliance into the outlet. "It'll cool off quickly."

"Hi, Tatty, I haven't seen you since I was in sixth grade and you came along with your grandfather whenever he visited Wolverine.

"The good old days," Tatty said. "You didn't know it, but Wolverine paid me to babysit you so he and Hanta could sit around telling lies."

"They paid you to take me to the movies and to buy ice cream?"

Tatty nodded. "I'll bet you thought I came along with Hanta because I was bored."

"I thought you enjoyed going to the movies." Christopher paused. "I saw Hanta this afternoon when I visited my grandfather. He said I should marry you because..." Christopher froze, realizing how uncomfortable a discussion of Tatty's wide hips and childbearing ability would be. "...you can cook."

Snorting, Tatty shook her head. "It's okay. I've heard Hanta tell men that my hips are perfect for bearing children."

"I...um..."

"It's okay. My hips are what they are." She paused, then asked, "Did he also say I was an old maid past my prime?"

"Wolverine said you are too old for me."

Tatty sat at the table. "I am too old for you. And, according to Hanta, I'm too old to marry men of a suitable age anywhere in Iqaluit."

"Hanta is trying to marry you off."

"Hanta has a bit of dementia and the once thin filter between his brain and his mouth is now gone. Whatever he thinks, he says."

"You're a Mountie now?"

"I'm a Royal Canadian Mounted Police Special Constable."

"What's the difference between a Mountie and Constable?" Christopher asked.

Tatty stood and unloaded groceries from the bags. "Special constables get police training, but our powers aren't as broad as Mounties. The RCMP uses us in situations where local knowledge, our Inuit heritage, and *Inuktitut* language skills are useful. The Mounties from Quebec and Newfoundland don't have a clue about Inuit traditions, so they sometimes inflame a situation by being culturally insensitive or overly aggressive when they should back off. That's when I step in, to calm the situation."

Dumbfounded, Christopher watched Tatty load eggs, milk, bread, and cold cuts into the refrigerator. "Um, why did you bring food?"

After emptying and folding the bags, Tatty sat in a kitchen chair. "Because you're staying here, and you'll need something to eat."

"Um, thanks. But why did *you* buy groceries for me?"

"Our grandfathers are roommates at the senior residence now. Wolverine told me you'd be staying here. He paid for the groceries. And I thought you might like to see a familiar face."

"I'm sorry to hear about Hanta's dementia." Christopher sat across the table, at a loss for other words.

"It's kind of frustrating because he can remember the past so well, but anything recent is lost or scrambled. When something gets stuck in his mind, he sometimes repeats the same question over and over for my entire visit."

"Hanta made you help me with my math homework, then he'd give you a couple of dollars and send us off to a movie or to buy ice cream while he and Wolverine talked about the old times." Christopher frowned. "I don't remember you after I started like sixth grade. You disappeared from our lives."

"You don't remember me after I stopped visiting with Hanta because I was quiet, plain, and four grades ahead of you in school. Then, I was in college while you were a high school student. I've been a special constable for three years while you've been away at university. I'm not married because I choose to be single, not because I'm past my prime."

"I didn't mean to dig into your personal life..."

Tatty's smile faded. "I need to warn you. Because of Hanta's lack of a mental filter, too many people are aware of your grandfather's plan to give you his land grant. Be careful."

"I don't understand."

Tatty leaned on the table and steepled her fingers. "Wolverine's land near the Soper River is valuable...more valuable than nearly any other section of land given to individual *Inuks* by the government. Because you've been going to college in Toronto, people have begun to think of you as an outsider. There are rumors that you'll sell the land and stay in Toronto. Other people think you'll keep the land and live high on the hog from the lease payments."

"What lease payments?"

"Wolverine has been bragging about the big money he makes leasing his land to outfitters who take tourists on Soper River rafting and canoe trips."

"Why would anyone care? The Soper is only usable for rafting or kayaking like three weeks out of the year and it's not like the kayakers have to pay to float the river. Right?"

Tatty checked her watch, then stood and pushed her chair against the table. "I've got to get back to work, so I don't have time to get into the details. Wolverine's land is the only flat area upstream of the best rafting areas. He owns the property where the outfitters land their planes and pitch their tents before starting their raft trips. No one knows for sure what they pay for leasing that spot, but everyone assumes it's a lot more income than most Iqaluits make in a year." She paused at the door. "Be careful. Lock the door when I leave."

"I don't remember the door ever being locked."

Tatty twisted a brass latch, covered with dark patina. It snapped. After two tries she got it to open and latch in place. "The lock works. Use it tonight and see if you can find the key."

"I think you're being overdramatic," Christopher replied.

Tatty stared at him as she weighed her words. "Christopher, you aren't the same teen who left Iqaluit three years ago, and Iqaluit isn't the same town you left. You've become an outsider, and the land grants have changed people. You grew up in a time when this was a homogenous community after the US Air Force closed their operations in the 1960s. There's...greed now. And drunks."

Christopher frowned. "Alcohol is illegal."

Snorting, Tatty shook her head. "If it wasn't for alcohol, I'd probably be out of a job. Alcohol or illegal drugs are involved in virtually every domestic assault call. People smuggle them in."

"You make it sound...like Toronto."

Tatty leaned against the door. "Every crime you've heard about in Toronto is in Iqaluit. Then, add suicides and missing *Inuit* women into the mix."

After searching Tatty's face for any hint of mirth, Christopher let out a sigh. "Your job sucks."

"Where's your head?"

"Huh?"

"You have a caribou in the headlights look. What's going on?"

"You already said it. I don't belong here. I'm not *from* here anymore. I should blow off tomorrow's celebration and fly back to Toronto."

Tatty walked to the table and sat. "I didn't say you don't belong here. I said people think you're not *from* here anymore."

"That's the same thing."

The knocking of her knuckle on the table startled Christopher. "Earth calling Christopher. Are you there?"

"What?"

"None of us are what we used to be. We've all changed. I used to be a quiet, nerdy high school student. Now I'm a constable who everyone hates but trusts. You went to college. You'll be something else after you graduate. Don't let the local rumors define you. Define yourself. You were born here. You belong here as much as anyone. Iqaluit needs educated people like you, who can return to make this a better place."

"My mom was white. My father was only half *Inuit*."

"That's how you want to define yourself? As three quarters white?"

"That's what everyone said in school."

A smile curled Tatty's lips. "Let me tell you a secret. Almost any single girl in Iqaluit would be flattered if you asked her out."

"What?"

"You're a good looking, smart guy who's got prospects beyond fishing, hunting, and drinking. You'll be quite a catch."

Christopher studied Tatty's round face and caramel-colored skin. "You'd date me?"

Rolling her eyes, Tatty said, "You're missing the point. I'm not hitting on you. I'm just trying to make you realize that the future is yours to mold." Tatty stood. "Go to the celebration tomorrow. Meet up with your old school friends. Catch up on what's going on in the community and see how it's changed since you left. See where life takes you."

"Tatty," Christopher called out as she opened the door.

"Yeah?"

"You should've been a social worker or psychologist."

"That's half my job."

"What's the other half?"

"Breaking up domestic assaults, arresting drunk drivers, and finding lost girls."

Christopher shook his head. "Are there many lost girls?"

"Too many. Right now, we're looking for a fifteen-year-old girl who disappeared from Cape Dorset a couple of days ago."

"Disappeared, as in kidnapped?"

"We don't know. Cape Dorset is a fair-sized town. Buniq Tingenek is the girl, and she might be staying with friends or hiding out with her boyfriend."

"Cape Dorset is that little artsy community off the north end of Baffin Island, right?"

"Yeah, it's on Dorset Island. The population is about one thousand. There are a lot of artists making *Inuit*-themed prints and carving walrus ivory and stones. I don't think anyone is getting rich, but that town has a lot more economic activity than most of Nunavut."

Nodding, Christopher said, "I suppose that also means there are more outsiders coming and going who might give a desperate girl a boat or plane ride out of town."

"The Mounties are checking on boat and plane traffic." Tatty looked around the small house. Every surface had a layer of dust, reminding her that the house had been unused since Wolverine moved to the Iqaluit Senior Lodge, or 'The Lodge,' as the local people referred to it. "I'm on duty so..."

Christopher nodded his understanding. "I'm good here. The heat is on, and you've left me some food. Thank you."

Tatty smiled and reached for the door.

"You're right, it is nice to see a familiar face. Thanks."

"I'll check in on you tomorrow. Get some rest, this is the first Canada Day since the creation of Nunavut. It's going to be a big celebration." She paused, then added, "And don't believe everything Hanta says."

"Tatty."

Peeking around the door, she stopped. "Yes?"

"Your hips aren't that wide."

As the door closed, Christopher heard her say, "Smartass."

Chapter 3

July 1 Canada Day

Christopher was half awake when someone knocked on the door. Pulling on his jeans and walking through the living room in his bare feet he thought, *in all the years we've lived here, the only visitors we've had were Hanta and Tatty. They walked in without knocking.*

He rattled the doorknob, then remembered the lock Tatty had set. The first thing Christopher saw when he opened the door was the word POLICE stenciled on the protective vest worn by the Mountie. The next thing he noticed was the officer's pink face. "Is this Wolverine Pokaik's house?"

"Um, yes. But he moved to The Lodge."

"You are?" The officer asked.

"I'm Christopher, his grandson." Half asleep and surprised by seeing a Mountie at the door, it never occurred to Christopher to ask why he was there, or to invite him inside.

Sensing Christopher's confusion, the Mountie asked, "May I come inside?"

Realizing that the officer was standing outside where it was only a few degrees above freezing, Christopher stepped back and held the door open. The officer's somber expression was concerning, and his somewhat nervous demeanor added to Christopher's unease. "I...um...would you like to sit down? I can make coffee."

The officer gestured to the kitchen table where Tatty had stacked the empty shopping bags. Christopher snatched them off the table and put them into the garbage before taking a chair across from the Mountie.

"I'm sorry, Christopher. Your grandfather passed away last night."

Unprepared for the news, Christopher said the first words that came to his mind. "Passed away?"

"Yes, I'm afraid he's dead."

Having seen his grandfather the evening before, Christopher was confused and surprised. "From what?"

The officer's smile was warm and genuine. "He was an old man. We think he died from a stroke." The Mountie glanced around the spartan, empty house. "Do your parents live here, too?"

"Um, my parents died when I was a kid. Wolverine raised me...here."

"Is there someone else we should notify?"

Tears welled in Christopher's eyes as the news registered. "No. There are...were just grandfather and me."

The officer nodded. "We're taking his body to the funeral home. You can contact them for a viewing and to make funeral plans."

Not knowing what else to say, Christopher looked around for a box of tissues. Not seeing any, he wiped his nose on the sleeve of his t-shirt.

"Will you be okay?" the Mountie asked as he stood. "We have a chaplain you can talk to if you'd like to speak with someone."

Christopher followed the officer to the door where they stood in awkward silence. "Um, not right now. Thanks."

"I'm really sorry to deliver this news. It's hard when the deceased hasn't been sick or anything."

As the officer turned to leave, Christopher was struck by a thought. "I have a friend who's a constable. Tatty Etok. Do you know how I can reach her?"

"We don't give out our officers' contact information. I'll ask the dispatcher to contact her for you."

"Thank you."

* * *

Christopher was pulling on clean clothes when there was another knock on the door. Still in bare feet, he rushed through the kitchen, running fingers through his hair, still damp from the shower. Tatty, wearing a black vest stenciled POLICE over her tan uniform, was standing on the steps, a pained smile on her face. "I got the news about Wolverine."

Christopher gestured toward the kitchen. "Yeah, a Mountie was here. He said Grandfather had a stroke and died."

Pulling off her police vest and coat, Tatty looked around the kitchen. "Have you eaten breakfast?"

"I hadn't thought that far ahead."

"Put your socks on. I'll make breakfast." Rattling around in the cupboard, Tatty found an electric percolator and a frying pan. She started a pot of coffee, then put a half dozen strips of bacon into the pan on the gas stove. As the percolator gurgled, she took plates out of the cupboard and set them on the table. Christopher sat down, looking numb as he pulled on socks.

Taking two cups from the cupboard, Tatty asked, "Are you okay?"

"Not really. I mean, I was supposed to meet Grandfather and go to the Canada Day celebration."

"Wolverine was excited about your visit. He told me he hasn't seen you in years."

"Both of you said something about his land grant yesterday. Tell me more."

Tatty flipped the bacon, then poured coffee into the mugs. "Wolverine received a land grant. He hoped owning land would bring you back to Iqaluit after your graduation."

"Iqaluit hasn't been in my plans."

Tatty set the steaming mugs on the table. "Most high school graduates move away from Nunavut. They see a better life for themselves in the bigger cities. We need people, smart educated people like you, to help mold this new territory."

Christopher took a sip of the strong coffee as Tatty moved the fried bacon to a plate and cracked eggs into the hot bacon grease. "There's not a lot to anchor a person here unless you're going to work for the Nunavut government or teach in Iqaluit or one of the remote towns. I have memories of growing up with Wolverine and some of my classmates. I also remember the bullying about being a half-breed. Toronto is more cosmopolitan and has much more to offer."

"I see two views on that. Young people see a life depicted on television and want to live elsewhere, places where food is cheaper and there are more jobs and cultural opportunities. Then there are the traditionalists who want to stay anchored in their *Inuit* heritage. They speak our native language, *Inuktitut*. They hunt caribou and seals, fish for turbot, and live traditional *Inuit* lives. Then there are the people starting businesses and working hard to form a Nunavut government, helping this new territory evolve into a special place."

Wrinkling his nose, Christopher said, "I have a hard time seeing myself hunting seals and lighting my igloo with a seal blubber lamp for the rest of my life."

Tatty flipped the eggs, then turned off the stove. "People don't live in igloos anymore. There's a whole group of us who live happy lives here in Iqaluit, never eating raw caribou liver or lighting our houses with seal blubber. It's not Toronto, but we shop in the grocery store and sleep in beds covered by blankets instead of seal skins." She set a plate of bacon and eggs in front of Christopher and sat down. "You lived in this house with Wolverine. I bought this bacon and these eggs in the grocery store, just like you do in Toronto. You need to understand how things are changing."

Stabbing an egg with his fork, Christopher watched the yolk ooze onto the egg white and bacon. "I'm not really hungry."

Leaning back and crossing her arms, Tatty said, "Eat something. You'll need energy to deal with today's tasks."

"What tasks?"

"I hate to be maudlin, but you have to make decisions about Wolverine's burial."

Christopher bit off a piece of bacon and considered Tatty's comments as he chewed. "I've never planned a funeral."

"Are you going to have an *Inuit* burial ceremony or an Anglican funeral?"

"I hadn't thought about it. My parents' funerals were Anglican. But Wolverine was never baptized. I suppose he would have chosen a traditional *Inuit* burial, like most of his friends."

"It's up to you."

Chewing a bite of egg, Christopher stared at Tatty. "What will you do when Hanta dies?"

"Hanta is an *angekkok*, an Inuit shaman. He will have an *Inuit* burial to free his spirits."

"That's probably what my grandfather would want too. He once talked about setting his spirit free to return as an owl."

"The funeral director will help you make arrangements for whichever tradition you choose."

Christopher dropped his fork and pushed the plate away. "I'm an orphan...again."

Tatty slid her chair next to him and put her arm around his slumped shoulders. "There are no *Inuit* orphans. We're all family."

"You don't understand. My parents died. Now my grandfather is dead. I don't have any parents, siblings, aunts, uncles, or cousins."

"Where is your mother's family? Where do they live?"

"She never spoke of them. She said her parents disowned her when she married my dad, an *Inuit*. I don't even know her maiden name or where she went to school. Based on their reaction to marrying my dad, I'm sure they wouldn't be excited about having a half-breed grandson or nephew knocking on their door."

Tatty touched her nose to Christopher's cheek. "Consider yourself my cousin. Okay?"

Christopher glanced at her. "I don't need to be your charity case."

"Hanta and Wolverine are like brothers. You're at least my cousin if not my little brother."

Digesting that thought, and reflecting on his Nunavut life, Christopher nodded. "Given the limited Iqaluit gene pool, we probably are cousins."

"There you go!" Tatty said as she stood and gathered their plates. "Now pull yourself together, cousin. I'll drive you to the funeral home."

"I'm not ready to deal with…"

"You're Wolverine's grandson. You're stronger than you know."

Chapter 4

Tatty drove Christopher to Iqaluit's only mortuary, where they met with the funeral director. Being an *Inuk* himself, Kenneth O'Keefe assured them that he could make the arrangements for a traditional *Inuit* burial. The specifics of the planning flew over Christopher's head, with Tatty agreeing to whatever was suggested while Christopher sat in O'Keefe's small office, feeling claustrophobic and overwhelmed.

"Do you have any other questions?" O'Keefe asked.

Christopher realized that the question was directed to him. "Um, I don't know how much money Wolverine has. I'm not sure how we'll pay for his burial."

O'Keefe's smile was reassuring. "The Nunavut government pays for all *Inuit* burials."

"Really?"

"What we're planning is modest. The cost will be covered. In a traditional *Inuit* burial, we place hunting and fishing items with the body before wrapping the deceased in a seal or caribou skin, then tying the wrap with leather laces. That way your grandfather will be able to hunt when he passes to the spirit world. Do you have anything you'd like to be buried with him?"

Christopher looked confused. "Do you mean, like his rifle?"

"Traditionally, the deceased are buried with a seal harpoon and a reel of fishing line."

"I...um...think those might be in the attic. I haven't seen them around the house. Wolverine wasn't into saving material things. Our family were nomads who kept only what they could carry."

Tatty put her hand on Christopher's arm. "Hanta left some things at my house when he moved to The Lodge. I can take care of this. Wolverine will have the things he needs when his three spirits leave his burial site."

"Thanks."

O'Keefe paused, then asked, "Would you like to view Wolverine's body? It might give you closure."

Panicking, Christopher looked at Tatty. "Would we?"

"It's okay," she replied. "Wolverine is at peace. He'll look like he's asleep."

After being directed to a large, refrigerated room, the funeral director led them to a black body bag laid on a cart. He carefully unzipped the bag far enough to expose Wolverine's face, then stepped back.

Wolverine's face was now waxy mottled gray. His eyes were closed, and his white hair was pulled back. Other than his skin color, Wolverine looked like someone whose eyes could pop open.

Being consumed with dread, guilt, and shock, Christopher was surprised when Tatty asked, "Is the coroner planning an autopsy and inquest?"

The director stepped forward and closed the zipper. "There's no need. The doctor said the cause of death was likely a stroke. Unless foul play is suspected, and in this case it's not, the coroner usually accepts the doctor's opinion. If the coroner accepts the attending physician's opinion, he doesn't request an autopsy and doesn't conduct an inquest."

* * *

As they drove away, Tatty glanced at Christopher, who was staring out of the windshield. "You look like a caribou in the headlights again."

"Sorry. There's so much to take in."

"There's still time to catch the end of the Canada Day celebration."

"Could we buy a hamburger somewhere away from the main activities? I'm not ready to face a crowd." A heartbeat later, Christopher grabbed his back pocket. "I left my wallet at the house."

Tatty smiled. "A true penniless college student. I can afford hamburgers."

"Really! I have money at the house."

Tatty laughed and patted his arm. "It's okay. I'm just kidding you."

As they turned away from downtown Iqaluit, Christopher watched the crowds of people gathering for the Canada Day celebration. "Don't you have to work? You've been with me all day."

"Let's say I'm doing my constable's job of serving the *Inuit* community. It's coincidental that we're cousins."

"Huh?"

"Part of being a RCMP special constable is dealing with the uniquely *Inuit* aspects of policing. I get called to mediate a lot of mental health meltdowns and domestic disputes."

"Those are uniquely *Inuit*?"

Tatty chuckled. "They are if the people involved are speaking our language, *Inuktitut*, and the Mounties who respond only speak English and French."

"Are there a lot of mental health calls?"

Tatty turned into the parking lot of a mom-and-pop café. "There are in the winter when the sun never shines. People get edgy and..."

"And what?"

"Depressed. Alcohol and drugs become more problematic."

"Are there a lot of suicides?"

Tatty let the question dangle as they got out of the car and walked into the nearly empty café. A waitress took their orders for hamburgers and poutine, then walked away.

"You didn't answer my question," Christopher said.

"The coroner often rules that a quarter of the winter deaths are suicides."

"That's a lot."

"Can we talk about something happier?" Tatty asked.

"Like what?"

"You've never said what year you are in college. What's your major?"

"I'm a senior, starting my fourth year. I'm majoring in teaching with a minor in indigenous studies."

"Are you coming back to Iqaluit to teach?"

"I suppose that's a possibility, if there are any openings. I'd been thinking about finding a job in Vancouver. It seems pretty and the winters are a lot warmer than Nunavut."

"I've heard British Columbia is beautiful. The winters are rainy. For me, that would be depressing in its own way."

They talked about college, plans, their grandfathers, and how uncertain the future was. After finishing the last pieces of poutine and their plates were taken away, Tatty looked earnestly at Christopher. "Are you going to be okay alone?"

"Why wouldn't I be okay?"

Tatty's expression softened, and she looked like a concerned big sister. "You've had a big shock, and I've kept you distracted all day, so you haven't grieved. I don't want you to melt down after I drop you off."

Christopher searched Tatty's eyes. "You don't want a suicide call at my house."

"I don't want you anywhere near that point." Tatty took out a business card and wrote a number on the back. "The number on the front is the RCMP office. If you're having a crisis, call them. The number on the back is my house. Call me if you need anything, or if you want to talk."

Reading the handwritten number, Christopher said, "The Mountie said they don't give anyone their home numbers."

"We're family. Okay?"

"Okay."

"If you want to get out of the house, walk around Iqaluit. The Canada Day celebration should be memorable."

"I'll think about it."

Chapter 5

The house seemed cold and empty. After pacing aimlessly for a few minutes, Christopher put on his jacket. As an afterthought, he put his wallet in a back pocket. He walked the few blocks to downtown Iqaluit where people were strolling among vendors selling food, hot chocolate, coffee, and commemorative buttons. A few of the people he knew from school spoke to him, most expressing their excitement about the *Inuit* people finally having their own homeland.

A hand on his shoulder caused Christopher to turn around. The smiling woman raised her eyebrows. "Christopher Pokaik?"

It took Christopher a second to recognize the young woman wearing makeup, with carefully arranged hair, and dressed professionally, "Connie?"

She nodded. "Hi Christopher, I haven't seen you since you left for Toronto."

Christopher was surprised to see how the shy girl he'd once dated when they were in high school had blossomed into an attractive, well-dressed young woman. "My grandfather invited me back for Canada Day."

Connie's smile was warm and sincere. "It's nice to see a familiar face."

Christopher immediately felt guilty. They'd spoken on the phone a few times after his move to Toronto, but long-distance calls were expensive, and he was a broke freshman living in the dormitory. "Did you get a television job like you'd talked about?"

Connie glanced around at the people surrounding them but shook her head. "It's hard to break into television without experience. I got a job at the radio station in *Pangnirtung*?"

"You're a celebrity!"

Connie shook her head, "I'm hardly a celebrity. I read the weather and news from four to ten in the afternoon while playing songs on a radio station that serves 1,200 people."

"That makes you a big star in *Pangnirtung*."

"A big star in a tiny town. Every fisherman wants to date me, but they all smell like turbots." Connie led Christopher to a booth selling coffee and hot chocolate. "I need something to take the chill off." After ordering hot chocolate, Christopher reached for his wallet. Connie handed the vendor five dollars. "My treat. Besides, I'm working and you're still a broke college student."

"I can pay."

Connie waved off his offer and took his elbow, guiding him into the crowded street. "It's nice to talk to someone who isn't starstruck and trying to hit on me."

Not knowing how to respond to that comment, Christopher sipped his hot chocolate and walked alongside his former high school girlfriend. He wasn't starstruck. Being with her felt comfortable, but also made him sad. "I'm only in Iqaluit for a few days. My grandfather invited me back for Canada Day."

"Am I keeping you from him?" Connie asked.

"Actually, he died last night."

Connie stopped and stared into Christopher's eyes. "I'm so sorry. Here I am, dragging you around Iqaluit and talking about my life as a radio broadcaster while you're grieving. I shouldn't keep you from your family."

Christopher looked away, then guided Connie back into the street where they followed the flow of the crowd. "I needed the distraction."

"Oh great, I'm a distraction," she kidded.

"I'm glad you stopped me. I needed to see a friendly face."

Connie cocked her head and looked at him. "I wish you'd called again. Did I say something wrong?"

Christopher felt red creeping up his neck. "You were talking about moving to

Pangnirtung and I was in Toronto. Calling you was expensive and...pointless."

"I wish you'd called me the summers you came home to Iqaluit."

"I couldn't afford to fly back. I stayed in Toronto and worked."

They turned a corner and joined a crowd gathering in front of a podium a half block away. Several people were seated behind a dais with a microphone. Connie pulled Christopher's arm and spoke loud enough to be heard over the crowd, "That's the new Premier of Nunavut, Paul Okalik," she said, pride evident in her voice.

"Do you think having *Inuit* leaders will make a difference in Nunavut? They're still politicians."

Frowning, Connie turned toward Christopher. "They're *our* politicians. They've experienced our culture. Their parents suffered through the 'sixties scoop' that removed *Inuit* children from their families and put them in residential schools. They understand our issues, culture, and problems."

"I'm struggling to get my head around Nunavut being its own territory. I can't believe that Canada let this happen."

"It happened. Believe it."

Okalik stood at the podium and addressed the crowd. "I'm honored to be the host of the first Canada Day celebration." Connie took out a small recorder and switched it on.

"Are you on the job?" Christopher asked as the crowd cheered.

"I'm reporting on this event. This will be the only six o'clock news item."

Seeing tears in Connie's eyes, Christopher cocked his head. "You're really proud of this."

Connie grasped Christopher's arm and pulled him close. Leaning her head against his shoulder she said, "I've never been prouder of my *Inuit* heritage. This is our new beginning."

* * *

After speeches by several dignitaries, the crowd dispersed. Connie turned off her recorder and led Christopher around the corner to a quieter area. "Just think, we were in Iqaluit for the very first Canada Day celebration in Nunavut!"

Christopher was more subdued. "I wish my grandfather could have seen it."

Connie reached out and touched Christopher's elbow. "I'm sorry about your grandfather." She paused, then added, "Call me If you're ever going to be in *Pangnirtung*. I could give you a tour." She dug in her purse and pulled out a small notebook and a pen. "Here's my number."

"I don't see myself flying to *Pangnirtung*."

Connie grinned. "There's not much there to see...except me."

A female voice behind them interrupted the conversation. "Are you going to introduce me to your friend?"

Connie was startled to see a woman in uniform standing behind them.

Seeing Connie's surprise, Christopher smiled. "Connie, this is my adopted cousin, RCMP Special Constable Etok. She goes by Tatty."

"It's nice to meet you, Connie. I had hoped Christopher would connect with some of his friends while he's in Iqaluit."

Connie took Christopher's hand and smiled. "We dated during our senior year in school. Christopher was one of the nicest boys in my class. And look at him now, a college student."

Feeling uncomfortable, Christopher added, "Connie is a radio broadcaster in *Pangnirtung*."

Checking her watch, Connie sighed. "I've got to fly back. It's nice to meet you, Constable Etok." Squeezing, then releasing Christopher's hand, she said, "Call me. It's been nice talking to someone who's interested in something other than carving ivory or the price of turbot. Seriously, you could visit *Pangnirtung*."

"I suppose I might go to *Pangnirtung,* someday."

Connie smiled. "Maybe I'll be discovered and be hired by a bigger radio station somewhere more interesting."

Smiling, Christopher kidded, "Bigger, like Iqaluit?"

Feigning disgust, she replied, "Who knows, maybe I'll find something closer to Toronto." Checking her watch again, Connie grimaced. "I really have to run. Take care of yourself." She turned to leave, then spun around and kissed Christopher. "Call me."

Tatty and Christopher watched Connie melt into the crowd. "Connie seems nice." Tatty faced Christopher and looked at him earnestly. "You *are* going to call her."

"Probably."

Tatty put her finger on Christopher's chest. "Call her. And maybe make a trip to *Pangnirtung* to see her."

He sighed. "What's the point? I'm in Toronto and she's in *Pangnirtung*."

"Christopher, people move. Their situations change. Connie seems very nice, and she obviously likes you. Call her."

Christopher rolled his eyes. "Yes, Special Constable Etok."

Tatty smiled. "You'd better do as I say, or I'll arrest you."

"I think you need a reason to arrest me."

"Not following an officer's direct order is an offense."

"What direct order?"

"Call Connie tonight."

"You can't arrest me for not calling an old friend."

"Are you sure?" Tatty kidded before walking away.

Wolverine's aging television received only one channel and Christopher found the evening movie sappy and stupid. The alternative was to try and sleep, but that seemed unlikely as a jumble of thoughts filled his head. He mulled over the planning of his grandfather's burial, Tatty's willingness to step forward with burial plans when he'd frozen, then Connie's smiling face. A knock on the door pulled him back from his thoughts. Thinking Tatty had come to check on him, Christopher was surprised to see a middle-aged white man in backpacking attire standing on his steps. "Are you Christopher?"

"Yeah. Who are you?"

The man offered his hand. "I'm Eric Curtis, a friend of Wolverine's. I came by to offer my condolences."

Dumbfounded by the stranger's sudden appearance, Christopher shook the man's hand, but said nothing.

"May I come in for a moment?"

"Um, sure," Christopher said, opening the door and letting the man pass. "You're a friend of my grandfather's?"

"Actually, I'm more of Wolverine's business associate. I lease his land on the Soper River. My company specializes in ecology and natural history experiences. During the summer, we take a few groups rafting or kayaking down the Soper River. We fly from Iqaluit to Mount Joy, then paddle down the river to Kimmirut.”

“What exactly did you lease from Wolverine?”

“His property has one of the few flat, rock-free areas near the river where we can land a plane loaded with tourists and gear.”

“Ah.”

Curtis waited for Christopher to say more. After a few moments of silence, he nodded. “Well, like I said, I wanted to stop by and offer my condolences. I liked the old guy.”

“Thank you.”

With his hand on the doorknob, Curtis stopped. “You seem confused about Wolverine’s land and the lease.”

“I only heard about the land grant yesterday.”

“I can come back tomorrow with maps to show you where Wolverine’s land is located.”

“Um, that would be helpful.”

Curtis looked past Christopher at the spartan house and the few dirty breakfast dishes in the sink. “I’ll come back at noon tomorrow. I can show you the maps of the Soper River trip we offer, then buy you lunch. Okay?” Curtis hesitated, “You could ride along on a raft trip. Think about it. I need to check out the river before I take the first clients down. You could ride along with me.”

Nodding, Christopher watched the visitor walk away. The black Suburban Curtis climbed into was a rarity in Iqaluit, where everything from cars to food were delivered either by ship, barge, or plane. He thought, *A Suburban would cost more than a year's wages here. And it would be frivolous to leave a Suburban in Iqaluit to be used a few weeks of the year. The river rafting business must be very profitable.*

Christopher had barely settled on the couch when there was another knock on the door. Hoping that Connie had missed her flight, he opened the door to two women, one middle-aged and the other a generation younger. They looked familiar, but he couldn't recall their names. The older woman carried an aluminum pan past him and set it on the table. "Christopher Pokaik, we heard about your grandfather and thought we'd bring you supper." She peeled off the aluminum foil cover allowing the lovely aroma of roasted meat, onions, potatoes, and carrots to fill the small kitchen.

The younger woman opened cupboards and drawers until she found a plate and silverware. She set them on the table and stepped back, smiling.

Standing awkwardly, Christopher said, "I'm sorry, I can't remember your names."

"I'm Mrs. Kilabuk and this is my daughter, Blossom." She gestured toward the table. "Please eat while it's hot." The older woman pulled out the chair in front of the place setting and held it, waiting for Christopher to sit. Seeing no alternative, he sat.

Blossom sat next to him and dished meat, potatoes, and vegetables onto the plate. "Mom and I were worried because you're staying all alone in this house. We thought you might be hungry."

Mrs. Kilabuk sat on the other side of Christopher and unzipped her coat. "We also thought you'd like to reconnect with some of your old friends and neighbors. Blossom was three years behind you in school. She has graduated now and is working in the Nunavut courthouse."

Blossom smiled but didn't speak. Christopher heard a foot slide across the floor, causing Blossom to jerk upright, having apparently been kicked by her mother under the table. "Um, yes. I'm helping in the court property room. We keep track of everything the Mounties seize until it's needed for a trial."

The mother nodded her approval. "It's a very important job, but she's buried deep in the courthouse, so she doesn't meet many people." The mother stared at her daughter, awaiting follow up comments.

It took Blossom a second to catch the hint. "Yes, my courthouse job made me more aware of some of the problems with many of the guys I've dated over the years. A lot of them have been in trouble with the Mounties."

Christopher ate the pot roast, pretending not to realize that Mrs. Kilabuk was trying to set him up with Blossom. "How interesting."

"It's not that interesting," Blossom said. She'd hardly gotten the words out before Mrs. Kilabuk kicked her under the table again. "Um, well, my job has its moments. I do get to bring things up to the courtrooms when they're going to be used as evidence in a trial." Blossom grinned. "How is the university? Are you moving back to Iqaluit after graduation?"

"The university is challenging but fun. As far as Iqaluit, I'm keeping my options open, too."

Blossom, obviously uncomfortable with her mother's matchmaking effort, stared at her hands. "I hear that Toronto is beautiful. Do you have a girlfriend there?"

"I've been too busy to date much."

Mrs. Kilabuk shook her head. "That's too bad. We were thinking about what Blossom should do when her vacation time comes. Would Toronto be a nice place to visit?"

"It's beautiful in the fall and spring. It's a wonderful place to visit. I feel sad that I'm so busy with school and my job at the library I wouldn't be able to show you around if you visited."

Blossom looked deflated. "Oh, that's too bad. If you don't have any plans tonight, *Star Wars* is playing at the Iqaluit theater."

Christopher pushed his plate back. "I appreciate your offer, but I have early morning plans and I'm going to bed shortly."

Mrs. Kilabuk looked disappointed as she gathered the aluminum pan and resealed the foil across remnants of the meal. "Perhaps a different night would work better."

"I'm still adjusting to the loss of my grandfather. I'm not making any plans."

Christopher escorted the Kilabuks to the door and held it open. "Thank you for the pot roast. It was very good."

After closing the door behind the women, Christopher leaned back and thought. *Tatty kidded that I'd be a catch, but this is insane.*

After fingering the piece of paper with Connie's phone number for a few minutes as he watched television, Christopher dialed the phone, hoping that he wasn't calling too late in the evening. Connie sounded breathless when she answered the phone. "Hello."

"Um, hi, it's Christopher. I wanted to make sure you made it back to *Pangnirtung*."

"Yeah. Like usual, the flight was late, but I got back in time for my radio slot."

"Can you tell if people enjoyed hearing about the premier's speech and the Iqaluit celebration?'

"The radio station phones never stopped ringing. I talked to a dozen people on the air. Each of them was excited and hopeful. I didn't expect the overwhelming response. People believe that Nunavut is really a new beginning for the *Inuit*."

Not wanting to express his feelings if Connie might not feel the same, Christopher said, "It was nice to see you. I didn't expect to meet anyone from school."

Connie's laugh made Christopher smile. "Meeting you was the best surprise I've had in a long time. I enjoyed talking to you."

Being an introvert and unaccustomed to conversations, he said, "Um, well, like I said, I just wanted to make sure you made it home."

"Christopher, I'd like to see you again."

Stunned, Christopher was speechless.

Reacting to the silence, Connie stammered, "I'm sorry if I've come on too strong..."

"No, it's just been a crazy day. I'd like to see you, too."

"Call me tomorrow. Who knows, maybe the radio station will want me to fly back to Iqaluit to interview the new premier...or something."

Almost as an afterthought, Christopher blurted out, "I'm staying at my grandfather's house. Here's his phone number."

* * *

In bed, Christopher's mind wouldn't shut down. His initial euphoria over talking to Connie faded, leaving him feeling more alone and lost than he'd ever felt before. Thoughts of people calling the radio station to express their excitement about the formation of Nunavut was both surprising and intriguing.

Then, the image of Wolverine's face in the body bag came to mind. Why hadn't Wolverine told him about his property and lease arrangement? Who was Eric Curtis besides being a man who could afford a big SUV? Who would attend Wolverine's burial? The *Inuit* belief that Wolverine's spirit would leave to become an animal was...unsettling. Wait! Tatty mentioned spirits going to different places. Did the *Inuit* believe that people possessed more than one spirit? He searched his memory for things Wolverine had told him about the spirit world. *Is there an* Inuit *heaven?*

Suddenly struck by his childhood Anglican Sunday school lessons, a prayer from his past came to mind. "Our Father, who art in heaven..." After praying, tranquility swept over Christopher, and he drifted off to sleep.

Chapter 6

A barking dog woke Christopher from his deep sleep. The all-night twilight had turned to morning sun, now leaking around the edges of the bedroom blinds. Because Iqaluit was just past the summer solstice, there was twilight all night long. Christopher looked for a clock but didn't see one in the bedroom. Wolverine believed in getting up and going to bed when his body said it was time, not when a clock dictated things.

Pulling on his jeans, Christopher walked to the kitchen, where the microwave clock glowed 7:12 in eerie red numerals. "It's got to be morning. I wonder how long I slept?"

After showering, Christopher searched the kitchen for breakfast options. A dusty carton of oatmeal in the cupboard caught his eye. Boiling the oatmeal gave him time to search the cupboards for a canister of brown sugar and a carton of rock-hard raisins. He threw a handful of raisins in the boiling cereal, hoping that they'd soften. Using a tablespoon, he scraped pieces off the solid brick of brown sugar.

With the steaming bowl in front of him, Christopher dropped brown sugar crumbs on top of the cereal and watched them slowly liquify. The simple breakfast reminded him of Wolverine and his daily admonition that Christopher needed something in his belly before he left for school. Today's oatmeal was comfort food. The eggs and bacon Tatty had prepared for him were great, but the oatmeal made him warm inside, bringing back memories of earlier. To his surprise, a mental image of his mother appeared in his mind, scurrying around the kitchen to prepare sandwiches for their lunch. His were for school, the others for his mother and father who were flying clients to a remote village. Christopher remembered them flying charters nearly every day. On their few days without a charter, his father did maintenance on their plane.

A knock on the door jarred Christopher from his memories and he wiped a bit of oatmeal from his lip as he walked across the tiny kitchen. Tatty, in her constable's uniform, stood on the steps, "I'm checking in."

Christopher stepped aside and gestured toward the table. "I made a big pot of oatmeal. Would you like some?"

"I don't suppose you made coffee to go with it?"

"Go ahead and make a pot. I'll dish up oatmeal for you."

With the percolator gurgling, Tatty pulled off her bullet-proof vest and coat, then sat down to the bowl of oatmeal. "Jeez, you put raisins into it."

"That's how grandpa always made it."

"I think putting raisins in anything is a crime punishable by ten days in jail."

Christopher smiled for the first time in a day. "You're funny."

Sliding the canister of brown sugar over, she poked at the solid mass. "How did you get any sugar out? It's a brick."

"You can scrape some loose with your spoon."

Shaking her head, but smiling, Tatty scraped at the brown sugar and sprinkled a spoonful on the oatmeal. The coffee pot stopped gurgling about the same time, so she took two clean mugs from the cupboard and poured coffee. Setting a mug in front of Christopher, she clucked her tongue. "You could have washed yesterday's dishes."

"Why? There were still clean dishes in the cupboard."

Chuckling, Tatty shook her head. "Spoken like a true college student. Never wash a dish if there are clean ones in the cupboard, and never wash more than one if only one is needed."

"Did you know that Mrs. Kilabuk and Blossom brought me supper last night?"

Tatty smiled. "No kidding? Did you have a nice chat with them?"

"I felt like a bug under a microscope. I must've passed the test because Blossom suggested that we go to a movie."

"Did you go?"

"I told them I was too tired. Mrs. Kilabuk also suggested that Blossom fly to Toronto on her upcoming vacation days."

Tatty's eyes lit up and a sly smile crept across her lips. "That sounds like fun. Did you make plans?"

Christopher snorted. "I said I was too busy with school and my library job to play tour guide."

"That seems cruel. The poor girl offered to fly all the way to Toronto to visit, and you refused to show her around. How are you ever going to find a wife if you turn down offers like that?"

"It gets even better! Mrs. Kilabuk kept kicking Blossom under the table, prompting her to make conversation. If Blossom's mom hadn't been here, the conversation might've died."

"How does Blossom compare to Connie?"

Suddenly uncomfortable with the conversation, Christopher set his spoon in the empty bowl. "Is my love life any of your business?"

Tatty leaned back. "Aren't you the man who said my hips were wide enough to provide a husband with many healthy children? I think statements like that mean all topics are open for discussion between us."

Smiling, Christopher shook his head. "Fine. We're even, but I'm not commenting on Blossom, Connie, or any of the other women who may, or may not, be part of my life."

"Come on, dish the dirt. It's not like I'm going to tell anyone."

Changing the conversation, Christopher asked, "Why are you here? Did you come just to needle me, or are you doing a wellness check?"

"I figured you'd be alive, but in need of company. So, did you call Connie like I told you to?"

Christopher felt red creeping up from his neck.

Tatty smiled. "Good. Did you get any sleep after you talked to her?"

"Some."

"Too many ghosts visiting you?"

Christopher turned somber and looked around the surroundings. "Wolverine is everywhere. I worried about his burial ceremony before I fell asleep. I smelled him on the towel I used this morning."

"Like your parents, he'll be with you forever."

"They're ghosts who visit me, like in Charles Dickens."

Tatty blinked at the sudden change in direction. "What?"

"Dickens' story, *A Christmas Carol*. I keep seeing the ghosts of the past and present. I need to see the ghost of Christopher future."

"Like it was for Mr. Scrooge, the future is yours to decide."

"What do you know about Eric Curtis?"

Tatty was confused. "Who's Eric Curtis?"

"He stopped here last night to talk about continuing his lease on Wolverine's Soper River land."

"Oh, him. He operates an outfitting service that takes tourists on outfitter's trips. He does some Soper River tours and has some other '*Inuit* culture' trips where customers stay with families in remote villages for a few days. He specializes in experiential tours where his clients get a real taste of the local culture."

"He only works in the summer?"

"He only runs summer tours in Nunavut. I think his company arranges tours all over the world the rest of the year. He's probably got people fishing in New Zealand during our winter months." Tatty paused. "He told you he has a lease on Wolverine's land grant?"

Christopher explained the value of the flat landing area. Tatty listened while finishing her oatmeal, then wiped her mouth on a tissue. "Don't agree to anything right away. You've got a lot of turmoil in your life right now. Weigh any life altering decisions for at least a few months."

"I think he wants a decision about the lease for this summer's raft trips. He offered to take me out to lunch and show me maps of his tour area."

"If you feel up to it, ask him what he paid Wolverine and then accept that for this season. We can do some research on the value of the lease before next season. That might give you leverage to negotiate a higher payment for next year." Tatty put their bowls in the sink and refilled their coffee mugs. "Are you considering his lunch offer?"

"I've got nothing else going on right now."

"Don't make many more plans. Wolverine's funeral is coming up and Connie invited you to *Pangnirtung*."

"Wow! The burial. Did we set a date?"

"*Inuit* funerals are usually held a few days after the death. I've got Hanta's spare seal harpoon and hand-fishing gear in my car. We can drop them off at the mortuary and set a burial time and date."

"Who conducts an *Inuit* funeral? I haven't been to a burial in years. Is there a minister or shaman who oversees it and prays? I can't remember."

"We should talk to Hanta. He can answer those questions."

* * *

Hanta was sitting at a dining room table with two other old men when Tatty and

Christopher arrived at The Lodge. He perked up when he recognized Tatty. "Ah, my granddaughter and her friend." Struggling to stand, he greeted Tatty with a *kunik* and took Christopher's right hand in his left. "Remind me, who are you?" he asked, his dementia having robbed him of yesterday's memory.

"I'm Wolverine's grandson. I need to know more about *Inuit* traditions for planning a burial."

Hanta blinked as he tried to recall Wolverine's death. "Come to my room, I have much I can tell you about burials, spirits, and traditions."

Tatty arranged three chairs so they were facing the window and took Hanta's hand. "Christopher is here to understand what plans should be made for Wolverine's burial."

Hanta's face clouded. "We do not speak the name of the dead until their name spirit has been given to a child. Has that happened?" Hanta paused. "I don't think so."

Tatty glanced at Christopher and raised her eyebrows. "We are learning, Grandfather. What else should we know?"

"Have you wrapped him in a seal or caribou skin yet?"

"Not yet."

"Do it soon and wrap his seal harpoon and fishing hooks with him. He'll need those to feed himself on his trip through *Adlivun,* the underworld, where his spirit will be purified." Hanta looked around, as if making sure no one was listening. "Tanaraq, get the knife from my top dresser drawer."

Rolling her eyes, Tatty sighed as she walked to the dresser. "Everyone calls me Tatty, Grandfather."

"Your mother named you Tanaraq, daughter of the Tundra. It's a strong *Inuit* name."

"And my friends call me Tatty"

Hanta frowned. "Doesn't tatty mean worn and of poor quality?"

When Christopher chuckled, Tatty glared at him. "It's a nickname, Grandfather. It doesn't *mean* anything," she replied as she ran her hand under the clothing in the top drawer, searching for a knife.

"Have you found my knife yet?"

"Why do you have a knife here?"

"Every *Inuk* has a knife to protect himself from evil spirits. Get mine for Christopher."

"You've never given me a knife to protect myself," she said, opening the second drawer and feeling around the clothing for the knife.

"You're strong, Tanaraq. You are able to protect yourself from the spirit world. Wolverine's grandson isn't schooled in the ways of the *Inuit*. He must be prepared for the spirits who will challenge him until he learns."

With Tatty busy, Hanta looked at Christopher. "There will be evil coming to you as your grandfather's spirit is reincarnated. You must carry the knife with you at all times, so you're prepared to defend yourself."

Frowning, Christopher said, "I don't think carrying a knife around Iqaluit is a good idea."

Nodding agreement with Christopher's comment, Tatty returned with a bone-handled knife in a scarred leather sheath. She handed it to Hanta, who passed it to Christopher. "Wear this on your belt, where you can reach it with your right hand."

"But..."

Hanta pressed the hilt of the knife into Christopher's hand. "I carried this knife for fifty years and it kept me safe."

Christopher tried to hand it back. "You should keep it..."

"I'm no longer in need of it. When the spirits come to take me, I will go with them. My time has come."

Tatty opened her mouth to protest but paused. "You may be with us for years."

Hanta shook his head. "I have taught you my knowledge, and now I've become a burden. I eat what's needed by younger people."

Having seen dozens of elderly people who'd committed ritual suicide during her few years as a special constable, Tatty was rattled. "There is plenty of food for everyone."

"Only until winter comes and the spirits move the caribou and fish out of reach. Then there will be hunger."

Hoping to break the somber discussion, Tatty turned to Christopher. "Teach Christopher the rituals of an *Inuit* burial."

Gazing at Christopher as if he had just recognized him, Hanta nodded. "You are so young and were raised as a Christian by Wolverine's son. I suppose you don't know how to proceed."

"It's been a while since I accompanied Wolverine to an *Inuit* burial. Remind me of how it's done."

Hanta leaned back and closed his eyes. "There is usually a five-day mourning period. The body should be washed, and his hair brushed back, as if he was going on a hunt. You should wrap his hunting and fishing gear with him in a seal or caribou skin. Bind it securely with rawhide to keep the scavengers away. After five days, take him as close to the place of his birth as you can and dig as deep as the permafrost allows. Then, place his body in the ground and cover it with stones. Place a white stone over his face so his spirit knows where to leave."

"Is there a shaman who comes to say prayers and lead us in...mourning?"

"All you need are strong men to carry the seal skin and women to bring the stones to cover the body." Opening his eyes after sensing Christopher's discomfort, Hanta added, "There's no need for your Anglican traditions. Your grandfather was a man who lived a clean life. His spirit soul will find its way to the underworld. Once it has been purified, it will go to *Qudlivun*, the happy land of the clouds and sky."

"Doesn't someone say a prayer?" Christopher asked.

Sensing that now wasn't the time for a theological discussion, Tatty stood. "Thank you, Grandfather."

Hanta stared at Christopher, then cocked his head. "Your beliefs will be torn but trust me. *Inuit* souls depart quickly, especially those who die violent deaths. Now go, knowing that the spirits will test you. They may be shapeshifters. Keep the knife close at all times, because you may not recognize them for the threat they are until they're upon you."

Hanta looked away, signaling the end of the conversation. Christopher followed Tatty silently until they got outside. "I'm confused."

"I'm not surprised. Hanta often speaks in riddles."

"Hanta said my grandfather's spirit would depart quickly, like those people who die violent deaths. Wolverine had a stroke."

Tatty shrugged and walked toward her car. "I suppose Hanta views a stroke as a violent death."

Inside the car, Christopher buckled his seatbelt. "I thought shamans interpreted the things they dreamt, then passed that knowledge on to us."

Tatty started the car and pulled out of the parking spot. "I don't understand all the shaman stuff. Like I said, Hanta sometimes speaks in riddles. Other times his dementia clouds his memories and jumbles his thoughts. Sometimes I figure out what he means. Other times, I scratch my head."

"Hanta gave me his knife. Does that mean he's going to die soon?"

Tatty shrugged. "He's not afraid of dying. That's pretty common among the elderly *Inuit*. They have been taught that the old, sick, and infirm are burdens on their families and it's their duty to die so the rest of the family has enough food."

"That's harsh."

Tatty glanced at Christopher. "You lived in Iqaluit for eighteen years? You know that life outside of town is a brutal test of strength, will, and hunting prowess. That reality has been bred into our *Inuit* beliefs for thousands of years. Life is a gift. Death is inevitable. The strong survive. The old die."

"You make the *Inuit* sound like a caribou herd. The strong survive. The lame and weak are eaten by predators."

"Who told you we weren't prey animals?" Tatty asked. Before Christopher could answer, Tatty pulled into a parking spot in downtown Iqaluit. "We need to drop the harpoon and fishing gear at the mortuary. Do you want to come in with me?"

Christopher froze. "I don't think so."

"Do you want to know whether they're going to wrap your grandfather's body in a caribou hide or a seal skin?"

"I have no opinion on that."

Christopher watched Tatty hustle across the sidewalk with the harpoon in one hand and the spool of fishing line in the other. *Yes, this is Dickens.* Christopher thought to himself. *I've just spoken with the ghosts of the past and present. I wonder when the ghost of my future will appear.*

Tatty opened the car door, startling Christopher. "Daydreaming?"

"I guess."

"Caribou."

Christopher turned toward Tatty as she buckled her seatbelt. "What?"

"The funeral director is using a caribou skin to wrap your grandfather. I guess they're pretty common and seal skins are hard to find this time of year."

"Um, okay."

They drove in silence. Passing the school, Christopher saw some children in the school playground. "Have they found your missing girl?"

"Not yet. It sounds like the Mounties have spoken to everyone who knew Buniq Tingenek from school or her neighborhood. No one offered a suggestion about where she might've gone."

"What do you think?"

"I've got no opinion. I don't know her or Cape Dorset."

"Why do young people disappear?"

"They think there's a better life somewhere else. They've given up on life here, thinking it's hopeless. Maybe they've fallen in love with someone their family doesn't like or approve of, so they run away."

"The hopelessness—do teens run away to commit suicide?"

"I wish you'd leave the suicide topic, Christopher. You're making me nervous."

"I'm not suicidal. It's just scary to think that teens think of that as an avenue out of here."

"Statistically, an *Inuit* teen is six times more likely to commit suicide than a white teen in the lower provinces. Part of that is the view that the rest of the world has it better than the life they're living in an *Inuit* village."

"What's the other part?"

"Death is less...scary if you're *Inuit*. If you believe that life is a cycle and souls move from people to other life forms, you're just moving to your next reincarnation when you die. Traditionally, the *Inuit* are nomadic, moving with the caribou herds, hunting, and fishing. If an old person couldn't keep up, the family would move ahead and hope that grandma would show up later. If she didn't, oh well. Her spirit would be in the next ptarmigan or caribou they saw."

"Let's back up for a moment. Hanta said my grandfather's soul departed quickly because he'd died a violent death."

"You're hung up on that."

"Are you sure my grandfather died of a stroke?"

"That's what his doctor said."

"Did his doctor actually examine him?"

Tatty glanced at Christopher. "He was old and in the bathroom. We see it all the time. An old person is trying to have a bowel movement, so they strain. A blood vessel in their brain pops, and they die. It happens. ALL. THE. TIME."

"But there was no autopsy."

"There's no need for an autopsy. All the evidence points to a stroke."

"But, Hanta said he died a violent death."

"Hanta sees visions, which he interprets. It's not like he witnessed someone shooting your grandfather. I assume Hanta dreamt that something violent happened. Maybe the violence was the ruptured artery in your grandfather's head. Or maybe Hanta's dementia created a memory of something that never happened."

Christopher digested the comments, then said, "I'd be more comfortable if the coroner had ordered an autopsy."

"Like the funeral director said, they don't do autopsies on elderly patients when the doctor lists a natural cause of death, like a stroke."

"Hanta said Wolverine's death was violent."

Tatty weighed her words. "The coroner deals with science, not an *Inuit* shaman's visions."

"Could you ask him if he'd do an autopsy?"

Tatty hung her head. "Christopher, I have a duty to be a competent officer of the law. Although a part of my job is helping the RCMP understand *Inuit* language and traditions, I'd have to put my personal credibility on the line if I told the coroner that a shaman with dementia had a vision that Wolverine's death was murder and not a stroke, so he needs to perform an autopsy."

Christopher blew out a breath. "It sounds worse when you say it out loud than when the idea is just bouncing around inside my head."

Tatty chuckled. "Yes, cousin, that's why I sometimes talk to myself. It's a way of assessing how reasonable, or stupid, something sounds before telling it to my boss."

Chapter 7

Christopher hadn't taken off his coat when there was a knock on the door. Eric Curtis was there, smiling. "Are you ready for lunch?"

"I, ah, just walked in the door."

"Perfect! The Suburban is warmed up and ready to go. What would you like for lunch? I'm partial to the pizza place downtown."

Christopher glanced at Hanta's knife on the kitchen table, then stepped out of the door and closed it behind himself. "Pizza sounds good."

Curtis chuckled. "I've never met a college student who disliked pizza."

The Suburban smelled new, and the dashboard looked like someone had just wiped it with Armor All. There wasn't a grain of sand on the floor, nor was there evidence that the drink holders had ever been used. "Nice ride."

"I need something classy when I pick up our clients from the airport and hotel. In my business, appearances are as important as the trip."

Hearing that, Christopher looked at Eric's expensive North Face jacket. The *Rough Water Adventures* logo of a red canoe going through river rapids, was embroidered on the chest. The same logo was on his matching, soft-brimmed hat.

"The Soper River trip isn't the only destination you offer, right?"

Eric snorted. "We offer trips fifty weeks a year. My guides are on the water somewhere every week except Christmas and New Years."

"Where do you find open water in the winter?"

"Primarily in the southern hemisphere. Argentina. New Zealand. We have a few trips on the Colorado River on the cusp of winter, but even the Grand Canyon is too cold in January."

"Really? It's in Arizona."

"It snows in the higher elevations there."

Eric circled the block twice to find a parking space, actually two parking spaces, to accommodate the long SUV. Walking the half a block to a busy pizza restaurant, Christopher thought about how quiet it had been when he and his friends ate there the last January he'd lived in Iqaluit. They'd slipped and slid down the sidewalk in the mid-day twilight with the temperature hovering around -20°C.

Eric pointed out a small table near the back, and they wound their way through the crowd. After ordering soda pop and a pizza with virtually every topping, Eric leaned back. "Have you thought any more about my offer to take you on a trip down the Soper?"

"I've got a funeral coming up and that might not mesh with the trips you've got scheduled."

Leaning forward, Eric smiled and pulled a map from inside his jacket. "I don't have anyone coming for two weeks. Because the landscape and river change each year, I like to make a run down the course before I take any clients. You know, to avoid unpleasant surprises like boulders that have fallen into the streambed. I thought you could join me on the checkout trip," he said as he spread the map on the table.

Quickly orienting himself to the map, Christopher pointed to the dot representing Iqaluit, on Frobisher Bay. "Here we are."

Eric slid his finger across the bay to a black line that started just past the opposite shore. "This is where the Soper River begins. It's not navigable until here, past Mount Joy. The green on either side of the river is Katannilik Territorial Park. We land the planes here, just outside the park boundary, on your grandfather's land grant."

"How far do you travel?"

"We float 38 kilometers of the river to Soper Lake, ending here at Kimmirut."

"When would we take the trip?" Christopher asked.

Curtis folded the map and put it back in his jacket. "I'm flexible. I'm lining up bush planes, food, and ice, so I'll be here until my first clients show up in two weeks."

"I've hunted in the hills around the river, but I've never actually been on a kayak or canoe on the river."

"We take an inflatable raft. It's easier to pack onto the plane than a rigid canoe or kayak, and it's more stable in the water."

"I can't go with you. I need to go to a funeral, then back to Toronto."

"You're a student, right? This must be your summer break."

"I've got a job in the library, and they expect me next week."

"Give them a call and tell them your grandfather died and you need to stay for his funeral." Sensing Christopher's continued reluctance, Eric said, "I'm offering you a $2,000 trip for free. Are you going to pass that up?"

"I suppose it would be interesting."

"Come on. Get into this. We're going on what most of my clients refer to as the trip of a lifetime."

"Great. This is the trip of a lifetime for a rich American or Canadian. I've been to the river before. It's probably not as magical for an *Inuk*."

Curtis leaned back as their pizza was delivered. "It's more magical than you realize. Your people hold the land in high regard, and you'll reconnect with your forefathers."

Christopher hesitated. Wolverine was his forefather. He knew nothing of his family any generations farther back than his grandfather. *Who were his forefathers? Were their souls in graves on the tundra? Or, as Hanta suggested, did they move into animals? Then there was the question of the name souls. Had a child been named Wolverine following his grandfather's death? Could that child be living anywhere in the world? Would that child have his grandfather's personality? Would he remember Christopher or his parents?*

"Are you okay, Christopher?"

Looking up, Christopher slowly focused on Eric Curtis' smiling face. "Sorry. Something you said made me think of other things."

"Wolverine owned an *Inuit* land grant. I was leasing the rights to use it as a landing strip for bush planes."

"Haven't you paid Grandfather for this summer's lease?"

"Your grandfather wanted you to be part of the lease negotiation."

"How much did you offer Grandfather for the landing lease?"

Wrinkling his nose and splaying his fingers, Curtis acted like whatever they'd discussed was insignificant. "We were talking about a couple hundred dollars."

Mental alarms went off in Christopher's head as he thought about Curtis' new Suburban and apparent wealth while he tried to remain nonchalant. "You're offering to take me on a trip worth several thousand dollars to discuss a lease that amounts to one tenth of that?"

"It's a gesture of good will. We're just rafting down the river to evaluate seasonal changes that might affect my trips with clients. I was making the trip anyway. You're just helping me paddle."

"Would you be willing to pay me a thousand dollars for the lease?"

Curtis leaned back. "That's a stretch from what I'd been paying the old man."

"You said there wasn't anywhere else near the river where the plane could land. That indicates that the lease is very valuable. Maybe I should talk to some of the other outfitters to see if they'd offer more."

"I'm actually negotiating on behalf of all the outfitters."

"So, we're not talking about just your two groups of clients. How many groups will be landing on the leased land?"

"It's dependent on the weather. If it gets cold too early, we'll cancel the late season trips." Curtis signalled for their waitress to bring the bill. "Let's continue this discussion on the river. I think that you'll feel differently about the situation after you're on the water."

"Why would I feel differently about the value of the lease?"

Curtis glanced at the bill and handed the waitress $100. "Keep the change." He stood and gestured toward the door. "I think you'll realize how important it is to share the experience of seeing your beautiful homeland with as many appreciative people as possible."

"Is that why you offer the trips? So you can expose more people to Nunavut?"

Curtis held the door for Christopher. "I specialize in eco-tourism with an anthropological component. I'm showing ecologically aware people places that are pristine and worth saving. I have them meet local people, and sometimes have them stay in the villages so they appreciate the value of cultural diversity and different lifestyles." As they walked toward the Suburban, Curtis added, "In New Zealand, we do the same type of trip, providing a view of Maori culture. In Chile, we hike to *Mapuche* and *Aymara* villages to experience local culture and view the breathtaking scenery."

"Are you an anthropologist?"

Curtis chuckled. "No, I'm just a guy who understands the value of exposing concerned people to native cultures that need to be appreciated and protected. Guiding a trip down the Soper River offers a Nunavut *Inuit* experience that provides hundreds of people a glimpse of your unspoiled homeland and the difficult life your *Inuit* brethren live."

Christopher stepped into the Suburban while he pondered Curtis' comments. "It seems like paying a thousand dollars a year for a lease to land planes would be a small price to pay compared to the other costs of your operation."

Curtis chuckled. "If you add up a lot of small items, they become a big number."

Looking around the interior of the Suburban, Christopher sighed. "A thousand-dollar lease is cheap compared to shipping a new Suburban to Iqaluit."

After turning onto the street, Curtis smiled. "From a business perspective, the Suburban is a depreciated asset that is deducted from my taxes. A lease payment in a cash payment out of my checkbook."

"But a deductible expense nonetheless."

"Are you studying to be an accountant?"

"No, but I've learned enough to know when someone's trying to take advantage of me."

"It's not personal," Curtis replied. "In the end, I'm a businessman who has to pay employees, rent office space, buy equipment, and manage groups of tourists who miss plane connections and resist my efforts to keep them safe and on schedule."

"I thought you were an altruistic ecologist who wants to expose people to places that need to be protected."

Curtis glanced at Christopher and chuckled. "I *do* want to share your homeland and culture with as many people as possible. But I don't run a charity. Canada and Nunavut don't pay me to run tours. If I don't make a profit, the tours end. Come with me on the river, then tell me that what I'm providing isn't important exposure for Nunavut and the *Inuit* people."

"You're giving me a trip that's worth thousands of dollars so you can negotiate a cheaper lease."

"Christopher, I'm inviting you to join me, Eric Curtis, on a raft trip. I want you to see and experience the wonder and cultural awareness that hundreds of people get from a Soper River trip. Your grandfather understood the inter-cultural value of these trips. That's why he offered me the lease at a fair price. He wanted concerned outsiders to understand the *Inuit* people in a way that didn't harm the environment."

Christopher looked at Curtis, trying to weigh the man's words against his expensive clothing and the Suburban.

"Come with me. After that experience, I'm sure you'll look at these trips and the value of the lease differently."

* * *

Returning to the mortuary, Tatty found the funeral director sitting in his office. Unlike the professional persona they'd seen while discussing funeral arrangements, the director was now sitting behind a desk without a tie and with his shirt sleeves rolled up. The brass sign on his desk identified him as "Kenneth O'Keefe.

"Excuse me," Tatty said, knocking on the open door.

O'Keefe pulled off his reading glasses and stood. "I wasn't expecting anyone, Constable." He gestured toward the guest chairs facing his desk.

"Something has been bothering me," Tatty said as she sat in a chair.

"Is there a problem with Wolverine Pokaik's funeral?"

"Did you notice anything...suspicious about the marks on Wolverine's face?"

O'Keefe leaned back and clasped his fingers. "To be honest, I haven't looked at the deceased other than to verify that he was dead, and when you and his grandson came to view him."

"Are petechial hemorrhages common in stroke victims?"

"Petechiae result from many medical conditions."

"Including strangulation and asphyxiations."

O'Keefe picked up a pen and tapped it on the paperwork he'd been studying. "Mr. Pokaik was elderly. His doctor signed a death certificate, noting a stroke as his likely cause of death. I have no basis for questioning his judgement."

"Were there petechiae around Mr. Pokaik's conjunctiva?"

"His eyelids were closed when he arrived here."

Tatty stood. "Let's look."

O'Keefe remained seated. "Constable, if you have some basis for questioning the doctor's statement, I suggest that you take it up with the coroner."

"Humor me. Let's take a look at Mr. Pokaik's eyes to see if there's bleeding in the capillaries."

"There are any number of circumstances that could cause petechial hemorrhages in his eyes. They found him collapsed in the bathroom. He could've been straining at the toilet and that could've caused his stroke and petechial hemorrhages."

"Mr. O'Keefe, I'm making a formal request to examine the body."

O'Keefe drew a deep breath and blew it out. He opened the lap drawer of his desk and picked up a keyring. "I hate to needlessly disturb the dead."

After walking down a short hallway, O'Keefe unlocked a door to a room that smelled of formaldehyde, and featured a stainless steel table and an array of tools that looked like torture implements. He opened a refrigerator door on the far side of the room and led Tatty into the cooler, where he flipped on the overhead lights.

The only trolley holding a body was in the center of the room. O'Keefe gestured toward the body, which was still enclosed in a rubberized body bag. "Do what you feel is necessary," he said, stepping back.

Tatty stepped up to the body bag and unzipped it. Usually able to remain distant and objective, she felt a pang of sadness when she looked at Wolverine's waxy face. Taking a pair of latex gloves from a box mounted on the wall, she reached out with her thumb and index finger and opened the old man's eyelids.

"Mr. O'Keefe, please step over and verify what I'm seeing." With O'Keefe looking over her shoulder, Tatty held Wolverine's eyelid open. "Would you say that Mr. Pokaik's eye is displaying significant petechial hemorrhaging?"

O'Keefe sighed. "Yes."

"Is this amount of hemorrhaging consistent with that you've seen in victims who've been suffocated, strangled, or hung?"

When O'Keefe didn't answer, Tatty turned to him.

"Well?"

"Yes, that's significant hemorrhaging and it's consistent with what I've seen in other victims of suffocation and asphyxiation."

"Thank you. I'll notify the coroner of our observations. Please don't do anything with Mr. Pokaik's corpse until directed to do so by the coroner's office."

O'Keefe nodded with resignation. "Yes, Constable."

* * *

Curtis chuckled as he turned onto Wolverine's road and saw the RCMP SUV idling in front of Wolverine's house. "It looks like they're looking for you."

"It's probably my cousin checking up on me."

"I didn't know Iqaluit had any *Inuit* Mounties."

Unbuckling his seatbelt as the Suburban stopped, Christopher shrugged. "I'm not sure I could find her on a family tree, but Special Constable Tanaraq Etok treats me like a cousin."

"Is she a female Mountie?"

"She's officially a special constable. But, yes, she works for the RCMP."

Curtis stared at the RCMP vehicle as Christopher got out of the Suburban. "Is there a problem?"

"No, she checks up on me to make sure I'm not suicidal."

"Is that a possibility?"

Christopher paused with his hand on the Suburban's door. "Not a chance."

"When would you like to take that trip down the Soper River?"

"I guess my grandfather's funeral will be in..." Christopher paused to do the math... "in four days. We can go after that."

Tatty walked back to the Suburban and Curtis rolled down his window. "I don't recognize you or this vehicle, sir."

"I'm Eric Curtis. I operate one of the outfitters offering Soper River trips."

"He's going to take me on a trip down the river after Wolverine's funeral. I just told him that we need to wait four days, until the funeral is over," Christopher explained.

"About that," Tatty said. "I just spoke with the coroner and the burial will be delayed. He's requested an autopsy, and it won't be scheduled until the pathologist's rotation to Iqaluit next week. She'll schedule a coroner's inquest after that to establish the official cause of death."

Curtis frowned, then looked at Christopher. "Didn't you say the old guy died of a stroke?"

"That's what the Mountie who informed me of Wolverine's death said."

Tatty weighed her words, unsure of Curtis' exact knowledge or relationship to Christopher. "I told the coroner we'd like an autopsy. He spoke with the funeral director, and they agreed an autopsy is appropriate."

Curtis frowned. "I thought *Inuit* tradition required that the burial was like within a week of the death, or the person didn't go to heaven."

Tatty suppressed her urge to roll her eyes. "Our tradition is to bury the person five days after death. In Wolverine's case, because his death was sudden, we believe that his soul went immediately to the spirit world in the clouds."

"Sounds like my Catholic catechism except you go to purgatory until St. Peter sends you to heaven or hell."

"There's no *Inuit* heaven or hell," Tatty replied. "Just a new incarnation of your soul."

"Oh, that's right. You can come back as a caribou or whale. That's why it's a big deal when you shoot an animal. It might have your grandma's soul." Curtis chuckled. "It must be difficult to eat grandma."

Closing her eyes, Tatty counted to three. "It's more complicated than that."

"Whatever," Curtis replied. He turned to Christopher. "If you don't have to hang around for a funeral, let's start that river trip tomorrow."

Christopher looked past Curtis to Tatty, who stiffened when she heard the proposal, but said nothing. "I suppose that would be okay. How long is the trip?"

"If we skip the usual tourist stops at the falls and things, we can be in Kimmirut in five or six days. That's probably before the pathologist will even get to the hospital."

"I suppose we could leave tomorrow. It's not like I have any plans. Right, Tatty?"

Not being able to verbalize why the offer seemed off, Tatty reserved her thoughts. "Well, I'm sure the pathologist won't be here until next week."

Curtis sat up straighter. "Perfect. I'll call the bush pilot, buy some groceries, and dust off the gear. I'll pick you up tomorrow morning."

Tatty walked across the road to Christopher, who was watching the Suburban drive away. "How well do you know Eric Curtis?"

"I only met him yesterday, but he's leased from Wolverine for years. He must be an okay guy."

"Do you need anything?" Tatty asked.

"No. I think I'm set up fine until Eric picks me up tomorrow. I'll probably spend this evening digging through clothes and packing a bag."

"Be sure to take Hanta's knife with you."

Christopher laughed. "To protect me from evil spirits?"

"Hanta says that not all demons appear as themselves until they have you in their grasp."

"I've read about shapeshifters who appear as friendly spirits, then reveal themselves as evil later. It sounded like Dracula to me." Christopher paused, digesting Tatty's words. "Don't worry, I don't think Eric plans to drink my blood and turn himself into a bat."

Tatty put her hand on his arm. "Be aware of your surroundings and pay attention to your dreams."

"My dreams?"

"Hanta has many visions that come to him in dreams."

Christopher laughed. "I don't remember most of my dreams." He paused, then blushed.

Tatty laughed. "You only remember the ones with pretty women in them."

Quickly shifting the topic, Christopher said, "I mostly remember the nightmares about missing math tests."

* * *

As he packed clothing for the raft trip, Christopher realized he didn't own anything for an outdoor adventure. Digging deep into Wolverine's wardrobe, he found gloves, a stocking cap, and long underwear. Although it was July, the overnight temperatures were still near freezing, and he realized he hadn't brought a jacket warm enough for the weather.

Standing in front of Wolverine's closet, a wave of nostalgia swept over him. Before him were a few shirts, pairs of pants, and his grandfather's coats. Having grown up living a nomadic life, Wolverine didn't collect *things*. He was a minimalist, and his wardrobe reflected how few items of clothing a person really needed. Christopher took a flannel shirt off a hanger and tried it on. He and his grandfather were about the same height, but Wolverine was a muscular man whose physique had shifted as his life became sedentary. The shirtsleeves were the correct length, but the shirt's girth was at least four inches too large. Closing his eyes, Christopher visualized the caribou hunting trip he'd taken with his grandfather the fall before he left for Toronto. Although Wolverine was forty years older, Christopher struggled to match the old man's pace. After they'd shot the caribou, they'd loaded the meat onto pack boards they carried back to Iqaluit. Staggered by the weight of his load, Christopher watched as Wolverine hefted a load at least forty pounds heavier than the one Christopher was carrying. His grandfather was amazing.

Blinking his eyes, Christopher focused on the closet. He chose a coat and well-worn flannel shirt from Wolverine's collection. With those items, his backpack was full. His mind was filled with thoughts about rafting the Soper River. *Was it a flat, easy float? Would they have to paddle the whole way? How rough were the rapids*?

He glanced at the phone as he turned toward the bedroom. *Connie is on the air. There's no point calling her now.*

Chapter 8

Soper River Day 1

A knock on the door woke Christopher from his sleep. Pulling on a pair of jeans and grabbing one of Wolverine's flannel shirts, he walked barefooted across the cold tile floor to the door. Eric Curtis was standing there, smiling. "Time to roll, sleepyhead."

Stepping back, Christopher gestured for Curtis to come in. "Give me five minutes and I'll be ready."

Curtis sat in a kitchen chair. "Take whatever time you need, but keep in mind the pilot will be ready to take off in half an hour, and I'm paying him by the hour whether he's flying or sitting in the hangar waiting for us."

Christopher pulled on socks and boots, then brushed his teeth. Seeing his *bed head,* he raked his fingers through his hair. He picked up his backpack and Wolverine's hunting coat.

Curtis stood when Christopher walked into the kitchen. "All set?"

Glancing around the room, Christopher's eyes were drawn to Hanta's knife. He picked it up and slipped it onto his belt. "A friend loaned this to me for the trip."

Walking to the door, Curtis said, "Yeah, that'll come in handy when you have to fend off a polar bear."

Ignoring the verbal jab, Christopher scanned the kitchen and living room one last time. Seeing the phone, he briefly considered calling Connie to let her know his plan. He dismissed that. *I wonder if she'll even notice that I'll be gone for a few days?*

* * *

The twin-engine Otter circled over a wide valley covered with blooming wildflowers. The Soper River's blue water turned into white froth in a narrow slot between two gray canyon walls. Curtis leaned close to Christopher as the plane's flight leveled out and they descended toward the plateau ahead of them. "This is your grandfather's land grant."

The view from the plane was incredible. Although Christopher had flown in and out of Iqaluit, he'd never seen this side of Frobisher Bay and the headwaters of the Soper River. "It's beautiful here, but why is this tract particularly valuable?"

"Look around. This is the only flat area that's not littered with rocks. This landing strip, within hiking distance of the Soper River, is unique."

"How many groups do you take here a year?"

"We can't get in until the snow melts in late June or early July, and we can't offer trips when the weather starts getting cold again in August. We usually book three trips a year."

"Can't you bring in a group every two or three days and just spread them out along the river?"

"We can't do that and advertise ourselves as eco-friendly. We have to bring in all our gear, food, and equipment by plane, then pack it all out again. If we land the plane too often and bring in too many campers, we'll impact the permafrost and make this area a sea of mud."

The plane bumped once before braking and taxiing to the end of the small open area. The pilot turned the plane toward the water and braked at the edge of the field closest to the Soper River. He took off his headset and looked over his shoulder. "You've reached your destination, the seatbelt sign is off," he joked.

Eric unbuckled his seatbelt and stood, hunched over in the small plane's aisle. "Give me a hand with the raft and camping gear."

Together, the pilot, Christopher and Eric pulled bundles of gear from the rear of the plane. A large rubber bundle was especially heavy. "What's in here?" Christopher asked.

"That's the inflatable raft. We'll camp here tonight, then pack our gear to the river. We'll start our raft trip in the morning."

Having completed his inspection of the plane's exterior, the pilot joined them near their pile of gear. "If you're all set, I'll take off."

Eric checked the pile of gear. "I think we're all set. We've got the raft, paddles, tents, food, and cookware. We'll see you in Kimmirut later in the week."

The pilot climbed back into the plane and started the engine. Watching the Otter lumber toward the flat area used as a landing strip, Christopher felt a wave of anxiety. This was it, the start of a river rafting adventure. No cell phone coverage, no television, no restaurants, no soft mattresses. They'd be sleeping in tents and paddling alone down the river. If there was trouble with the inflatable raft, no one would be there to rescue them. They were truly on their own, as Christopher's forefathers had been.

Christopher's concentration was broken by Eric's voice. "Give me a hand. We'll inflate the raft."

"We're like a mile from the river. Why inflate it here?"

Eric released buckles and pulled away the packing straps. "It's easier to pack our gear in it and slide it like a toboggan into the river, than to carry all this gear on our backs."

They unrolled the Raft from its durable case. "Please tell me we're not going to blow this up like a balloon."

Eric chuckled as he grasped a metal ring hanging from one side of the raft. "There's a CO_2 gas cartridge in this tube." He jerked the handle, unleashing a hissing sound that caused the raft to unfurl as the sides inflated.

"Whoa. That's awesome."

"That's probably the last time you'll be impressed with technology on this trip. Everything else we'll do or see is a throwback to your *Inuit* ancestors."

"We're sleeping in Nylon tents. That's hardly *Inuit* tradition."

Removing a bright yellow bundle from the pile of gear, Curtis handed a similar blue bundle to Christopher. He unrolled a tent and assembled the support rods. "You're welcome to sleep under the stars if you'd prefer to be rustic. Personally, I like a foam mat, sleeping bag, and tent when the temperatures dip down to 10°C."

Christopher shivered at the prospect of sleeping in the open with the temperature only a few degrees above freezing. "I'm not interested in a full *Inuit* camping experience. A sleeping bag and tent sound good to me."

With tents pitched and camp set, Eric pulled food and cooking utensils from a box. An ice-packed cooler held plastic zippered bags filled with pre-measured portions of food. Sitting on his haunches, Christopher watched. "I thought we were roughing it."

"My clients expect a wilderness experience, while dining like they're in a restaurant that won a Michelin star."

"That seems wrong."

Brushing oil on a pan, Eric spoke while continuing his meal preparation. "They pay a couple thousand dollars apiece for the trip. I try to make them feel like they're getting their value. None of them would be happy if I prepared meals of freeze-dried hamburger casserole."

"Do you cook like this for every meal?"

Eric snorted. "I'm using up the heaviest ingredients and the fresh meat tonight. The remaining meals will be more...mundane. At least until we get down to where we can catch fish. It's hard to beat a meal of arctic char fillet cooked over a willow fire."

Meat sizzled in the pan over the Coleman stove. "I serve them local food. We have caribou, goose, and ptarmigan."

"They won't have the real Nunavut experience unless they've tried seal and whale meat."

Curtis laughed. "There are limits to what my guests are willing to eat. Many of them would object to eating whales because they think of them as endangered species."

Christopher nodded. "I suppose your clients think seals are too fuzzy and cute to eat."

Eric pushed the meat portions to one side of the pan as he added flour and seasonings to the browned bits left in the pan. "I assume you've eaten seals and whales. Would you choose that over caribou?"

Christopher wrinkled his nose. "I think my ancestors ate what they hunted. The flavor of the meat and tough texture aren't considerations when your belly is empty, and your children are starving."

After thickening the gravy in the pan, Eric coated the meat and ladled servings onto aluminum plates. He sliced a slab of bread from a hearty looking loaf and set it on top of the meat. "Your dinner is served."

After his first bite, Christopher leaned back. "You should've been a chef. This is like the best caribou steak I've ever eaten."

"Working in a kitchen night every night is tedious and boring. I'd rather whip up something out here than standing at a stove cooking the same menu over and over." Eric nodded toward Christopher's plate. "There are no leftovers in camp. Save a bit of the bread to mop up the last of the gravy."

After supper, Eric washed the dishes in the clear Soper River water while talking about his clientele and their interest in environmental issues. Christopher listened, at some point realizing he was getting a sales pitch. Now curious, he waited for the salesman to close the sale.

"What do you want, Eric?"

The outfitter seemed surprised. "Want?"

"You didn't fly me here to tell me about the land."

Eric spread his arms and gestured broadly. "This is a special place that deserves to be shared with the world. I bring people here who appreciate its natural beauty and serenity here. I understand that you've made a home in Toronto. I think we could come to an understanding that would allow me to continue protecting the environment here, and sharing this place with ecologically aware people, while providing you an income commensurate with the value."

There it was—money was on the table. "I'm living in Toronto, but I am *Inuit* and this land is part of my heritage."

"My clients are curious about your heritage and this beautiful uninhabited land. They're respectful and live by the adage, 'Take only pictures. Leave only footprints.' We carry out everything that we bring in, leaving the river, campsites, and land as we found it."

"That sounds nice, but you're making a living off my *Inuit* heritage and land."

"There are people in Nunavut more interested in the income than maintaining this undisturbed land and their Indian heritage."

"We're *Inuit*, First People. Not Indians."

Eric ignored the correction. "My company is sharing your...*Inuit* history with the rest of the world. That's to your advantage, both historically and financially."

Christopher stared at the sun as it neared the horizon. "My grandfather gave me this land."

"You have an aunt who's disputing that."

Christopher froze. "I don't have any living relatives. Whoever that woman is, she's an imposter."

"I was approached by a woman who claims to be Wolverine's daughter. She's very interested in collecting lease payments."

"I don't have an aunt, period. Besides, my grandfather transferred his land grant to me."

"Your grandfather died before he transferred the land to you. The ownership will be decided by the Crown Court."

"I think you've confused the Canadian legal system with the Nunavut system. Land ownership is paternal. I'm my grandfather's only male heir. The land belongs to me regardless of some unknown woman's wishes for income."

Eric stared into the distance. "Your blood quantum is only twenty-five percent *Inuit*. Your aunt is full *Inuit*. She believes that the elders will remove you from the membership rolls if she protests. That means the land goes to her, a full *Inuit* with a one hundred percent blood quantum."

The bullying Christopher experienced at school welled up inside him. His grandmother was an American worker at the Air Force base after WWII. Grandpa claimed to have swept her off her feet, giving him his first and only son. That son, Christopher's father, had married a French/Canadian woman from Quebec he'd met in flight school. Together they'd started their own bush air service. Their business involved flying tourists and supplies around what was then the Northwest Territories. Their service sometimes included making emergency medical flights to bring sick people from remote villages to Iqaluit for treatment...until they'd crashed. They'd left him, their only child, who was one quarter *Inuit*, with a white mother and grandmother, living with his *Inuit* grandfather.

"You got as quiet as a cigar store Indian, Chris."

Christopher stared into the outfitter's eyes. "My name is Christopher and I'm *Inuit*, not Indian."

"Oh, that's right. Canadian Indians like to be called First Nations people."

Bristling at the outfitter's lack of understanding or sensitivity, Christopher sat quietly while composing his thoughts. The extrovert outfitter couldn't stand the silence. "You're not Indian enough to be anything but a bastard half-breed. Your tribe will cast you aside."

"My *Inuit* membership has never been an issue."

"That was before money was involved. When everyone is poor, it's easy to be charitable and share. Money changes people...so does living in the city. I doubt you can move back to Iqaluit after experiencing all that Toronto has to offer."

"You've talked the whole circle. First, you tell me what a great ecologist and cultural teacher you are, then you try to buy my friendship. After that, you try to intimidate me by saying my unknown aunt is going to inherit the land. Then, you insult my *Inuit* credentials before trying again to entice me with money. Are you done?"

Eric's smile turned to a sneer. "Whatever it takes, I'll have a lease here. Either you go along with my offer, or your aunt will."

The sun set, leaving the plateau in eerie twilight. Christopher closed his eyes, wishing his grandfather was there to guide him. A sudden thought struck him, something Hanta said nibbled at the edge of his memory.

"Grandpa didn't want to renew your lease," he blurted out.

The outfitter shrugged. "He planned to give you the land and let you negotiate the lease agreement."

"You killed him!"

The outfitter looked wounded. "How can you even suggest that? I'm a respected businessman who dealt fairly with Wolverine."

Christopher stood and started pacing. "Grandpa was happy about Canada Day. He was going to transfer the land grant to me. Then he died. His roommate said something about a demon coming from the Northern Lights to kill him."

Eric chuckled. "Hanta is crazy. He drank too much fire water in his day. His brain is fried. I bet he sees pink elephants too."

Christopher stopped walking. Thinking about Hanta, his dementia, his visions, and Eric's attributing them to liquor, he said, "Take me back to Iqaluit."

Chuckling again, the outfitter shook his head. "The plane isn't coming back. There's no way to contact him. The only way home is to paddle down the river for five or six days to Kimmirut where the bush pilot will pick us up...unless you plan to walk across a hundred kilometers of tundra to Iqaluit."

Christopher's blood ran cold. Reflexively, he reached down and touched Hanta's knife in the leather sheath. Hanta's last admonition to him was to always wear the knife.

After he crawled into his sleeping bag, Wolverine's warning of many years ago gnawed at him. "You never know when the demons will attack." That was a nightmare inducing comment when Christopher was a child. As a teen, he'd written off the old man's advice as *Inuit* folklore. As a young adult, he'd reconsidered many of the things Wolverine said, rethinking them from the perspective of *Inuit* spirituality, rather than demons who slept under your bed and jumped out at you in the dark. Demons came in many forms and sometimes shifted between forms, making them difficult to discern until you were in their grasp. And now, Christopher realized, that grasp might take many forms. Physical danger was easily discerned and avoided. Harder to identify was depression, or addictions like alcohol and drugs. Even more insidious and hard to resist were the siren's call of vanity, money, beautiful women...or perhaps Wolverine warned him about the comfortable college life provided by a scholarship. Now, as he lay in his tent near the greedy white man, he realized that a demon might arrive in a shiny Suburban wearing a North Face jacket.

He drifted off to sleep thinking about an attractive redhead who sat next to him in his psychology class. She always smiled at him and said hello. He never knew what to say, so his usual response was a smile and head nod. Was she a demon sent to lure him to some other pitfall? The redhead's memory slipped away as Connie's smiling face came to him. He fell asleep remembering how they'd held hands as they'd walked through Iqaluit.

Chapter 9

Soper River Day 2

Plagued by unsettled thoughts and the chilling temperature, Christopher tossed and turned for hours in his sleeping bag. Once sleep came, it was fitful and filled with swirling dreams about the Iqaluit school, Toronto, Connie, and Tatty. He awoke curled in a ball, his head inside the sleeping bag. Slowly unzipping the sleeping bag, he peeled it back. The cold immediately seeped into his clothing, damp from his sweat.

"The elders slept naked under their seal skin blankets," he said to himself as he crawled free of his bag. I always thought it was because they were sharing their partner's body heat. He remembered teenage boys whispering the elders slept naked so they could have sex without having to remove heavy clothing. Wolverine explained that he slept naked so he could dress in dry clothing that would warm quickly. Christopher remembered that advice as he pulled a dry t-shirt from his backpack. After pulling on his dry, albeit cold, jacket, he unzipped the tent and stepped out. The scents of frying bacon and perking coffee filled the crisp air.

Eric Curtis was hunched over a two-burner camp stove. Seeing Christopher, he gestured toward the coffee pot. "There's a cup for you next to the pot."

Squatting down to pick up the cup and pour coffee, Christopher fixated on the skillet filled with sizzling bacon. "It looks like your breakfasts are as gourmet as your dinners."

"Paddling a raft takes a lot of energy, so we pack a lot of high calorie food. Our guests pay a lot of money for the trip. They expect the river trip to test their skills. They expect the food to be commensurate with the price." Eric pushed the bacon to one side of the pan, opened a cooler, and took out a carton of eggs. "How do you like your eggs?"

"Scrambled without any runny whites."

Eric cracked six eggs into the pan and stirred them in the puddled bacon grease with a spatula. "I'll make some pancakes after the eggs are done."

"Wow! I usually eat cereal for breakfast."

Eric laughed. "I bet you don't burn 5,000 calories a day sitting in class. Believe me, your stomach will be howling by the time we stop for lunch."

"I thought we'd be eating freeze-dried meals, like when I hiked."

"We strap coolers into the raft, so there's plenty of fresh food for the trip. I might even whip up a dessert tonight."

Christopher sat on the ground and accepted the plate of eggs and bacon as Eric poured pancake batter into the skillet. Looking at the sparse landscape in the valley around them, Christopher struggled to reconcile his meal with the harsh *Inuit* life his ancestors had once lived here.

"What's wrong?" Eric asked as he put two pancakes on Christopher's plate.

"I'm trying to understand why I'm here, eating this wonderful food while the *Inuit* people struggle to catch fish and shoot caribou to eke out a living from this land."

Eric dished up a plate for himself and poured maple syrup over the pancakes. "Yeah, the Eskimo life is tough."

Bristling at the racially insensitive comment, Christopher paused. "Eskimo is a white man's name for the *Inuit*. We don't use that term ourselves."

The slight smile on Eric's face hinted that he was testing Christopher. "I thought maybe you consider yourself more of a 'White Canadian' than an *Inuit*. Your blood quantum is only twenty-five percent."

"I'm a member of the *Inuit* nation. Like I said, blood quantum is something dreamt up by the Americans to test whether First Nations people are pure enough to deserve government handouts."

Eric chuckled. "The tribes seem to think it's a pretty good way to measure who gets casino profits, too."

Christopher set his half-eaten breakfast on the ground. "Did you drag me out here just to needle me about being less than full *Inuit*?"

Hesitating before he responded, Eric took another bite of pancake. "I thought maybe you could take a joke."

"What ethnicity is Curtis? Are you English? Do people kid you because you're not fully English?"

"Good guess. My family emigrated from England to the U.S. and became part of the melting pot there. Your *Inuit* relatives fight to keep from integrating themselves with the rest of the Canadian people."

"We're not immigrants, Eric. We are First People. *Inuit*s were living in Canada while Saxons and Gaels were still Roman subjects."

"You're quite a history student." Nodding toward Christopher's plate, Eric said. "Eat up. You'll burn every calorie on that plate later this morning."

After breakfast, Christopher and Eric broke down the tents and stowed their gear into the inflatable raft. Eric carefully secured coolers and gear inside the raft, then handed Christopher a life jacket and paddle. "You can wear the life jacket if you want. We won't run any rapids today."

Stepping into ankle deep icy water to push the raft from shore, Christopher leaped over the raft's inflated tube and settled in among the coolers and packs. The raft rocked as Eric jumped in and sat on the opposite side.

"How hard do we paddle?" Christopher asked.

Eric sat on top of the tube and surveyed the water ahead of them. "In this stretch, we only need to paddle enough to keep the raft from getting hung up on a sand bar or the shore. It'll be tougher when we get to the rapids."

"Are life jackets necessary there?"

Eric chuckled. "It all depends on your perspective. Nunavut requires them on any vessel carrying passengers. Personally, I don't see the need. We're not going to sink or get swamped, so it's not an issue. Besides, the water is so cold you would die of hypothermia before I could gather enough wood for a fire to warm you."

After glancing at Eric, who wasn't wearing a life jacket and was sitting on top of the inflated tube, Christopher asked, "Should I try to start a fire if you fall off the tube?"

"First of all, I'm not going to fall off the tube in flat water. Secondly, if I *do* fall into the river, you can just keep paddling because I'll be dead before you could get this raft back to me, pull me out of the water, get me to shore, and start a fire large enough to warm me up before my heart stops."

"Really? *Inuit* fishermen have survived overturned kayaks in freezing sea water."

"They were dressed in layers of sealskin that kept them warm and dry. In our cotton clothing, we'd be lucky to survive fifteen minutes in this icy water."

Mulling over that information, Christopher looked into the crystal-clear water and realized it was runoff from snow melting on the nearby hills. As if that wasn't cold enough, it drained across the permafrost. He dangled his fingers into the water, verifying that it was indeed as cold as the snow.

"Hey, Chief, you've got to keep paddling."

Bristling at the outfitter's cultural insensitivity, Christopher dipped his paddle deep and corrected the drift that was carrying them toward the shore. Getting into a mindless rhythm, he reflected on his grandfather's stories of whale hunters who'd been knocked from their kayaks and were never seen again.

* * *

Christopher's departure with the outfitter troubled Tatty as she patrolled Iqaluit. The outfitter had been too willing to show Christopher the land grant. And Christopher had been too willing to jump into a plane with a man he'd just met for the river trip.

Announcing her stop at The Lodge to her dispatcher, Tatty backed into a parking spot and walked through the lobby and into Hanta's room. Wolverine's empty bed was a stark reminder of the man's death. Walking past Wolverine's empty bed and dresser, she saw Hanta asleep. When she touched her nose to his cheek in a traditional *kunik,* kiss, his eyes popped open.

"Did you think I was dead?" he asked as he stretched.

"I don't think a pack of wolves could kill you, Grandfather."

Hanta pushed himself up, so his back was resting against the pillows. "It is good that you know that."

Tatty sat in the guest chair near the foot of the bed.

Hanta frowned and said, "You are troubled."

"Wolverine's grandson left with the outfitter to see the land grant."

Hanta, who was both an elder and shaman, nodded. "I had a vision. The spirit *Agloolik* overturned a boat, Christopher was not in it."

"Christopher and the outfitter flew to the river in a bush plane. He's not in a boat."

Hanta nodded, closing his eyes. Tatty, sure the old man had fallen asleep, stood. Before she could take a step, he spoke. "The airplane trip is no threat to Christopher. The danger lies in the Soper. *Agloolik* is unhappy and will take his fury out by upending their boat."

"Why would the spirit of the water be angry with Christopher?"

"Why is *Agloolik* ever angry? His moods are not for me to understand. But in this case, Christopher is the victim, but not the target of *Agloolik's* anger."

Knowing that many older Innuits believed in animism and shamanism meant they believed that the ills that befell a person or village were due to demon spirits. Being a college graduate and working in law enforcement, Tatty knew that most "bad luck" could be attributed to changing weather conditions, movement of the game herds, and often alcohol use leading to stupidity. Unwilling to argue Hanta's religion, world view, or visions, Tatty nodded.

Seeing the skepticism in Tatty's eyes, Hanta put out his hand. "Come to me, child."

Tatty sat on the edge of the bed and held Hanta's hand. "What is it?"

"You feel the same unease about Christopher's journey, but we perceive it differently. I see the challenges he'll face as his path to enlightenment and manhood. You fear the unknown. Together we believe Wolverine's grandson is facing danger."

"What should I do?"

Hanta shook his head slowly. "I can not answer that question for you. Only your spirit knows the answer to that question."

"I don't believe..."

Shushing her, Hanta squeezed her hand. "Your spirit is connected with Wolverine's grandson."

"I knew him as a child. I hardly know him now."

"Your spirit knows him in ways your mind doesn't. Follow your spirit."

"He hasn't been reported missing, so there's nothing I can do."

Hanta intertwined their fingers and gently squeezed. "You're confusing your job with what your spirit knows. A policeman might not be ready to look for Christopher. A true friend with a concerned spirit will act."

"But..."

"I'm tired now. Let me know what you've discovered tomorrow."

Tatty pulled the covers over Hanta's shoulders after he lay down. Sitting on the edge of the bed until his breathing slowed, she stared at his bony hands, scarred by fish hooks, frostbite, knives, and fire. Rolling his hand over to examine his palm, she saw a long scar across what a palm reader would call Hanta's lifeline. He snorted, and pulled his hand free, rolling over. Her career was filled with events that defied the principles of criminology. Justice was sometimes meted out without a courtroom. Lifelong criminals showed neither remorse nor contrition after they were sentenced. Innocent people were hurt, often without recourse.

Tatty stood and stared at the old man's gray hair. "Perhaps I've relied on my head too much and my spirit too little."

Leaving The Lodge, she drove to the Iqaluit RCMP office and parked in a spot reserved for police vehicles. The clerk, wearing a tan RCMP uniform without a badge, looked up and smiled when Tatty walked in. "How can I assist my favorite special constable?"

"Tell me there weren't any suicides or domestic assaults last night."

Carole McKittrick held out a pink slip. "None of those, but someone left a message for Special Constable Etok."

Tatty accepted the slip and read the brief message. *Please call Connie Kootoo.* Recalling that Connie was the person Christopher introduced to her at the Canada Day celebration, Tatty sat at her desk and dialed the number on the message slip. The phone was answered on the first ring. "Hello."

"Ms. Kootoo, this is RCMP Special Constable Etok. You left a message for me."

"Thank you for calling me back. Um, I expected a call from Christopher last night or this morning. When I didn't hear from him, I called his house, but didn't get an answer."

"He's gone on a river rafting trip with a local outfitter. They'll be gone for a few days."

"Constable Etok..."

"Please call me Tatty. Okay?"

"Um, Tatty, I have a bad feeling about this. Christopher and I have been talking about his grandfather's burial and plans of things we might do together. He never mentioned going on a raft trip. This seems so abrupt. I'm worried."

Tatty sighed. "He told me about it, but to be honest, I'm not thrilled about him taking off with this outfitter. The guy wants to negotiate a lease with Christopher. The whole suggestion of the raft trip seemed to come from nowhere."

"Tatty, I haven't seen Christopher for a couple of years, but when we spoke, I felt a connection. I didn't say anything to him, but he was the only person from our high school class who treated me with respect. I felt that again when we met. I mean, I felt connected. Now, I feel uneasy. Something isn't right."

"I'm sure Christopher will be safe and will come back to us in a few days."

"Tatty, are you sure he got on the plane with the outfitter?"

"I wasn't at the airport, but there's no reason to believe Christopher didn't get on the plane and fly off on a rafting trip."

"Something is very wrong. I can feel it. Is there some way you can contact him and warn him?"

"Connie, I'm sure he's fine."

"Please check on him. Please."

"I don't know of any way to contact him, but I'll try. Okay?"

"Tatty, Christopher is special."

"He's special to each of us. I'll check."

Tatty walked across the room. "Hi Carole, I'm filing a missing person report."

Carole turned in her chair and clicked her computer mouse to change screens. "Who is missing and where was the person last seen?"

Calmed and inspired by Hanta's words, Tatty sat in the only guest chair. "Christopher Pokaik flew away with an outfitter and a bush pilot yesterday."

"The pilot, outfitter, and your friend are all missing?"

Weighing her words, Tatty paused. She might be risking her career by filing a false report resulting in a large rescue operation. "This is an informal investigation right now. Christopher Pokaik and Eric Curtis, the outfitter, haven't been seen since the plane dropped them off at the Soper River yesterday."

Carole turned. "Do you have reason to believe they're in danger?"

"I do."

As Carole typed, she said, "You know we usually wait 24 hours before starting search and rescue operations."

"I know."

Sensing the earnestness of Tatty's request, Carole finished typing and turned. "I'll submit the report, but you know that there are only a hundred Mounties covering all of Nunavut. I'll contact Kimmirut, but the Mountie there may have something more pressing to deal with." As she typed, the clerk paused and looked at Tatty. "You started this process with Heidi Price in the Katannilik Park office, didn't you?"

"I was afraid foul play was involved, so I came here first."

"Every Katannilik Park visitor is required to register when they leave and again when they complete their trip. The registration form will tell you where the charter dropped them off and when they expect to reach Kimmirut. Heidi can look at their permit and tell you exactly where they are."

"Good suggestion. I'll stop by the park office."

As Tatty stood, Carole stopped her. "Tatty, your friend should be okay. There are tours on the river every couple of days this time of year. If he's in trouble, someone will see him and help."

"I wish there was a way to reach him."

"A lot of Katannilik Park is in a valley. Even if he has a satellite phone, he might not get reception."

"I'll check with the park office."

The clerk nodded. "They can notify new groups flying in. They can at least watch for them on the river." Carole frowned, accenting the worry lines on her forehead. "I'll ask the bush pilots to look for your missing men when they overfly the area."

* * *

The young *Inuit* woman refilling slots with travel brochures was startled when she looked up and saw Tatty's uniform. Initially unsure of whether to ignore the officer or to address her, the worker froze.

"Feeling guilty, Kammi?"

The woman nervously jammed all the remaining brochures she was holding into one slot. Her tension was palpable, and a sheen of sweat appeared on her forehead. "No. I'm just...working."

"Working as in serving your sentence."

Kammi drew a breath and let it out. "You know that I am."

"Did Eric Curtis file a registration package for a Soper River rafting tour?"

"Not today."

"He flew out with Christopher Pokaik yesterday."

"I wasn't working yesterday."

Although her personal history with Kammi was filled with legal confrontations, it was Kammi's poor choices that led to her repeated arrests for drug use and abandonment of her children while she partied. Tatty contained her frustration. "Could you check the file to see if he registered for a trip yesterday?"

Kammi crossed her arms. "I'm not sure how to do that."

"Where would you file a new registration?"

Glancing at the only desk in the small office, Kammi said, "I suppose I'd put it in the tray on the desk so Heidi could file it when she came in.”

“Could you look in the tray to see if there’s a registration form there?”

Kammi walked slowly to the desk and flipped through the sheets of paper in the tray. “You know I’ve been clean for three weeks now, right?”

“That’s a start, Kammi.”

Dropping the sheaf of papers back into the tray, Kammi looked up. “There aren’t any registration forms there at all.”

“Do you think Heidi might’ve already filed it?”

Shrugging, Kammi said, “I don’t know.”

“Could you look?”

“I don’t know which file it would be in.”

“Sit down at the desk and open the file drawer. Look for a thick file that is labelled registrations.”

Kammi glared at her but did as Tatty suggested. “You don’t have to be snotty about it.”

“I’m not being snotty, Kammi. I’m asking you to do your job.”

“Well, I don’t know exactly what my job is. The judge dumped on me and sentenced me to volunteer hours.”

“Heidi trained you.”

After rolling her eyes, Kammi separated the files, reading the labels. “It’s not like I paid attention. Once I do my fifty hours of community service, I’ll be out of here.”

Tatty walked across the room and pulled a chair in front of Kammi. "Listen to me. Heidi will fill out an evaluation when you've completed your hours. When you apply for a job after this, the people who hire you will probably want to see Heidi's recommendation letter."

"Why would anyone care how well I sorted brochures and answered the phone if I'm going to end up in some shit hole washing dishes?"

"It never occurred to you that doing a good job here and receiving a glowing recommendation from Heidi might lead to something other than a shitty job washing dishes?"

Giving up on her search, Kammi slammed the file drawer shut. "This is a small town. Everyone knows I was busted for using drugs a couple of times. Why would they hire me to do anything but wash dishes?"

"You can change what people think. You don't have to hang around with Derrick. Stay home and watch television with your mom and kids."

"Derrick feeds me."

"He also gave you the drugs you've been busted for, and he's the one who pimped you out when he was broke."

Kammi turned away. "There's no registration file here. Call Kimmirut to see if Curtis filed one with their office."

Tatty stood and stared down at Kammi, who refused to look at her. "Listen, sister. The point of this community service isn't to punish you. It's to give you a new start."

"Maybe I'm not looking for a new start, Ms. Mountie. Maybe I'm happy with my life as it is." Kammi paused, then added, "It's not like I'll ever be anything but Kammi the druggie in Iqaluit."

Tatty walked out and thought, *Especially, if being a drug user is all you ever aspire to. I pity your kids. Or maybe they'll take after their grandma, who's caring and reliable.*

Chapter 10

Soper River Day 3

Dinner was stroganoff over wide egg noodles, its lush aroma of the herbs and spices caused Christopher's stomach to start growling as he set up his tent. Spreading his pad and sleeping bag on the ground allowed him a few moments away from Eric. There wasn't a lot of conversation between them, and Christopher hadn't initiated any of it. Most of the outfitter's comments were what must've been his standard guide banter, pointing out changing landscape and reciting the geological history of Baffin Island. The natural history lesson made Christopher feel like he was back in elementary school.

The rattling of aluminum plates broke Christopher's thoughts. "I'm dishing up your supper," Eric yelled as Christopher climbed out of the tent. "Stroganoff over noodles with honey carrots on the side."

After collecting his plate, heaped high with food, Christopher sat on the ground and scooped up a forkful of stroganoff. The meat was tender, the noodles al dente, and the sauce creamy and savory.

"Aren't you going to compliment the chef?" Eric asked.

"It's good."

"That's it?"

"I like it."

"I don't get your people. Most *Inuit* live solitary lives. I'd think you'd jump on a chance to have a conversation with someone."

Christopher considered Eric's comments before replying. "I only talk when I have something to say. There's not much point to small talk."

Eric seemed surprised by the frank response. "Okay, tell me about school."

"I'm taking summer classes between my third and fourth years. I'm writing a paper this summer on the US Air Force base that became Iqaluit."

"Huh. The U.S. Air Force built Iqaluit?"

"The United States needed a fueling stop between Newfoundland and Greenland for their intermediate range planes during World War II."

"What was there before the Air Force showed up?"

"Iqaluit means the place of many fish, so it was a fishing village during the summer."

"What did the residents eat in the winter?"

"You know the history as well as I do. My people were nomadic, going wherever there was food. They hunted seals, whales, and caribou. During the summer they fished.”

Eric chuckled. “And because they were competing with the polar bears for food, the hunters sometimes became the hunted.” When Christopher didn’t respond, Eric smiled. “Mother nature is cruel.”

“Cruelty implies intent. Nature isn’t cruel, it’s unforgiving.”

“Nah, Mother Nature is a cruel bitch. There’s no three strikes and you’re out here in the Arctic. You mess up once and you end up dead.”

After helping clean the plates and cookware, Christopher stared at a small Dutch oven sitting on a low burner. “What’s that?”

Eric made a show of looking at his waterproof watch. “In two minutes, that’ll be the best peach cobbler you’ve ever eaten.”

“I never ate peaches when I was growing up.”

Eric laughed as he turned off the stove and lifted the lid off the Dutch oven. “I suppose you get a few berries if you beat the birds to them.”

“We get the same fruit as you do at the Iqaluit grocery store,” Christopher replied. “Grandfather didn’t like peaches.”

Eric made a show of dishing up the steaming cobbler onto two plates. After handing a plate to Christopher, Eric patted a canister of bear repellent spray on his belt. “I hope your bear spray is handy. The polar bears love peaches."

"You can save the bear attack stories for your tourists. The bears hunt seals along the coastline. I've never seen one more than a mile from the ocean."

Eric's smirk was his only answer.

* * *

At the end of her shift, Tatty called Connie. "I'm chasing down every lead we have, but I don't have any information about Christopher."

Connie sighed. "I feel hollow, like I've lost my connection. Do you know what I mean?"

"My grandfather is a shaman. He often has visions and feelings that later turn out to be true. Hang in there."

"Please don't tell Christopher this; I felt butterflies when I saw him on Canada Day. It was like something I'd been missing was returned."

"Let's assume he's just rafting down the river and everything is fine. I'll keep chasing down people who might be able to verify that." Tatty paused, "There's something you could do for me."

"Name it."

"Buniq Tengenek is missing from Cape Dorset. Could you ask people to be on the lookout for her?"

"Sure. Give me her description. I'll make an announcement during my radio show."

Tatty warmed leftover pizza for supper. The CBC news was depressing. Jean Chretien, the Prime Minister, was berating the House of Commons over their reluctance to press ahead with the Canadian Environmental Protection Act. Grimacing, Tatty wondered what that meant for Nunavut. The *Inuit* people were one with the environment, but sometimes acted in ways that were contrary to the law. Hunting and fishing were now confined to seasons and bag limits. Although an individual *Inuk* didn't harvest more than he needed and always shared his bounty with his relatives and neighbors, his seasons were defined by the availability of game and fish, not the territorial laws or calendar.

Tatty reflected on Hanta's old memories of the U.S. Air Force building the Iqaluit airfield. Due to the times and the necessities of war, the airmen polluted the ground with gasoline, antifreeze, cleaning chemicals, and sewage. Supplementing the Air Force crews were *Inuit* workers who'd never dealt with airplanes, trucks, or support equipment before, so they were unfamiliar with the hazards presented by the machines, fuels, and chemicals.

Iqaluit was built where a fishing village was situated. In 1943, the new town was filled with young airmen who were far from home, unaccustomed to the weather, and ignorant of *Inuit* customs, language, or beliefs. The Air Force hired *Inuit* hunters and fishermen to feed the men posted at the base, as well as the air crews ferrying planes to Europe. The result was a culture clash of epic proportions with a near extinction of the local caribou herds. A variety of unfamiliar diseases were transmitted to the *Inuit* population, along with chaos involving alcohol, theft, rape, jealousy, pregnancies, and a few murders. One of Tatty's teachers likened the 1940s in Iqaluit to the American Wild West. Luckily, most of the Americans left shortly after the war, and a new normal came to Iqaluit that was a blend of American, Canadian, and *Inuit* cultures. The *Inuit* elders hoped to retain the best of all the cultures. The reality was a mixed bag of the good and bad from each.

The beeping microwave jerked Tatty's thoughts back to supper. Removing the pizza slices from the microwave, she reflected on Christopher. A man, yet a boy. School smart, but not worldly. Torn between two cultures without acceptance in either, with a potential girlfriend who was very concerned about him.

Shaking her head, Tatty spent a moment reflecting. *I wish I'd been raised a Christian, with a loving God who listened to prayers. Instead, I live in Hanta's world of mean, shapeshifting spirits who punish rather than save people. Christopher, I hope it's your Anglican God who's looking over you,*

*helping to ward off Agloolik, who wants to
overturn your boat and Anguta, who wants
to steal your soul.*

Chapter 11

Soper River Day 4

Christopher slept fitfully. He'd never recalled his previous dreams, but he woke several times during the night to vivid dreams filled with colors and smells. At one point, he awoke to the smell of bread baking in his mother's kitchen, feeling her presence everywhere, but unable to find her.

Later that same night, he'd awoken to a sound outside the tent. Grabbing Hanta's knife, he'd unzipped the tent to find nothing but the lingering twilight of the Nunavut July night. He'd scanned the area, thinking that Eric was playing a trick on him, but then heard snoring in Eric's tent some ten meters away. A chill ran over him as he thought about Eric's reminder about polar bears. The knife in his hand would be useless against a bear. The chill of the air made him shiver and the onslaught of hungry mosquitoes made him retreat to his sleeping bag listening for the sound he'd heard in his dream.

Hours later, Christopher awoke to the smell of perking coffee. At first, he was sure it was another dream, then he heard the sound of the skillet being set on the camp stove. The coffee aroma melded with the smell of frying bacon as he stepped out of his tent and pulled on his jacket.

"Good morning, Chief. I thought you were going to sleep through breakfast."

Christopher picked up a cup and poured himself a cup of coffee. After a sip of coffee, he said, "*Inuits* don't have chiefs."

Eric smiled. "It was an honorary title I bestowed upon you."

Shaking his head, Christopher sipped his coffee, trying not to be baited by the outfitter's comments, yet making it clear that his slurs were unwelcome. "Do you tell your clients that the *Inuit* have chiefs?"

"I generally discuss the hunting and fishing prowess of the *Inuit* people. We don't usually talk about your class structure or politics."

"What class structure would that be?"

Eric slid the bacon onto two plates, then poured pancake batter into the pan. "You know, how the male elders rule over the tribes. How the medicine men, like your grandpa, pray to your spirits."

"We have families, not tribes. There is some geographical segregation of *Inuit* groups that's resulted in different dialects of our language. Grandpa was a shaman, an *angekkok* who meditated to hear the spirits. The *Inuit* don't have medicine men."

Eric snorted. "What do you practice? Are you an *Inuit* shaman too? Is being able to meditate with the spirits something that's passed down from one generation to the next? The Irish have this belief about the seventh son of the seventh son having second sight. It is like that with you people?"

"I think that's a rhetorical question. You know the answer."

Curtis grinned. "I might know more about the *Inuit* people than you do. Wolverine told me you grew up in the Christian church. You believe in heaven and hell."

Christopher accepted the plate of pancakes and bacon, then poured maple syrup over the stack of cakes. "A friend told me that I practice religious syncretism; a mixture of Anglican and *Inuit* spirituality."

"Ah, you're a half breed in blood and religion."

Feeling baited again, Christopher focused on his meal. Finishing his pancakes, he decided to change the topic. "The shoreline along the river is changing. There are a lot more hummocks and swampy areas here."

Taking Christopher's plate and silverware, Eric nodded. "The landscape was rockier where we landed. Tonight, we'll camp in an area where there are willows in a valley. It's a unique ecosystem to Baffin Island, found only in that small area."

Swatting at a black fly that was biting his ankle, Christopher cocked his head. "There's a grove of willows along the river?"

"There are a couple of spots that have microclimates where willows grow. Some willows are nearly two meters tall. They're the tallest plants in Nunavut."

"You're joking."

Eric shook his head. "There are even more flies and mosquitoes there than there are here. They'll suck you dry in an afternoon if you don't spray on some bug juice and wear a head net." Eric paused. "One of my *Inuit* guides said mosquitoes are proof that there is no loving God, only *Inuit* demons who allow the mosquitoes to suck the blood and life spirit from you."

Once in the raft, Christopher mulled over the outfitter's comments about his Anglican God versus the *Inuit* spirit world. While his Sunday school lessons talked about the loving miracles Jesus had performed, the Old Testament lessons were closer to the spirit world stories told by Wolverine. The Old Testament God was vindictive and punitive. Much like the demons in the northern lights, the God of Moses demanded sacrifices and his believers had to kill or be killed. Noah, who built an ark, saved only two animals of each species while the rest of the world flooded. The Old Testament God sounded more like an *Inuit* spirit than the loving God of the New Testament.

"You're pretty quiet, Chief."

"My grandfather taught me that I had two ears and one mouth. They should be used in that proportion."

"That's deep philosophy for an old *Inuit* hunter."

"The old hunters have a lot to teach us if we open our minds and listen. You've been so busy spouting facts that you found in an encyclopedia that you've forgotten to listen to the spirits around you."

Eric snorted, then continued paddling. "What do you think about the land?"

"I don't know what you mean."

"The *Inuit* people were nomads. I don't think they owned land. They wandered between sites as they hunted and fished."

Christopher sensed more in the question than was spoken. "I think the *Inuit* collectively *owned* all of Nunavut. That's what the Canadian government recognized in the land grant that created Nunavut Territory."

"That's a pretty grand statement, the tribe owning a whole territory."

Christopher tried to understand Curtis, his motives, and the question. "First of all, there is no Inuit *tribe*. We are a people, who now have our own government. But we are different from the First Nations like the Cree and Blackfoot tribes. We are First People, not First Nations. There is a difference."

Curtis waved off Christopher's comments. "You're all descended from the same genes. All of the North America native people are members of some tribe. Don't you have a membership card that identifies you as an *Inuit* tribe member?"

"You seem to know more than I do about my heritage," Christopher said, deciding against further argument, rather than agreeing with Curtis' view of native people.

The monotony of the river left Christopher's mind time to wander. He thought about Tatty, who spoke with the voice of an older sister, and Connie, whose smile made his heart flutter and whose voice made him forget his sadness. On the other hand, Eric Curtis' culturally insensitive remarks were starting to build a wall between them. No matter how many facts Eric quoted about the river, geography, and animals, his prejudice against the *Inuit* people was becoming clearer and more irritating.

Eric's voice pulled Christopher back from his thoughts. "A stream comes in from the right after we go around this bend. We'll have to paddle hard to avoid being pushed into the opposite bank."

"Um, sure."

"After the stream, we'll hit the first set of rapids. They're small, only Class I, but it'll prepare you for the later, more challenging stretches. Remember, the rocks are hidden where the water swells. The white-water breaks past the rocks. We'll paddle between the swells to keep the raft in the deepest part of the channel and off the rocks."

"Is there anything else I should know?" Christopher asked as they passed the mouth of the stream.

Paddling to keep them near the center of the river, Eric replied, "Yeah. If you hear the raft scraping on a rock, hang on. The current will whip the raft around and we'll be floating backwards in the blink of an eye."

"That sounds bad," Christopher replied.

"The raft doesn't know front from back. Just turn so you're paddling downstream."

"Is there anything else I should know?" Christopher asked as the white froth of the first rapids appeared ahead of them.

"The water is damned cold. Don't fall out of the raft."

As directed, Christopher paddled for the areas between the rocks, the current pushing them along in a rush like a carnival ride. Paddling for control, not propulsion, was different and difficult. Eric shouted out directions as they splashed through the short rocky stretch of rapids. Surging with adrenaline, Christopher took a deep breath after they cleared the last rock. "That was epic!"

Snorting, Eric replied, "If you think that was exciting, just wait until we hit the Class II rapids closer to Kimmirut."

"What are the most challenging rapids you've ever been through?"

Eric paused. "I think the Class IV rapids on Idaho's Snake River are the toughest I've ever experienced. We wear helmets and life vests, and even then, we strap everyone into the raft. The old guides told us that if we fell overboard, we should keep our feet in front of us so we could push off the rocks. That trip through the rapids was a rush like nothing else I've ever felt."

"You said we're going through Class II rapids downstream. They won't be tough?"

"As a rookie, they're all the challenge you'll need."

* * *

After patrolling Iqaluit and encountering no speeders or crime, Tatty parked outside The Lodge. Hanta was sitting in a chair looking out of the window. The bare second mattress in the room reminded her that Wolverine was gone.

Walking behind Hanta, Tatty put her hands on his shoulders and leaned close to rub her nose against his cheek, giving him a *kunik*.

"Tanaraq, I've been expecting you."

Tatty pulled a straight-backed chair from the room's small desk and sat across from Hanta. "Did you have a vision of my visit?"

"No. There are things you need to do, so I need you."

Thinking of all the issues that arose with Hanta's sometimes inappropriate behavior in The Lodge, Tatty braced herself. "What do I need to do?"

Hanta stared into her eyes, preparing to give an earnest declaration. "They serve us too much chicken."

Stifling a laugh, Tatty smiled. "What's wrong with chicken?"

Hanta wrinkled his nose. "Man was not meant to eat birds raised in cages."

"Doesn't it taste good?"

"They prepare it many ways; fried, creamed, in casseroles, but it's still chicken. I'd rather have caribou or fish. I'd love to have a bowl of your grandmother's caribou or even ptarmigan stew. The whole house filled with the aroma of her stew when it cooked."

Reaching out, Tatty took her grandfather's hand. "Grandma is gone, and so is her stew recipe."

"Didn't she teach you how to make it?"

"Grandma was very secretive. I cut up meat and onions for the meal, but she never showed me her secret seasonings. It's too bad she never wrote down the recipe."

"Her fried grayling was wonderful."

Tatty's involuntary grimace made Hanta smile.

"What's the matter, Tanaraq. Don't you like fish?"

"Fish is just fine. I don't like eating the entire fish, guts and all."

"Aah, child, eating the whole animal is what keeps us healthy. The white fur traders who came to buy seal skins ate only the meat from the caribou. They grew weak and sick until we fed them raw liver and seal brains."

Tatty shuddered. "I can't believe that you ate raw seal brains, Grandfather."

"The shamans taught us that the health provided by the liver and brains leaves with the cooking smoke."

"Yeah, we were taught in school that cooking destroys the vitamins in our food. But still, I'm not going to carve off a slab of caribou liver and eat it raw."

A hint of a smile crossed Hanta's face. "This talk about raw caribou liver is making my mouth water."

"I can assure you that the cook won't serve raw caribou liver for supper. Eat your chicken and take your vitamin pills. You'll be healthy."

When Hanta gazed out of the window and seemed to mentally drift away, Tatty cocked her head. "I'm sorry you don't like eating chicken."

Without looking back, Hanta said, "Wolverine's grandson is in trouble."

"What kind of trouble?"

Hanta shrugged. "The spirits came to me last night. They told me that it was important for him to have the knife nearby."

"I don't know what that means."

"An *Inuk* always carries a knife. There are demons in the northern lights chasing our spirits across the sky. An *Inuk* needs a knife to defend himself."

"You told me that the spirits in the northern lights played ball with a walrus skull."

"That's when they're happy. When they're unhappy, they are demons who come looking for *Inuit* spirits to steal. If you're unprepared, they'll steal your spirit and play ball with your skull."

Tatty clasped her hands and wondered what she was being told. "I don't understand. What demons are chasing Christopher?"

"He will never know until he's facing them," Hanta said. After a moment, he added, "Demons are shapeshifters. Some appear friendly until you let your guard down. Those are the most dangerous kind."

"Are you saying that Christopher is going to be confronted by a demon who appears to be a friend?"

Hanta scoffed. "If I knew that, I would've warned him. The truth is, Christopher won't recognize the demon until it bares his teeth. He'll need to have his knife ready before he knows the nature of the demon, or it will carry his *iñuusiq*, his life spirit, away before he can pull his knife."

"Tell me more."

Hanta shifted his weight forward in the chair and pushed himself up. "Help me to my bed. I need to rest."

Holding Hanta's arm, Tatty walked across the room with her grandfather. "Christopher has a girlfriend who has called me. She's worried."

"I saw that cloud in his sky."

"What does that mean?"

"Shapeshifters sometimes appear as women. They will steal your spirit while they're warming your body."

Tatty chuckled. "I think most people refer to that as stealing your heart."

"It's the same thing. They leave you surrounded by children who need to be fed and cared for."

"Some men want that."

"It's a burden to have so many spirits dependent on you."

"What should I do about Christopher?"

Hanta sat on the bed and stared at the floor. "Christopher will face his demon alone. You can warn him, but it is up to him to defend himself."

"Will Christopher win?"

Hanta lay back and stared at the ceiling. "That story is yet to be written, Tanaraq."

Mulling her grandfather's words, Tatty walked out of The Lodge. *Where are you, Christopher? Are you prepared for the demon?* Sitting in her police car, she searched for some way of warning Christopher. What threat was he facing?

She drove to the small private charter terminal and walked inside. Unlike the main terminal, where the two scheduled airlines had counters with service people, the charter terminal offered chairs. A part-time manager served all of the outfitters and bush pilots who flew from Iqaluit to the outlying communities.

Charlie Ma, the terminal manager, was sitting at the desk reading a magazine. He glanced up when he heard Tatty walk in but didn't set his magazine aside. "What's up, Tatty?"

"I'm looking for the pilot who flew an outfitter and one client to the Soper River two days ago."

"I don't keep track of who's flying when or where. I just connect people with their pilots."

Tatty leaned on the desk, her face only a foot away from Charlie's. "You have the memory of an elephant, Charlie. Don't bullshit me."

A smile crept across Charlie's face, and he sat up. "You're looking for whoever flew Eric Curtis and his client out. Eric is the only one who's chartered a flight to paddle the Soper in the past few days."

"That sounds right. Who was the pilot and is he around today?"

Charlie pulled out a dog-eared notebook and flipped through the pages. "I think Wes Sharp is in his hangar working on his plane. Do you want me to give him a call?"

"Tell me where his hangar is. I'll walk back and talk to him."

Glancing at Tatty's constable badge, Charlie hesitated. "A lot of the guys would prefer that I call to tell them there's a visitor rather than having someone walk back to their hangar." After a pause, Charlie added, "It's sometimes unsafe to be around the planes and tools while they're working on them."

Knowing that some of the bush pilots occasionally delivered alcohol to communities with liquor bans, Tatty knew why the pilots wouldn't want a constable walking unannounced into their hangars. "Fine, give Wes a call and tell him there's a constable here to see him."

Charlie picked up the desk phone and dialed a number from memory. It took several rings before the call was answered. "Hey, Wes, there's a constable here in the terminal who wants to talk to you." After listening for a moment, Charlie looked at Tatty. "She didn't say why she wanted to talk to you. Do you want me to send her back to your hangar, or would you rather talk to her up here?"

Smiling, Tatty waited for the pilot's reply.

"Um, no. She's listening to my conversation, so telling her you're not here is not an option." After a few more seconds, Charlie hung up the phone. "He'll be right up after he cleans the grease off his hands. Can I get you a cup of coffee or tea?"

"If you think he'll be more than a minute or two, I would love a cup of tea."

Rising from his chair, Charlie stretched. "If Wes was deep into his engine, it might take him more than a couple of minutes to clean the grease off his hands."

Tatty followed Charlie to a small counter with a coffee maker equipped with a hot water spigot. "The tea options are in the box to your left. I'll draw a cup of hot water."

The tea choices were surprisingly diverse, probably reflecting the variety of passengers served by the bush pilots. Tatty chose an English breakfast tea packet and tore it open as Charlie ran hot water into a ceramic cup with a Cessna logo.

"I don't suppose Wes is one of the pilots who transports illegal booze to the communities with alcohol bans."

Charlie handed Tatty the cup. With a look of pure innocence, he said, "I wouldn't know anything about that."

"There's a teenage girl missing from Cape Dorset. I don't suppose you saw her get off one of the bush planes returning from there."

"I don't think any of the pilots have been to Cape Dorset recently. How long ago did she disappear?"

Tatty dunked her tea bag and smiled. "You know damned well that she disappeared last Thursday. It was in the newspaper, there are posters on the board in the waiting room, and it's the hot topic of conversation in the cafés."

A look of recognition swept Charlie's face. "Oh, her. I don't think any of the pilots would fly a girl away from her village."

"Her parents are worried."

Charlie nodded. "I imagine her father has no one to beat anymore, now that she's gone."

Tatty dropped the tea bag into a wastebasket and sipped the steaming brew. "What makes you say her father won't have anyone to beat anymore?"

"Like you said, her disappearance is the hot topic in town. People say she ran away from an abusive situation."

"If that's true, there are social services to deal with her home situation. Kidnapping her from her parents is a crime, regardless of what's happening in her parents' house."

Charlie looked out of the window as a plane landed on the nearest runway. "It's a shame the kids in those remote villages think the rest of the world is heaven. I suspect that the life of a runaway is more hellish than the escape to Disneyland they expect when they leave home."

"So, you don't know what happened to her?"

Charlie shook his head. "I'm afraid I can't help you, Tatty."

"Can't help, or won't?"

Charlie sat at his desk and stared at Tatty. "I'm not in the human smuggling business. I feel sorry for some of those kids, but I'm not the one who's solving their problems by relocating them."

"And you don't know of anyone who is?"

"Nope."

A door opened in the back of the terminal, and a rail thin man with a short military haircut walked in. His greasy coveralls were either a great disguise, or he had actually been working on his plane. He offered his hand to Tatty. She noticed the odor of Go-Jo grease remover. The grease stains ground into his fingertips and along the edges of his fingernails were evidence that he was a hands-on mechanic and pilot.

"I'm Wes Sharp."

Tatty introduced herself, then gestured toward the small terminal's dark corner farthest from Charlie's desk. "I'm trying to locate Christopher Pokaik. I think he flew out of here for a Soper River rafting trip, but the outfitter didn't file a trip registration form with the Territorial Park office."

"I've got nothing to do with filing paperwork for the outfitters."

"I understand that. I'm trying to confirm when and where they flew."

Sharp ran his hand over his short hair. "I dropped them off at Mount Joy. Eric told me he'd call from Kimmirut when they arrived there."

Tatty took out a notebook and wrote, Mount Joy. "When did you drop them off and when do you expect to pick them up?"

"I dropped them off two days ago, and I expect to pick them up on Friday or Saturday. Eric said their pickup date would depend on the river conditions."

"Did everything seem okay between the two passengers?" Tatty asked.

The pilot shrugged. "I guess. We unloaded Eric's gear, and I took off."

"Christopher didn't seem reluctant to go?"

"As far as I could tell, they were fine. They were hauling gear out and getting ready to set up camp."

"Where would you expect them to be after two days on the river?"

Sharp shook his head. "I'm not a river guide."

Tatty nodded. "I understand that, but you do fly over the entire river. What's the halfway point?"

"The Livingstone River feeds into the Soper about halfway to Kimmirut."

"Is the river any more dangerous after that point than it is in the early part of the trip?"

"None of it is very dangerous. I mean, the early part is placid and slow. There are some rapids farther down the river, but they're not like the ones you see on TV. There's a small set of falls just before the river enters Soper Lake, but they portage around that area and get back into the raft after the falls."

Tatty's mind flashed to pictures she'd seen of the falls entering Soper Lake. They weren't like Niagara Falls, more like a set of steps as the river dropped in altitude. "Thanks, Mr. Sharp." Tatty closed her notebook, then looked up. "You wouldn't know anything about the girl who disappeared from Cape Dorset, would you?"

Sharp's posture stiffened. "If you're asking what I think you're asking, I'm not in the business of flying runaways."

"Do you know anyone who would fly her out of Cape Dorset?"

"Listen, the bush pilots may be a little loosey-goosey on their flight logs, and some are downright crazy, but we're not human smugglers. None of us."

Tatty smiled and stood. "That's good to hear." As she walked away, she thought, *I hope that's the truth.* Her cell phone rang as she approached her vehicle. Struggling to get the phone out of her pocket before it rolled over to voicemail, she nearly dropped it. "Hello."

"Constable Etok?"

"Yes."

"This is Jerome Kinsey. You asked me to notify you when I'd scheduled the coroner's inquest for Wolverine Pokaik."

"Yes. I apologize for not answering formally. My mind was elsewhere."

"That's okay. Most people aren't expecting a call from the coroner. There's been a complication."

"What kind of complication?"

"Because of your suspicion about Wolverine's death, I delivered his body to the hospital for a post-mortem exam. Since the pathologist only flies to Iqaluit one day a week, I can't schedule the inquest until his office confirms which day he'll be here. Perhaps you can help me out. I've been trying to reach Wolverine Pokaik's grandson, to notify him that the burial will have to be delayed. His cell phone rolls over to voicemail. Do you have another phone number or some other means to contact him?"

"He's on a week-long river rafting trip."

After a pause, the coroner added, "I can't find a secondary contact."

"I suppose I'm the backup contact for Christopher."

"Can you reach him?"

"He'll be out of contact for several days. Wolverine raised Christopher, and his grandson is the primary contact." Tatty paused. "Have you notified the RCMP of your post-mortem and inquest plans?"

"I spoke with Sergeant Carson a bit ago. She dispatched someone to collect the bedding and towels from Wolverine Pokaik's room for forensic analysis."

"Thank you for taking this seriously. My grandfather is Wolverine's roommate and we're concerned."

"Constable Etok, be careful. It sounds like you may be too close to this investigation to be objective."

After ending the call, Tatty thought, *The coroner may be right. I can't be objective anymore. The Pokaiks are my extended family.*

* * *

Hanta was away from his room when Tatty arrived. Wolverine's side of the room was bare. His bedding was gone, and his dresser drawers were ajar, as if someone had searched them, but not closed them completely afterwards.

She found Hanta sitting in a sunroom chair with his eyes closed. Tatty gave him a *kunik* on the cheek, causing his eyes to pop open. "Granddaughter, I was just thinking about you."

After pulling a chair alongside Hanta, Tatty sat. "Why was I on your mind?"

"I had a vision of you married, living in a small house, with five children seated at the kitchen table."

"Why would I marry someone? I'm a strong woman with a good job."

Hanta seemed surprised by the question. "Who hunts and fishes for you? Come winter, who warms your bed?"

"I earn enough to buy food and heat my own house."

Frowning, Hanta shook his head. "It's not a woman's role to be the head of the household."

"We've had this discussion before. Just because I'm not married doesn't mean that I'll starve or die lonely. I prefer my own company to a bossy husband and a pack of rowdy children."

Hanta shifted in his chair, obviously unhappy with the discussion. "You seek my counsel but ignore my advice."

"I didn't come here for relationship advice. I came to talk about Wolverine."

Sighing, Hanta shook his head. "For some reason, Wolverine's spirits are troubled. They're unable to pass into the cloud world."

"What do you see when you look for Wolverine's life spirit?"

"I see the underworld with pots of boiling sea blubber. His spirit needs to be freed."

"I spoke with the coroner. He said Wolverine didn't die of natural causes. The Mounties are investigating."

Hanta snorted. "I knew he didn't die of natural causes."

Stiffening, Tatty put her hand on Hanta's arm. "You knew that Wolverine was killed?"

"Of course, I knew. His teeth were on the table."

"I'm confused about his teeth. Tell me more."

"Wolverine was vain. He never rose from bed without putting his teeth in."

"He was found on the bathroom floor. Why would he put his teeth in to go to the bathroom?"

"You are not hearing my words. Wolverine went nowhere without his teeth. Nowhere."

"Did you see someone in the room before he died?"

Folding his hands, Hanta closed his eyes. "I saw many things the night that Wolverine died. *Anguta*, the spirit of death, visited me in a dream. I thought he'd come for me, but I awoke still alive."

"Did you see any *humans* in your room?"

Hanta's watery eyes looked at Tatty and whispered, "There was a woman wearing a black vest."

Tatty edged closer. "She wore a black vest. What else was she wearing?"

"I don't recall. I just remember her vest said, 'POLICE.'"

Rolling her eyes, Tatty leaned back. "Did you see RCMP Sergeant Carson when you woke up?"

"Yes. She was in the bathroom with Nurse Gustafson. They were kneeling over Wolverine's body."

"Did you see anyone in the room before that?"

Hanta shook his head. "No, but I felt *Anguta's* presence. The evil one who steals spirits must've come for Wolverine."

Tatty stood and was struck by a sudden thought. "There's a girl, Buniq Tingenek, who's missing from Cape Dorset. Ask the spirits about her."

Hanta scowled. "I don't ask the spirits. They come to me when they want me to know things."

"Have the spirits said anything to you about Buniq?"

Turning his head so he could look at Tatty, Hanta said, "Do not worry about her."

"Her family is concerned."

"The girl's life spirit is happy. Tell them not to worry."

Tatty froze, knowing that an *Inuit* life spirit can be happy in a good way, eating well, being warm, and enjoying happiness. Or a shaman like Hanta could see her life spirit being happy because it was freed from her physical body and moved to a different physical form, either as another child, or as an animal. "Is she happy as the child she was, or is she happy in a new form?"

Considering the question, Hanta continued to stare at Tatty. "It is not for me to know which form she has taken. I can only see a happy aura around her life spirit. Tell her family not to worry. Her life spirit is happy."

"Her life spirit is happy. But she's alive?"

Hanta raised his eyebrows. "That's hard to say. Life spirits in Qudlivun are sometimes happier than when they're suffering among us."

Tatty grimaced. "So, is she among us, or has her spirit moved to the cloud realm?"

Nodding his head, Hanta answered, "Yes, she's in one or the other."

"Which?" Tatty asked.

"Some things are not as clear as a special constable might want them to be. With time, all will be answered."

As she walked away, Tatty considered Hanta's somewhat infuriating view of spirits and their happiness. *I'm pleased the missing girl's iñuusiq spirit is happy. But the RCMP would like to know if her physical body is somewhere safe, or if her iñuusiq is happy because her life spirit has been released from her physical body and is at peace in death.*

Chapter 12

Soper River Day 4

After breakfast, Christopher and Eric loaded the gear into the raft for another day of paddling. The river moved more slowly than it had during the previous days. The landscape changed; the shore less swampy than it had been farther upstream. They beached the raft on a small spit of sand adjacent to a rocky slab and Eric unpacked bread and cold cuts from the cooler.

"No gourmet lunch today?" Christopher asked.

"I'm trying to move along so we can finish the trip tomorrow." Eric pointed to the stream that flowed into the Soper just past the point where they'd stopped. "I take our clients up to the waterfall here, but after you've seen one waterfall, you've seen them all. Besides, the mosquitoes will just about carry you away walking upstream."

"Don't your clients complain about the mosquitoes?"

Curtis laughed. "They are part of the Soper River ambiance."

"Do you mind if I walk to the waterfall while you prepare lunch?"

"Squirt some repellent on your arms and face before you go."

Christopher enjoyed the solitude of the walk without Curtis' constant chatter. Once at the waterfall, he sat on a rock and watched the frothing water splash over the rocks and continue downstream. With his mind free, he stared at a small rainbow in the mist. His thoughts drifted to times he and Wolverine had hunted the tundra. Most times they walked in silence, but Wolverine sometimes used their time together to share stories of his life and the spiritual beliefs of the *Inuit* people.

"I wish I'd listened more carefully to your stories, Grandfather. There's so much I don't know."

Closing his eyes, Christopher choked back tears. A passing shadow caused him to look up. Searching the sky, he saw a hawk circling above, and Wolverine's voice came back to him, "A circling hawk means you should look at your life from a higher point of view. Look beyond the present to what your life is meant to be."

But I don't know what my life is meant to be.

Feeling a pang of hunger, Christopher retraced his steps to the river where Eric had arranged sandwiches and apple slices on metal plates. "Did you find the falls?"

Christopher nodded, thinking the falls were hard to miss when following the Livingstone River upstream.

"They're not much after you've seen Angels Falls or Niagara Falls."

Christopher decided not to share his visions and thoughts with Curtis. "They were nice enough." As he ate, Christopher tried to look at his life from a higher point of view. *Did Wolverine ask me to come back for something more than the Canada Day Festival and the land transfer? Was this trip meant to make me see my life from a different perspective?*

After packing up their lunch scraps, the two men paddled around a big bend in the river. "Just ahead are the tallest trees on Baffin Island," Eric said.

"They wouldn't have to be very tall to be the biggest." Christopher replied. An open area was filled with wildflowers and willows that appeared to be about two meters in height.

"There they are. The biggest trees on the island."

Christopher pointed beyond the trees. "Those are the first caribou we've seen."

"There's a pool just past the willows where we can catch a couple of arctic char for supper."

Christopher looked around the raft. "You didn't bring any fishing rods."

"I have clients who like to bring fly fishing gear. I let them have their fun. But in reality, the fish here react to anything flashy in the water. A dry fly will catch a fish on about every cast. I could drop a can opener with a hook over the side and I'd catch a fish here."

"That would be more in line with *Inuit* tradition. I've never seen an *Inuk* with a fishing rod or lure."

As predicted, a flashy gold hook on a monofilament line was sufficient to attract a char large enough to feed the two of them. Eric dropped the fish onto the floor of the raft and unhooked it. "We'll clean and cook it about a mile down the river."

Christopher closed his eyes and asked forgiveness from the fish's spirit.

"Are you napping?"

"Just asking for the fish's spirit to forgive us for killing him."

Eric chuckled. "What other traditions do you have about fish?"

"My ancestors believe it's healthy to eat the entire fish."

"And my clients are accustomed to having a filet served to them on a plate. I'll save the fish liver and other entrails for you if you'd like to eat them."

"I'm not that deep into tradition. They'd also eat the fish raw. I prefer mine cooked."

"A lot of your ancestors suffered from worms and nasty parasites after eating raw fish and game. I want to make sure all my clients are healthy and happy when the trip is over."

Christopher had forgotten about those discussions in school. Nearly ninety percent of the *Inuit* population died in the 1800s, primarily from tuberculosis, smallpox, and other diseases introduced by the first

English and French explorers. But even before the Whites arrived, most *Inuit* didn't live past the age of 35-40. When graves were excavated and mummified *Inuit* remains examined, many died of trichinosis, worms, starvation, suicide, or because they froze to death. *Inuit* history said many men went hunting or fishing and never returned.

"You got quiet again, Chief."

"I was just thinking."

"Thinking about what a great life you could have in Toronto spending your lease payments?"

Maybe thinking about how interested you are in signing a lease before I have a chance to determine how much it might be worth.

* * *

Tatty walked into the RCMP building, distracted with worry about Christopher. She nearly bumped into Sergeant Geraldine Carson. "Whoa, Tatty. Be careful or I'll bowl you over."

"Sorry, my mind was elsewhere."

Directing Tatty to her office, Carson offered Tatty a chair, then sat behind her desk. "Actually, I was going to have the dispatcher contact you. I have the bedding and personal items from Wolverine Pokaik's room. You'd requested that the bedding be sent to Ottawa for testing and that an autopsy be performed on the body."

"I went to the mortuary and checked the body. He has petechial hemorrhages that may be indicative of asphyxia."

Carson leaned back, "I responded to that call. It appeared Wolverine died of natural causes."

"Did you see the hemorrhaging in his eyes?"

Carson leaned back, trying to visualize the death scene. "As I recall, the nurse closed his eyelids before I arrived."

"Do nurses usually do that?" Tatty asked.

"Um, no. The staff usually leave the victim's eyes open until the mortician arrives."

"Don't you find that suspicious?"

"I didn't, but you raise some interesting points. On the other hand, I hate to waste money testing pillowcases and conducting an autopsy when the death was caused by a stroke or heart attack."

"I spoke with the coroner. He agreed to delay the inquest until after the pathologist flies into Iqaluit to conduct an autopsy."

Carson pinched her nose. "You've been busy. I wish you'd spoken with me before talking to the coroner."

Tatty leaned close. "Gerri, there are things about Wolverine Pokaik's death that don't add up. He told my grandfather he was going to transfer his land grant to his grandson on Canada Day, which was the day after he died. He'd been negotiating with an outfitter over a lease in the days before his death, and now his grandson is rafting down the river with that outfitter. I'm...suspicious."

"Is Wolverine's grandson his only surviving heir?"

"As far as I know, Christopher is Wolverine's only surviving relative."

Carson drew a breath and let it out. "Check the birth and marriage records. Verify that the grandson is the only heir."

Tatty crossed her arms and pressed a knuckle to her lips. "I can do that. But, in the time of our grandfathers, adept hunters were revered as sports superstars are today. People lived in small family groups and my grandfather said that many hunters left behind a pregnant girlfriend or common law wife when they left to fish in the spring. Some returned to their 'wives'. Others disappeared, either dying or moving on to other family groups. Many of those seasonal relationships were never recorded as marriages, nor were the children's births in remote igloos recorded with the government."

"So, we have no idea if, or how many, common-law wives and children Wolverine had?"

"I'm afraid that's the reality of *Inuit* life. Anglican marriages and births were recorded. Until recently, most *Inuit* marriages weren't recorded."

"I wonder if Wolverine left a will?" Carson asked.

"Wills aren't an issue for nomadic people, like the *Inuit*. There is no tradition of owning real estate, and their most prized possessions, like hunting equipment, are either buried with them or left to their children." Tatty paused. "I'm concerned about Wolverine's grandson. He left with the outfitter on an unregistered trip down the Soper River. It's almost as if the outfitter didn't want a record that Christopher was with him."

"I imagine they'll arrive in Kimmirut and be chastised by the Territorial Park authorities for not submitting a permit."

"My grandfather, Hanta, gave Christopher a knife to protect himself against the spirits he was going to encounter on his trip."

Sergeant Carson frowned. "I don't see the connection."

"Hanta thinks Christopher is in danger. I think we should dispatch someone to check on them."

"Tatty, we don't send Mounties out to check on people based on a shaman's suspicions. Right now, my primary concern is finding Buniq Tingenek."

"I asked one of the bush pilots if someone might have flown Buniq out of Cape Dorset. He got very defensive and told me that none of the bush pilots were into human trafficking."

"I doubt anyone would admit to abetting her disappearance, especially if she was being transported for...something illegal."

"He seemed sincere."

Carson's look was skeptical. "When did you develop the ability to read minds?"

"You know what I mean. He didn't beat around the bush, and he answered quickly, without considering his response. He sounded sincere."

"Tatty, the accomplished liars are the ones who pose the greatest risk."

"Still..."

"The Cape Dorset Mountie interviewed the girl's friends and neighbors. Buniq was unhappy at home and some people felt that her father was...overly aggressive with physical punishment. Her closest friends thought she might've run away with a boy from Kimmirut."

"The guy who operates the airport terminal said there's a rumor that Buniq was escaping from her father's abuse. I think it's unlikely that she fled to be with a Kimmirut boy. Kimmirut is like 300 km away."

Carson shrugged. "Young love."

"How would she even meet someone who lived that far away?"

"The girl's friends think her boyfriend is an artisan in Kimmirut and they met when Buniq and her father went to Kimmirut during tourist season to display some of his walrus ivory carvings."

"I assume the Kimmirut Mountie is looking for her, too."

"He is, but we don't have a boyfriend's name, and there are a lot of artisans in Kimmirut." Carson paused, "And her friends may be throwing us a red herring. Keep your ear to the ground here in Iqaluit, too."

"I'll mention it to the local artisans. I think it's unlikely that she'll turn up here."

"I know. Too many *Inuit* women disappear and are never seen again. They don't run away to Iqaluit, and if they did, someone would report a homeless girl in town or would recognize her from the posters we put up. Iqaluit isn't like Montreal or Quebec where a girl could melt into the mix of people who don't know each other."

Tatty stood, then paused. "It's like the Greenland oral history of their aged and infirm people being set adrift on ice floes. They just disappeared into the fog."

"That's an easy way to dispose of a body."

Reflecting on Hanta's comments about the girl's spirit, Tatty weighed telling the sergeant. "My grandfather says Buniq's spirit is at ease."

"What does that mean?"

"She's in a place where she feels safe...or she's dead."

Carson leaned back. "There's a lot of space between those two options. Did your grandfather expand on that?"

"Um...no. He sometimes talks in riddles."

Carson stood. "Let's hope that she's in a happy place."

Chapter 13

Soper River Day 5

After a biscuit and sausage breakfast, Christopher packed up his gear and tent while Eric washed and stowed the cookware. The weather was consistent with that of previous days, cold mornings with high clouds. A warm southwesterly breeze blew into their faces as they pushed the inflatable raft into the river.

Within half an hour, they reached an area where gray cliffs rose along the riverbanks, creating a small fjord. The river narrowed and the current pulled them along faster. "Keep us centered!" Eric ordered as they approached the white froth of another set of rapids.

"This looks rougher," Christopher replied as he paddled to keep the raft in the center of the current.

"Yes, these are Class II rapids. They'll get your heart pounding."

The inflatable raft was tossed from side to side as Eric shouted paddling and steering commands. They scraped across a rock before being sucked down a chute between two sets of white water. Christopher let out a whoop when they'd cleared the rapids and the current slowed. "That was epic!"

Eric smiled as he removed a spool of fishing line from a rubberized bag. "We'll hit a longer stretch of rapids this afternoon. First, we'll catch and cook lunch."

The hook had hardly touched the water when Eric jerked the line. "I've got a nice one." Pulling in the line hand-over-hand, he fought until the fish was alongside them. He reached over the inflated tube, pulling a large silver fish into the raft. It flopped wildly as Eric laughed.

Christopher looked at the fish that lay still on the raft's floor with its gills pulsing. "This one will be plenty for the two of us. A second one would give us enough to feed a family."

"The river is full of them." Eric held out the spool of line. "Catch one for yourself. I'll cut it up and we'll throw the pieces into the river to feed the other fish."

Christopher leaned over and touched the head of the fish. "You won't go to waste. Your soul can move on."

Eric laughed. "You prayed over the last fish, asking his forgiveness. You're telling this fish that he'll be reincarnated?"

"Animals have souls. This fish may have the soul of an ancestor."

Snorting, Eric kicked the fish aside while picking up his paddle and steering them toward the shore. "I've got news for you kid, fish and birds are soulless creatures, just like the flowers on the bushes over there."

Christopher looked at the fish, now inanimate in the bottom of the raft. "Yes, your soul is now departed. Rest assured that we'll make good use of your body."

Later, Eric gutted the fish, then cut the fillets into pieces that he fried with onions and potatoes. Christopher watched the meal preparation, which was mechanical for Eric. Not honoring the fish, nor a gift of food supplied by the animal, the fish was only food to Eric. Only business. *Eric is as soulless as the fish he's cooking,* Christopher thought to himself.

"Grab a couple of plates and forks out of the gear," Eric said after sprinkling salt and seasoning over the contents of the frying pan. "There's nothing like a fresh fish shore lunch."

Christopher ate silently, savoring the flavor of the fresh fish while feeling guilty about how poorly Eric treated it after pulling it out of the river.

"You're pretty quiet, Chris. Cat got your tongue?"

"I prefer being called Christopher."

Eric snorted. "You didn't like being called Chief, either."

"My mother named me Christopher. That's what my friends and family call me."

With a dismissive wave, Eric said, "Whatever blows your sails." He ate silently for a moment, then pointed at a trail leading through the wildflowers. "I'll show you the lapis field after lunch."

"Lapis field?"

"There's a spot where lapis is just laying around on the ground. I suppose some sort of geologic phenomenon pushed it up out of an old volcano or something."

After cleaning up after lunch, Eric handed Christopher a bottle of insect repellent. "Slather this on your hands and arms. I'll give you a net to wear over your head."

Taking the bottle, Christopher rubbed the liquid on the backs of his hands and arms. "I'd forgotten how bad the bugs get out here."

"Yeah," Curtis said, pulling soft-brimmed hats with netting attached to the edges from a pack. "The bugs will eat you alive where we're going."

A trail wound through the wildflowers, then on through an area where the bluffs were broken into boulders. Beyond that, they came to an open rocky area. As predicted, the insects swarmed around them. Eric reached down and picked up the brightest blue stone Christopher had ever seen.

"This is lapis lazuli," Eric explained, handling the rock to Christopher. "It's all over this area. If you're lucky, you'll find a chuck of green pargasite embedded in a piece of hornblende."

Dropping the rock, Christopher followed Eric. "It's like God decided to scatter these beautiful gems here."

Eric chuckled. "Which one of the *Inuit* gods is responsible for rock scattering?"

"I don't recall hearing about any *Inuit* spirits who cared about rocks. Most of them were focused on making *Inuit* life difficult."

"Your *Inuit* gods are all evil?"

Sighing, Christopher said, "They're not so much evil as they are unhelpful. They make the game and fish scarce, and tip over boats."

Eric bent down to pick up a fist-sized piece of lapis. "Here's a chunk you could bring back to impress your girlfriend."

Christopher didn't reach out to take the rock being handed to him. "I can't take that."

"Why not? It's just laying here."

"First of all, if we take it, there will be less lapis for future visitors to see. Secondly, whose land is this? Do you have permission to remove gems?"

Ignoring the question, Eric froze. "Look. There's a piece of pargasite." He picked up the piece of stone with a finger-sized green crystal extending from the top.

"I'm not familiar with pargasite."

Wiping a bit of dirt from the green crystal, Eric held it out to Christopher. "It was first identified in Parga, Finland. There are only a few places in the world where it's found, and this is the biggest crystal I've ever seen. It's probably worth a couple hundred dollars."

"I'm sure the landowner will be pleased to have it."

Eric looked at Christopher. "I have approval for my clients to pick rocks."

"Really? Do you pay the owner more than my grandfather for his lease?"

"It's not much and I tell my people to only take one stone per trip."

"Who is the landowner?"

"This is Nunavut *Inuit* Grant land. There isn't a single person who owns it."

"No one has granted you permission to pick gems here."

"No. It's public land. Anyone can pick stones here." Seeing Christopher's unease, Eric asked, "Do you have a problem with that?"

"I do. *Inuits respect* the land. I can't believe anyone would let you pick lapis or pargasite here without a permit or some documentation."

"Fine. Don't take anything. Let's go back to the raft." They walked silently until the river was in sight. "There's one more set of rapids before the falls into Soper Lake. We'll slide the raft around the falls, then start across the lake in the morning before the wind comes up."

"We'll be in Kimmirut tomorrow afternoon?"

"With mild breezes and a little luck, we'll be able to paddle across the lake in time for lunch in Kimmirut. I'm sure it'll be a letdown after my gourmet cooking."

Christopher thought about the removal of lapis. "How many groups do you take down the river each year?"

"I usually take two or three. It's somewhat dependent on the weather. Some years there aren't that many people who are interested in taking a near-Arctic adventure, so we only bring two groups."

"How many people are in each group?"

"It varies. Sometimes there are as few as six people. Other groups are a dozen."

"And everyone brings home a piece of lapis?"

Eric stopped. "Why are you hung up on the lapis? There are a million pieces of it just laying around on the ground."

Christopher let out a sigh. "How much were you paying my grandfather for the lease?"

"I've been giving him ten dollars per person."

"How much is that a year?"

Eric started walking. "Like I said, it depends on how many groups we get through and how big the groups are."

"How much did you pay Wolverine last year?"

"I don't remember the exact figure, but he was happy to have me lay a couple of hundred-dollar bills in his hand."

"You're driving your clients around in a forty-thousand-dollar Suburban, and you're paying a couple of hundred dollars for the lease to access the river?"

"Your grandfather seemed pleased about that arrangement."

"The price is going up."

Eric stopped. "Why?"

"Your clients are paying a couple thousand dollars each for the trip."

"Hey, there are lots of expenses. You've seen the quality of the food I serve, and I own all the gear. Those inflatable rafts aren't cheap, and they don't last forever."

"I think two hundred dollars per client would be a fair price."

"No way! That's ten percent of my gross."

Christopher kept walking. "Okay, what's fair? Is five percent of your gross a fair number? How much would that be each year?"

"Listen, kid. If you push me too hard, you'll get edged out of the deal."

"How would I get edged out? You told me that Wolverine's land was the only flat spot without rocks that was near the river. If you didn't land there, how far would you have to drag your gear?"

"You don't get it, do you?"

"Get what?"

"Your Auntie Sos has a claim on that land grant, too. If you're unreasonable, I'll deal with her."

Christopher stopped. "I don't have an aunt."

Eric chuckled. "The old man never told you he sired a love child?"

"What are you talking about?"

Eric began walking. "The winters around here are cold and lonely. The old man took comfort under the seal skin with a cute *Inuit* girl when he was a handsome young caribou hunter. He knocked her up, and your aunt was born."

"You're lying."

"Nope. I spoke with your Aunt Sos, and she's interested in continuing the lease deal I had with Wolverine."

"I don't believe you. Wolverine promised me the land."

"Like I said, your Auntie Sos seems to think she might have a stronger claim on the land grant than you do. She's the old man's first kid and one hundred percent *Inuit*. You're just a grandson from a later wife. And you're only one quarter *Inuit*. Auntie Sos says she might file papers with the *Inuit Tunngavik* to protest your *Inuit* membership. You might be ineligible to inherit the land."

"Where are you getting this?" Christopher asked, trying to get his head around the disturbing information.

Eric snorted. "Auntie Sos and I have had several discussions. She's fired up to claim Wolverine's heritage, edging you out."

"I don't believe any of this."

"Believe what you want. If you're not willing to accept a continuation of the old man's lease, I can help your auntie find a lawyer to file paperwork taking away your *Inuit* membership and making her the old man's legal survivor."

"That's what this whole trip is about? You're blackmailing me to accept Wolverine's petty lease payments or else you're going to help some...fake aunt?"

"There's nothing fake about her. I'm sure she'd be able to take a DNA test or something, to prove she's the old man's kid."

Christopher jogged ahead and grabbed the outfitter's arm. "I'll bet she doesn't have a birth certificate naming Wolverine Pokaik as her father."

Eric stopped and stared at Christopher. "Back in the days when the old man was a hotshot hunter, there was no government office around the corner to register marriages, births, and deaths. Your Auntie Sos was born in an igloo somewhere south of Iqaluit about fifty years ago. The old man probably never knew the girl he'd been *kuniking* under the seal skin had a bun in the oven when he left in the spring."

"This is," Christopher threw up his arms, "insane. I don't have any aunts, uncles, or cousins."

Eric marched off leaving Christopher to ponder the possibility that Wolverine had a daughter from a relationship before marrying his grandmother. *Do I have cousins?*

*** *** ***

Tatty walked to the RCMP clerk's desk. "Hi Carole, have you heard anything back on the missing persons report on Christopher Pokaik and Eric Curtis?"

"Not yet. I'll email a reminder to Keith Young in Kimmirut. You should call too, so he knows it's a priority."

Tatty nodded and was about to walk away when Carole whispered, "What do you think about the missing girl from Cape Dorset? Do you think she could be in Kimmirut?"

"None of the roads in Cape Dorset extend beyond the city limits, so there's no way she left there in a car. I'm sure there are trappers' trails running to Kimmirut, but I don't see a teenage girl taking off on a 300 km trek across the tundra. That leaves planes or boats as her only means of departure. I've already spoken to a bush pilot who claims that none of them would smuggle a girl out of Cape Dorset."

Carole nodded. "I suppose a fisherman might've taken her somewhere."

Tatty sat in Carole's guest chair. "I keep coming back to the question of why someone would help her escape? I mean, even if her home situation is bad, who would take the risk of helping an *Inuit* teen run away knowing that every Mountie in Nunavut will be looking for her?"

Carole made sure no one was listening to them, then whispered, "You think she's dead, don't you?"

The stark reality of Carole's comment struck Tatty in the gut. "Probably."

Carole nodded. "She's the fifth missing *Inuit* woman in two years. That's a big number in Nunavut."

"It's not like Quebec or Ontario where a girl could hitchhike to another province and disappear. All the towns in Nunavut are isolated, with planes, ATVs, dogsleds, or boats being the only way to get from one to another."

"I suppose she could've jumped in a kayak and paddled away."

Tatty considered that possibility, then shook her head. "The nearest town is Kimmirut, and that is hundreds of kilometers away. Any other direction, she'd have to paddle across a hundred kilometers of open sea to reach another town. If she tried that, it's more likely she would die of thirst, exposure, drown, or be eaten by a polar bear than actually paddle her way to another settlement."

"Like I said, maybe she's dead."

Chapter 14

After a silent supper, Christopher walked to his tent. Zipping himself in for the night, he reached down and touched the sheath of the knife Hanta had given him. *You said this was to protect me from evil spirits. Has a shapeshifter taken the form of an outfitter?*

Listening to the wind and the sounds of the night, Christopher struggled to sleep. Every hoot of an owl or gust of wind made him grasp the hilt of the knife. When he finally dozed off, his dreams were vivid and his sleep fitful. In his dreams, the northern lights danced across the sky in steaks of pulsating green. Spirits without faces played ball with a walrus skull and the voices of unsettled souls called out for help.

Christopher woke with a start certain he'd heard something outside his tent. With the knife in one hand, he unzipped the tent and peered out into the eerie half-twilight. Nothing was moving, then a rodent skittered through the nearby bushes. The noise seemed loud in the silent night. Christopher was about to close his tent when air whooshed above his head. He ducked as an owl flew past before swooping in to grab the lemming he'd just heard.

The lemming's death screech seemed loud and ungodly in the still night air. As quickly as it had arrived, the owl was gone with the lemming dangling from its talons. *What souls do lemmings have? Are they released when the owl kills it?* A moment later he thought, *The owl was an omen, but of what?*

Snug in his sleeping bag, Christopher considered what he'd dreamt and seen. "Wolverine and Hanta, tell me the meaning of all this," he whispered. "Am I the lemming, about to be crushed and carried away by an owl?"

* * *

The sounds of Eric making coffee woke Christopher, who felt like he'd only slept a few minutes since seeing the owl. Crawling out of the tent, he made sure the knife was on his belt as he pulled on his coat and zipped the tent.

"Did you hear the owl kill the lemming last night?" Christopher asked as Eric handed him a cup of coffee.

"I sleep like the dead after a day of paddling," Eric replied. He poured pancake mix into a bowl, then scooped river water into it as bacon sizzled in the cast iron skillet. "Today we traverse the last set of rapids, then paddle on to Soper Lake. Your people call it *Tasiujajuaq*. The name refers to the meromictic nature of the lake that is a mixture of fresh and saltwater. The tides are so high in Kimmirut they reverse the river flow and push ocean water into the lake."

Eric dished bacon and pancakes onto an aluminum plate, then handed Christopher a plastic bottle of maple syrup. "Have you reconsidered the lease arrangement?"

Uneasy after his dreams and seeing the owl grab the lemming, Christopher decided it was prudent to soften his position about the lease. "I think you've been getting a bargain on the landing lease. Make me a better offer."

A smile curled the corners of Eric's mouth. "Your auntie would be happy with what I'd been paying the old man."

"You said it would take time and the cost of an attorney to make her the heir. Make me an offer and save that time, money, and effort."

Being a cagey businessman, Eric asked, "What number did you have in mind?"

"I think it's worth $100 per client to you."

Eric snorted. "That would cut my profit to almost nothing."

"Raise your prices. It appears your customers are affluent enough to afford an extra $100 for the trip."

"There are price points that make the trip too expensive. If I charge $1,999 for the trip, it seems more reasonable than $2,100.

It's psychology. If I go too high, people will opt to take cheaper trips to Alaska, the Yukon, or British Columbia."

"Sell your Suburban and buy a van to transport your customers back and forth."

"How about $40 a head? I could make that work and it's four times what I was paying the old man."

Mopping up the last syrup with a bite of pancake, Christopher said, "I think $100 is a nicer round number."

Eric took Christopher's plate. "Work with me. Negotiation means that each party gives a little. I can go as high as $50. Besides, I just treated you to a $2,000 raft trip."

Acting nonchalant, but feeling queasy about the negotiations and his dreams, Christopher paused to make it appear he was considering the offer. "If the last rapids are as thrilling as you've promised, I'll probably be willing to take $60 per person for the lease."

Eric packed up the cookware as he thought. "I might be able to go that high. Let's talk about it again when we get to Kimmirut."

* * *

The northern lights had flashed across the sky in Christopher's dreams. The demons had been playing ball with a human skull in the dancing green lights. That bad omen had been followed by the death scream of the lemming caught in the owl's talons. *Were those a message for me?* Christopher asked himself as he packed his gear, rolled up the sleeping bag and mat, then broke down the tent. *I wish my grandfather was here. He'd be able to interpret those signs.*

Standing next to his pile of gear, Christopher watched Eric packing up the cookware, coolers, and his gear. "Were you one of the faceless demons playing ball in the northern lights, Eric?" he whispered. "Whose skull was being used as the ball?"

Eric and Christopher pushed the raft from the riverbank into the swift current. Paddling only to keep the raft centered the river, they made fast progress. The sound of the rapids preceded their appearance as they rounded an elbow in the river. The sight of frothing water ahead made Christopher's heart pound.

"Remember, the white water is *after* the rocks. We need to paddle to keep the raft in the chutes between the smooth water."

Despite his deep strokes, the raft drifted to the right, where the water surged over a large rock before splashing into a froth. Christopher leaned over the edge of the raft, trying to use the blade of his paddle to push off the boulder visible just below the surface. The scraping of the rubber raft against the surface of the boulder preceded the violent spin. With the right side of the raft hung up on the boulder, the left side was whipped around by the swift current, spinning the raft 180 degrees.

Christopher was thrown against the rubber tube by centrifugal force. Gripping his paddle to keep it from flying out of his hand, he slid on the wet floor and tube. A sharp pain jabbed his ribs as he fell over the edge of the raft into the water. Eric pushed him away with the end of the paddle as Christopher reached for the slippery wet surface of the tube.

Thrust into the water, Christopher was twirled as the current hurled him through the river. His elbow struck a rock, then his back was scraped by a boulder. He struggled to get his head above water to breathe. As soon as he'd taken half a breath, the current flipped and tumbled him. Striking a rock, the crushing blow caused air to rush from his lungs. Seeing stars as the last oxygen in his brain was used, his head popped up and he drew a deeper breath before being sucked under again.

Mercifully, the tugging and rolling gave way to a gentler, steady current. Above, the blue sky shone through the water, and Christopher kicked until his head broke through the surface. Drawing a deep breath, he felt the sudden rush of oxygen to his brain and muscles. He drew repeated breaths occasionally sucking in a gulp of water that caused coughing fits. Eventually, the current slowed, and he was able to tread water, breathe, and evaluate his situation.

Looking around, he realized that he was past the rapids and near the center of the river. Spinning around to look downstream, he saw Eric paddling away in his raft.

"Hey! I'm here!" Christopher shouted.

Eric glanced back. After a moment of surprise, he smiled, then waved before turning and continuing to paddle away.

Suddenly aware of the cold water, Christopher swam toward the nearest shore. The rocky river bottom banged his knees and scraped his hands as he scrambled out of the current. With water dripping from his hair and clothes, he crawled onto the riverbank and collapsed. Chills ran over his body, and he shivered like he'd never shivered before. Christopher pulled his knees to his chest, trying to conserve whatever body heat he could muster. Wracked with shivering and chattering teeth, he felt suddenly warm. Memories of his parents and Wolverine came to him, and he felt at ease. Then he lost consciousness.

* * *

After patrolling Kimmirut, Mountie Keith Young stopped in the *Mirnguiqsirviit* office, headquarters for the Nunavut Territorial Parks. A young *Inuit* woman was dusting off soapstone carvings crafted by the local artisans.

"Good morning, Palatok."

The woman smiled. "What can I do for the RCMP?"

"We received a missing person report. Two rafters were dropped off at Mount Joy and haven't been seen since."

The woman opened a drawer and pulled out a file of park permits. "I was asked to look for a permit a couple days ago. Is one of the missing men Eric Curtis?"

"He's one of the people. The other is Christopher Pokaik."

"If they're in Katannilik Park, they're illegal. They didn't file a permit or fill out the polar bear warning acknowledgement."

"Does that happen often?"

"We get a couple hikers a year who are unaware of the permitting requirements. But the outfitters who fly customers in are diligent about filling out the forms. Eric Curtis has been an outfitter who's hosted tour groups for years. He's always filled out the permits in the past."

The Mountie chuckled. "As far as you know, he's always filled out the permits."

"We monitor the trails and lakeshore carefully. I don't think anyone has slipped by without a permit, or a warning that they did not fill out a permit."

"If they were dropped off three or four days ago, I'm not surprised that they're not here yet. The tourist trips take seven days, with their hikes to the falls and other sights. Even if they rafted down without any side trips, it'll take them at least four days. The earliest I'd expect them to show up is today."

"Let's keep our eyes open. Please advise your people and anyone hiking from here that we're missing a pair of rafters. Let us know if they show up."

"I've got two groups of hikers on overnight camping trips and another two groups going out shortly. There's no way to reach the people already on the trail. I'll ask the new groups to look for your missing men."

* * *

The Iqaluit RCMP dispatcher radioed Tatty and asked her to call the office. She'd been walking downtown, so she stepped into a coffee shop to use the pay phone near the door.

"Hi Carole, what's up?"

"I got a call from the hospital. The pathologist flew in unexpectedly a couple of hours ago. Her assistant said she's got tissue samples to examine this morning, then she's planning to do an autopsy on Wolverine Pokaik this afternoon. They asked if anyone from our office wanted to attend the procedure. Gerri said this is your case, and you can decide whether you want to be there, or if you'd rather talk with the pathologist when she meets with the coroner after the autopsy."

Tatty thanked Carole and hung up. *Do I want to see the pathologist cut Wolverine, or can I just meet with her and the coroner after the procedure? I think the coroner's meeting will be fine.* Tatty thought to herself.

Chapter 15

In his dream, Christopher was being crushed by two rocks. They pressed against his chest making it hard to breathe. Working his right arm free, he pushed against the rock in front of him.

"I think he's coming around," the rock said.

Hearing a demon rock speaking English startled him and his eyes popped open. The bearded face in front of him was too close to focus on. "Who are you?"

"I'm one of the guys trying to save your life by warming you between our bodies."

A shudder passed through Christopher as he felt the cold deep in his core. "Where are we?"

"We're in one of the Katannilik Park shelters, about seven kilometers from Kimmirut."

"How did I get here?"

"Bud and I found you soaking wet and curled up by the river. We carried you up here, stripped off your wet clothes then pressed you between our bodies."

"Who are you?"

"I'm Larry. Bud is my hiking buddy."

Turning away from Larry's whiskers rubbing against his face, Christopher asked, "Am I going to live?"

"The jury was out on that when we found you. The odds are better now that you're awake and talking to us. We were wondering if there was any hope when you were blue, and your breathing was raspy." The man paused, then asked, "What's your name?"

"Christopher Pokaik."

"Did you fall out of a kayak or something?"

With his brain function slowed by the cold, the question was beyond Christopher's mental grasp. After a moment of consideration, snippets of memory returned. "I was...in a raft. We were going through the rapids... Did you see a rubber raft with another guy in it?"

"There was no raft in sight when we found you."

Bud rolled away from Christopher and pressed a sleeping bag against his back. "I'm going to heat some water. It'll help warm you from the inside out."

Moments later, wrapped in sleeping bags, Christopher sat up and accepted the cup of steaming liquid from a lean, bearded man. "Thanks."

"Don't thank me yet. From what I learned in first responder classes, this will warm your core, which will set off a round of unpleasant shivering."

Christopher sipped the coffee that seemed so hot it burned his lips. He pushed the cup to Bud "It's way too hot."

Bud shook his head. "It's barely warmer than your body. It won't burn you; I promise."

Forcing himself to drink the coffee, Christopher felt the warmth radiating in his core. Almost immediately, he started shivering violently. Larry looked at Bud. "By God, you *did* remember something from that first responder course."

"I also remember how to tie a tourniquet around your leg if you're bleeding to death."

"Great. You remembered the two random life saving skills, but you forgot the moleskin to deal with my blisters."

"I told you to wear two pairs of socks!" Bud replied.

"Not until the second day when I already had the blisters."

Christopher's shivering stopped and he held out the cup. "Can I have some more coffee?"

"Focus Bud. We're trying to save...Christopher's life. Arguing is not helpful."

"Find those chocolate bars that you hid in your backpack. They'll give him a jolt of energy."

"How do you know about my chocolate bars?"

"I can smell them on your breath after you eat them. You know, polar bears are attracted to the scent of chocolate."

"That's bullshit and you know it."

Christopher sipped the second cup of coffee as the playful banter went back and forth. "Polar bears can smell a seal from ten miles away."

"Great!" Larry replied, as he unwrapped a candy bar. "We're attracting any bears within ten miles."

After eating the chocolate, Christopher took a deep breath. "I need to get to Kimmirut."

Bud put his hand on Christopher's shoulder. "Listen, pal. Your legs are going to feel like they're made of rubber for the next few hours. We'll spend the night here, filling you with warm liquids and food. Then, we'll see if you can walk tomorrow."

"But I need to get to Kimmirut."

"Is someone expecting you there today?" Bud asked.

"Not really. But there's a constable in Iqaluit who needs to know where I am, and that someone tried to kill me."

"Whoa. Someone tried to kill you?"

"Eric Curtis pushed me overboard with his paddle while we were going through the rapids. He said that people die from hypothermia if they fall into the icy water."

Bud nodded. "He was almost right about that. I thought we'd be dragging your body back to Kimmirut."

"Can you carry me there today?"

Bud and Larry exchanged a look. "Listen, Christopher. We're willing to interrupt our hike to save your life, but if you're no longer in danger, we're not carrying you anywhere since you'll be able to walk on your own tomorrow. Besides, it'll be sunset in a couple of hours. Walking the trails in the twilight is challenging."

Bud nodded. "I also think the bears are less active in the daylight."

Christopher looked at Bud skeptically. "I think they're actually more active in the daytime. They're visual hunters. They can follow a scent like a bloodhound, but they'd rather hunt in the day."

Larry arranged the sleeping bag that slipped off Christopher's shoulder. "Kimmirut is a long one-day hike. We're not starting at twilight. Okay?"

"Fine."

* * *

The hospital conference room featured a rectangular table that seated twelve. With additional chairs lining the perimeter walls, the room seated close to thirty people. It seemed like an echo chamber with only three people at the meeting. Tatty, the coroner, and the pathologist were all seated at one end of the table.

Dr. Kara Wilkenson handed single sheets of paper to Tatty and the coroner.

"The hospital transcriptionist will send you a full autopsy report later this week. The copies you have are my brief notes and opinion."

Tatty stared at the outline of a body drawn on the paper in front of her. The body outline she'd seen from past autopsies showed the location of stab wounds or bullet entry and exit points. This drawing was blank, much as she'd seen after drowning autopsies and heart attacks. The doctor's handwritten notes filled in blanks, like the date and time, along with technical details. Most interesting were her barely legible notes.

Setting aside her glasses, pen, and sheet of paper, the pathologist turned to the coroner. "My examination suggests that the victim was murdered. The manner of death was asphyxia caused by the face being covered with a cotton covered material, like a pillowcase. I recovered white cotton fibers from around the victim's mouth, nose, and eyes."

Looking tired, the coroner leaned forward and spoke to Tatty. "The RCMP recovered the victim's bedding and sent it to Ottawa for testing. Is that correct, Constable Etok?"

"Yes, Mr. Kinsey. I believe the bedding was shipped to Ottawa the day after the victim died."

Kinsey nodded and looked at the pathologist's notes. "Did you note any defensive wounds, Dr. Wilkenson?"

"I took scrapings from the victim's fingernails, but there were no bruises or other signs of physical trauma visible on the surface of the body to indicate there'd been a struggle."

Tatty cleared her throat. "I spoke with the victim's roommate. He indicated that the victim was extremely vain and never left his bed without putting his dentures into his mouth. His dentures were on the nightstand when Sergeant Carson arrived at the scene."

Kinsey nodded and stared at the sheet of paper, apparently deep in thought. "Based on your observations, Dr. Wilkenson, I assume we don't need to conduct a formal coroner's inquest to declare this a murder."

"That would be my professional judgement, Mr. Kinsey."

"Constable, please advise Sergeant Carson that I'm turning the case over to the RCMP for a murder investigation."

Tatty nodded and stood. "I'll ask the sergeant to open a formal investigation this afternoon." She turned and left the conference room feeling like a weight had been lifted.

Kinsey was a step behind her, "Constable?"

Tatty paused. "Yes, sir."

Kinsey smiled. "You were right to request an autopsy. But don't rest on your laurels, our work has only begun."

Suppressing a smug smile, Tatty walked out of the hospital and drove to the RCMP building. Carole looked up when Tatty walked in the door. "Well?"

"Tell Gerri we have a murder to investigate."

Carole nodded toward the closed door behind her. "You can tell her yourself. She's through with her phone call to Ottawa."

Not waiting for her knock to be answered, Tatty opened Carson's office door just far enough to put her head through. "The coroner says we have a murder to investigate."

Carson, who'd been drafting an email, looked away from her computer. "How quickly will we have the pathologist's report?"

"It's being transcribed now and should be in our hands tomorrow."

"What was the cause of death?"

"Asphyxiation, probably caused by something covering the victim's face. There were white cotton fibers, like from a pillowcase, around the victim's mouth and nose."

"I'll notify Ottawa and ask them to prioritize the bedding analysis. I assume they'll find saliva on the pillowcase. That won't tell us much because it'll be there naturally. It's too bad we can't recover fingerprints from the fabric."

"I'll go back to The Lodge and ask if anyone saw a stranger in the hallway around the time of death."

Carson nodded. "Requesting an autopsy was a good move. I'll put a commendation in your file." She paused, then added, "I assume you'd prefer that we not do anything more formal."

Tatty froze. "I can't imagine anything more uncomfortable than having Mounties patting me on the back and congratulating me."

Carson smiled. "Consider yourself officially thanked."

Walking away from Carson's office, Tatty glanced at Carole who was standing around the corner where she'd listened to the conversation. Carole gave her a thumbs-up gesture, causing Tatty to blush.

In her car, Tatty smiled. "Thank heaven for Gerri Carson. I finally have a sergeant who understands my wish to stay out of the limelight."

Chapter 16

Christopher slept fitfully, with vivid dreams of drowning and being chased by a polar bear. Dressed in their warm dry clothing, the two hikers continued to sandwich him in an effort to warm his chilled body. Thrashing to free himself from the clutches of a bear, Christopher awoke to find Bud shaking his shoulders.

"Wake up. You're having another nightmare."

Shivering, Christopher pulled a sleeping bag around his shoulders. "Sorry, I ah..."

Larry lit their propane stove and set a pot of water on top of it. "No need to apologize to us. We've seen and experienced a lot of scary things on our hikes, and your hypothermia is at the top of the list of scary, almost killed somebody events."

Bud nodded. "This was scarier than when that guy slipped into the crevasse when we were hiking Mount McKinley."

"How are you feeling, Christopher?" Larry asked.

"I'm still cold, but better."

Bud handed Christopher another cup of coffee. "I stirred a couple teaspoons of sugar into this to help your body generate its own heat. You need to realize it's going to take several days before you've fully recovered from hypothermia."

"I'm ready to start hiking," Christopher replied.

Bud glanced at Larry. "If it was just the two of us, we'd be able to make it to Kimmirut in a long day of hiking. I'm not sure Christopher is ready for our usual pace."

Trying to show how well he was doing, Christopher stood, which caused a bit of vertigo. He swayed, and Larry grabbed his arm. "Don't go crazy on us. Let's set a pace that suits you, and we'll let nature determine how far we go today."

"But I need to get to Kimmirut," Christopher protested.

Larry stroked his graying beard and smiled. "When you're experiencing the outdoors, mother nature determines the route and pace. We'll do what makes sense, and no more."

"But..."

Bud, who was packing up the stove and gear glanced over his shoulder. "It's better if you arrive in Kimmirut alive."

"I'm fine!" Christopher protested.

Bud stopped packing their gear and addressed Christopher. "Listen kid, you're not fine. If we hadn't found you yesterday, the ravens would be pecking at your carcass today. Your body suffered deep trauma. You were literally chilled to the bone. It takes time to overcome that."

"But I *need* to talk to the Mounties in Kimmirut."

Bud nodded. "If you take it easy, you will get to Kimmirut. But only after you listen to your body. I suspect that your endurance has been affected, as have your balance and reasoning."

Christopher sighed but resolved to fight on and show these two old men how tough he was. "What do you two do for a living so you can hike the Arctic and climb mountains?"

Bud pulled a huge backpack onto his shoulders, handling the weight with apparent ease. "We're Thunder Bay firemen."

"Ah, that's why you know first aid and you're in such good shape."

Larry shouldered a slightly smaller pack. "You should've seen us fifteen years ago. We could hike a hundred kilometers a day with fifty-kilogram packs."

Bud laughed. "Yeah, uphill and into the wind all the way."

Bud started walking down a poorly defined trail through the bushes and wildflowers. Christopher followed behind him, keeping the pace for about one hundred meters before feeling his legs start to wobble.

Larry stepped up next to him and steadied his shoulders. "Hey, Bud, take it down a couple of notches. Our patient isn't up to speed walking."

Even the slower pace was challenging for Christopher, and they took frequent breaks. Bud gave Christopher a chocolate bar from his backpack at their second break. "You're doing pretty well."

"I feel like I've been run over by a herd of caribou."

"Tell us when you need a break or when we should stop for the day."

Christopher cocked his head. "I'm messing up your hike."

Larry shrugged. "Each hike presents its own challenges and rewards. This will give us great stories for the fire hall."

"A hike and a rescue," Christopher replied. "Are you guys married?"

"Yup," Bud replied. "Larry and I go on a wilderness trip and our wives go shopping in New York and attend Broadway plays."

"That sounds expensive."

Larry chuckled. "They don't like camping out, and we don't like the big city. In the end, their trip to New York is much cheaper than a divorce."

"Do you have kids?"

"Larry's got two teenagers and I've got three who are late teens and in college. What's your story?"

"I'm going to University in Toronto. I'm originally from Iqaluit and came home for Nunavut's Canada Day celebration."

Shouldering his pack, Bud asked, "How did you end up in the river?"

"It's a long story."

"You might as well get into it. We're going to be hiking together for at least another day."

Christopher started the explanation with the story about growing up with his grandfather, then transitioned to his time in college and the request for him to return to Iqaluit for the Canada Day celebration. He was telling them about the outfitter's lease proposal when a pair of caribou appeared ahead of them. Bud stopped and gestured toward the cow and calf.

"My people believe the caribou are a sign of life and regeneration."

The caribou, 200 meters away, stared at the trio of hikers for a few moments, then walked away.

Larry stepped next to Christopher and tapped his elbow. "Maybe they're a sign that you're going to survive."

Walking ahead, Christopher nodded. "My grandfather would probably agree with that. He was a shaman who liked to interpret the things we saw and experienced."

A short time later, Bud stopped and pulled his backpack off. "Lunch time. I think a bowl of hot soup is on the menu."

Exhausted, Christopher sat on a flat rock. "Are we halfway to Kimmirut?"

Larry pulled a map from the side pocket of his pack and unfolded it. After spending a moment to orient it to their location, he knelt beside Christopher. "Here's where we found you by the river, and this is the shelter where we warmed you up." Pointing to a spot farther west, Larry said, "We're here."

"That's hardly a quarter of the way to Kimmirut from where we started!" Christopher complained.

Folding the map, Larry smiled. "Like I said, mother nature is going to determine the route and pace of our trip. Your body isn't ready for a faster pace, and there's no shorter route...unless you've got a boat stashed ahead on the lakeshore."

Sighing with frustration, Christopher shook his head. "I don't have a boat, canoe, or kayak stashed anywhere near here."

* * *

Tatty walked from table to table as the residents of The Lodge ate lunch. At each table, she greeted the residents, introduced herself, then asked if anyone had seen a stranger walking in the hallway the night of Wolverine's death. Most everyone was asleep during the murder or hadn't looked in the hallway when getting up to use the toilet.

A woman at a table near the kitchen frowned when Tatty asked about strangers in the hallway. "I don't recall which night it was, but I walked to the nurse's station when she didn't answer my call light."

"Did you see a stranger in the hallway?"

"I was having heartburn and I needed my heartburn medicine."

"I see. Did you see a stranger while you waited for the nurse?"

"She was on her break. The aide said I'd have to wait until she got back because only nurses can hand out medicine."

Having dealt with many *Inuit* people who often answered questions indirectly, or after lengthy introductions, Tatty listened politely, asking for clarification as the woman told her story.

"There was a man in a dark colored jacket. I thought it was odd, since it was the middle of the night. Who would wear a jacket?"

"Did you recognize him?"

"No. He was too young to be someone here. He moved quickly. The residents here shuffle."

Her curiosity piqued, Tatty urged the woman to expand on her description.

"He wasn't tall, and he was kind of skinny."

"Did you see him go into a room?"

"No, he was leaving. I saw him go out of the exit door at the end of the hallway."

"He went out the emergency exit and not the front door?"

The woman frowned. "That's what I just said."

"Did he come from the direction of Wolverine's room?"

The woman thought for a moment, then clocked her head. "Yes, Wolverine and Hanta live down that hallway, the one the man came through." The woman paused. "You should talk to Nurse Gustafson. She saw him, too."

The last table was Hanta's. He'd been quietly watching Tatty work across the room. When she arrived, he looked up. "So, have you found Wolverine's killer?"

"I never told you I was looking for a killer."

Shaking his head, Hanta looked sad. "You have no faith in my powers of observation. If this was a social call, you would be smiling. Bring over an empty chair and sit with me."

The other men around the table slid their chairs aside to make room for Tatty. Smiling, they nodded a greeting without speaking.

Once seated, Tatty studied Hanta, reminded that he was no longer the vibrant middle-aged man she'd grown up around. "You look old and tired, Grandfather."

One of the men coughed to hide his laugh. Hanta gave him a disgusted look, then turned to Tatty. "You used to show your elders greater respect."

"You used to be younger and better rested."

"It's unwise to engage in a war of wits with a man as worldly as me. Even if you win a battle, you will lose the war." He paused, letting his words sink in. "Have you learned who killed Wolverine?"

"One of the women saw a skinny man in a dark-colored jacket leaving The Lodge late one night. She wasn't sure if it was the evening of Wolverine's death."

"The man who argued with Wolverine about the lease of his land grant was skinny and wore a green jacket."

Tatty removed a notebook from her pocket and wrote Eric Curtis' name. "There are many men in Iqaluit who wear dark-colored jackets."

"Not many have green jackets with Rough Water embroidered on the back."

"You didn't see a man with Wolverine late that night."

"Not with my eyes."

"What does that mean, Grandfather?"

"I was asleep when the man came. My eyes were closed, but I knew when Wolverine's spirit journey began. The spirit of the man in the Rough Water jacket was nearby."

"His spirit was nearby? Was he physically here? Was he the killer?"

"It doesn't matter if the man who argued with Wolverine was the same man who ended Wolverine's life. It was his spirit who willed Wolverine's death."

Tatty leaned back, confused. "So, a man wearing a green jacket argued with Wolverine. That man's spirit willed Wolverine dead but he may not have been the person who was the killer."

"Yes."

"Grandfather, you're talking in riddles."

Hanta sat quietly, staring at each of the other men seated around the table. "You think like a white Mountie, not an *Inuit*."

"I'm an *Inuit* special constable. There are strict rules of evidence I have to follow to identify and convict a killer in court. I can't arrest someone because you say their spirit willed the death of another person."

"Too bad your rules are so rigid that you can't deal with a killer when we know who it is."

Tatty closed her eyes and counted to ten before responding. "I'll let you, as a shaman, deal with the killer spirit. I'll continue my quest to find the living person who ended Wolverine's life."

"I don't think that will be a good use of your time."

"Why not?"

"Wolverine didn't fight his killer."

Tatty thought back to the pathologist's comment that there weren't any defensive wounds and none of the attacker's skin under Wolverine's fingernails. "Why wouldn't Wolverine fight his attacker?"

Hanta shrugged. "Why would he? The demon was there to free Wolverine's spirit." Hanta paused, "He knew young Christopher had passed his ordeal."

Confused by the sudden change of topic, Tatty frowned. "What?"

"Christopher's ordeal has passed. He'll return soon to help bury Wolverine's body."

Long past questioning Hanta's visions, Tatty nodded. "The Mounties are looking for him."

"It is Christopher who will find the Mounties, not the other way around."

"But he's still lost."

"Not lost. Just not where you think he should be."

"Where is he?"

Hanta chuckled. "I thought I'd taught you patience. Things happen in their own time, not when you think they should."

Tatty stood. "I have to talk to Nurse Gustafson."

"Again, patience will serve you well."

"What?"

One of the other men laughed. "Betty Gustafson only works the night shift. She'll probably be here at about eleven o'clock."

Hanta nodded. "Patience, child."

"I'm still looking for the missing girl, too. What have the spirits told you about her?"

"You're looking in the wrong place."

"She's not in Cape Dorset?"

Hanta closed his eyes. "Her *anirniq*, breath spirit, has been set free to find another body. Perhaps she's now a seal, fish, or hawk."

"She's dead?"

Without looking up, he shook his head. "She didn't escape the demons set upon her by *Agloolik*, who overturns boats."

"She's with *Sedna*, the spirit of the sea?"

Hanta raised his eyebrows. "If you open your mind, you'll hear more."

Tatty closed her eyes, wondering how much of Hanta's advice was oral history or teaching, and how much was his dementia. "I wasn't blessed with your vision, Grandfather."

"Tanaraq, your gift is as strong as mine. You only need to listen to the spirits when they speak." Hanta paused, "It's difficult for young people today. There are so many noises that interfere with the voices of the spirits. It's much easier to listen when you're alone with nothing but the sound of the shifting ice and wind in your ears."

Tatty walked to her car and started the engine. Was Hanta right? Did she not hear the spirits because there were so many things pulling at her? Co-workers, radios, televisions, people in the stores, all made distracting noises. What would she hear if she sat on the edge of the sea and listened to the sounds of nature and the spirits?

She stiffened when she recalled Hanta's words about the missing girl. He'd mentioned *Agloolik*, the dreaded spirit who overturns boats, drowning whale hunters and fishermen. Was the girl in a boat that sank? Or was Hanta telling her what she wanted to hear?

She drove to the RCMP headquarters and found Carole shutting down her computer. "Is there a boat missing from Cape Dorset?"

"I haven't seen anything about missing boats."

"My grandfather said the missing girl was taken by *Agloolik*. That's the spirit who overturns boats and downs fishermen."

Carole shrugged. "Like I said, I haven't heard anything. That doesn't mean there isn't a boat missing. It just means that no one has reported a missing boat. You could check with the coast guard."

Tatty shook her head. "Or maybe the old man just misheard the spirits."

Carole laughed. "I think there's a lot of static on that spirit communication line." She paused. "Would you like me to call the coast guard?"

"Would you? The request would seem more formal if it came from the RCMP office than from a special constable who walks into their office worried about a shaman's vision of a spirit overturning a boat."

Carole made the call, and after explaining the request, nodded and thanked the person who'd answered the phone. "There haven't been any distress calls, nor have they been asked to watch for any missing Cape Dorset boats."

"This is a bit out there. Will you call the Mountie in Cape Dorset and suggest that someone reported that the missing girl might've been on a boat."

Carole considered the suggestion, then dialed the phone. "We got a tip that your missing girl was on a boat that left Cape Dorset." She listened, then added, "It's a tip from a usually reliable source."

"Well?" Tatty asked as Carole hung up the phone.

"He's going down to the docks to put up posters and ask if anyone saw the girl."

"I hate to bother them with one of Hanta's visions."

"To be honest, the Cape Dorset Mountie is out of ideas. I think a walk around the docks might be the most interesting thing he has to do tomorrow."

Chapter 17

The dreams that haunted Christopher the night before didn't return. He woke to gentle shaking and Bud's voice. "Hey, kid. Rise and shine." The aroma of coffee filled the air in the tiny opening in the tundra where they'd spent the night.

"Thanks," Christopher said, pulling his arms free of the sleeping bag to accept the cup Larry held out to him.

"Nothing like a cup of instant coffee with three heaping teaspoons of sugar to get your heart started."

After sipping the cloyingly sweet coffee, Christopher smacked his lips.

Larry shook his head. "I can't believe that you're enjoying Bud's coffee. We don't let him brew firehouse coffee."

Rolling his eyes, Bud dumped instant oatmeal into a boiling pot of water. "If you don't like my instant coffee, you can make your own."

"Nah," Larry replied, "Even you can't mess up a cup of instant coffee. One teaspoon of coffee into a cup of hot water. How do you ruin that recipe, Bud?"

Bud snapped his fingers. "It's a teaspoon of coffee per cup, not a tablespoon."

"You idiot," Larry said, throwing the dregs of his coffee into the bushes.

Winking at Christopher, Bud smiled as he stirred the oatmeal. "I never understood that teaspoon versus tablespoon thing. They both start with a T and end with spoon."

Larry held out his cup for a serving of oatmeal. "I hope you did better with the hot cereal recipe. I don't want to chip a tooth because you only added a tablespoon of water when you should've used a quarter cup."

After stirring brown sugar and raisins into the pot, Bud poured the thick oatmeal mixture into Larry's cup. "Listen, if you don't like the way I cook, you can buy the food and do the cooking on our next trip."

Larry scooped up a spoonful of steaming oatmeal and blew on it. "There's nothing I like less than grocery shopping."

Bud took Christopher's empty coffee cup and spooned the thick oatmeal mixture into it. "Are you going to complain about my cooking too?"

"My usual breakfast is a bowl of corn flakes. Oatmeal is a step up."

Bud ate a spoonful of oatmeal directly from the pot, apparently to keep from dirtying another dish they'd have to clean. "How are you feeling this morning, kid?"

"I slept better, so I feel...refreshed."

"You should be at a near normal body temperature today. That should help with your endurance and reduce your confusion."

"I was confused yesterday?"

"You kept demanding that we get you to Kimmirut, although you never explained the motivation for the rush."

"I've been seeing a lot of demons with dark messages."

"What kind of demons?" Larry asked.

"They're mostly faceless. I've been seeing them dancing in the northern lights."

Larry looked at the sky that was brightening as the sun broke over the eastern horizon behind them. "There haven't been any northern lights. The lingering overnight twilight is too bright to see them at this latitude in summer."

"They're there in my dreams. I saw the spirits playing ball using a walrus head."

Bud scowled. "I have a Cree friend who says the northern lights are signs of happiness and good fortune."

"For the *Inuit*, the northern lights are signs of demons and impending bad fortune. They're filled with demons who often cause famine and death."

"You saw multiple demons?" Larry asked.

Setting aside his empty cup, Christopher wiggled free of the sleeping bag and pulled on his jacket. "Some were faceless. Others were demons I knew. *Anguta*, the demon who steals spirits, was chasing me."

"I think you're out of the soul thief's reach now," Bud said as he folded up the stove and put it into his backpack.

"Yes. I think he found someone else to chase."

"You make him sound like a wolf who's chasing a herd of caribou. He chases until the weakest or the lame lag behind the herd, then he pounces on the weakest victim."

Christopher pulled on his hiking boots while considering Bud's comment. "I think you've summed up the life of an *Inuk* in that statement, Bud. We're each trying to not be the caribou who lags behind the herd." He rolled up the sleeping bag and tied it. "Which of you gave up your sleeping bag for me?"

Larry took the sleeping bag, rolled it up, then tied it to the bottom of his pack. "Bud figured mine had the fewest fleas."

Christopher ignored the attempted humor. "That was a kind gesture for a stranger."

"Are there any kind *Inuit* spirits, or only demons?"

"There's *Eeyeekalduk* who lives in a grain of sand and heals sick people."

Bud pulled his backpack onto his shoulders. "There you go. Think about him."

Following Bud onto the trail, Christopher added, "*Eeyeekalduk* heals sick people, but if you're not sick and you stare at him, he'll make you sick."

Walking behind, Larry commented. "Your *Inuit* spirits are really a mess. Even the good one can be bad."

"Like I said, an *Inuk's* life is tough."

Larry chuckled. "Especially if everyone is a pessimist being chased by evil spirits who want to kill you, starve you, or make you sick."

"Don't forget the spirits like *Agloolik* who overturns boats and drowns people."

Bud glanced over his shoulder. "He sounds like a real gem. Is *Agloolik* the reason so many of your people disappear while they're fishing and seal hunting?"

"*Agloolik's* name is whispered when someone doesn't return from a fishing or hunting trip on the ocean."

Walking over the crest of a small hill, Bud paused. "The trail is...poorly defined ahead of us. I'll pick a line that looks hopeful, but we may have to backtrack."

Larry stepped alongside Christopher. "You don't seem as panicked about reaching Kimmirut today."

"Something has changed. I can't explain it, but whatever was drawing me to Kimmirut has been resolved without me."

"What about the guy who knocked you out of the raft?"

A dreamy look swept over Christopher. "He was a shapeshifter."

"What does that mean?" Larry asked as they followed Bud.

"He seemed to be good but turned out to be bad. He will be seen for what he is."

"You need to report him when you get to an RCMP station."

"I will, but I sense there are other spirits who'll deal with him."

"That's heavy. Are you saying the demons are going to kill him?"

"I don't think so, but I feel like he's no longer a factor in my life."

"I'd be out to get a guy who tried to kill me, then left me for dead."

"There's a story my grandfather told me about an old woman whose child was teased by the local people. Only one man, Kiviuq, treated her child well. When the old woman can no longer stand the bullying and abuse, she changes Kiviuq into a seal who swims out into the ocean. The bullies jump in their boats and chase the seal, planning to kill it. The old woman conjures up a storm that flips all the boats and drowns the bullies. Kiviuq swims back to shore where the old woman turns him back into a person."

"So, even when there is good to be done, the *Inuit* spirit used a bad event to punish and kill people?"

Christopher walked in silence while he pondered the question. "I guess you're right, Larry. The whole *Inuit* spirit world is full of negativity. No wonder we're all pessimists."

"Maybe you should start a new *Inuit* story about two firemen who are good spirits who come to rescue a hypothermic college student who's about to die."

Christopher raised his eyebrows. "Who would believe a story like that?"

Tatty called The Lodge as soon as she got up, hoping to catch nurse Gustafson at the end of her night shift. The tired voice answering the phone sounded haggard and at wits end. "This is Betty, how can I help you?"

"Is this Betty Gustafson, the night nurse?"

"You've got her. What's up?"

Tatty explained who she was, and that Wolverine's death had been ruled a murder by the coroner. "Did you see anyone unfamiliar in the building around the time of Wolverine Pokaik's death?"

"Oh dear!" the nurse exclaimed. "I feel terrible. Wolverine pulled the call cord in his bathroom. I was busy, so I didn't respond immediately. When I found him on the floor, he was already...gone. I assumed he'd died of a stroke."

"He pulled the call cord?"

"Yes, there's a cord next to the toilet that activates a light in the nurses' station. I was assisting a different resident when he activated the call. I don't know how long the light had been on before I went to check on him."

"Did you see someone come out of his room or maybe in the hallway?"

"I didn't see anyone come out of his room, but there was someone at the other end of the hallway."

"Can you describe the person?"

"Not really. I mean, there was someone there, but the lights were dimmed at night and the person was dressed in dark clothing."

"Was it a man or a woman?"

"I only saw him from the back...the person moved like a young man."

"Please describe his clothing."

"It was dark. I suppose he might've been wearing jeans. He wore a dark-colored jacket."

"Did you notice a logo or writing on the coat?"

"I...don't know. Um, I don't think so."

"What color of hair did he have?"

"I didn't notice...wait...he was wearing a cap."

"Can you remember anything else at all about the person you saw?"

"He kind of reminded me of a person who'd visited Mr. Pokaik."

"You don't start work until what, eleven o'clock?"

"Yes, he was here really late. Everyone was already in bed, and I was surprised to see someone talking to Mr. Pokaik. I asked him to leave."

"Who was it?"

"Hang on. Let me check the visitor logs." After a pause the nurse returned. "Tanaraq Etok and Christopher Pokaik signed in on July 8th. No one else signed in to visit Mr. Pokaik after them the day of his death."

"Can someone get in without signing into the log?"

The nurse chuckled. "It's an honor system. Anyone could walk past the desk and not sign the log."

"What did he look like?"

"He was middle-age and slender."

"Was he *Inuit* or white?"

"He was white. He apologized for visiting so late, then he shook hands with Mr. Pokaik and left."

"Do you remember what he was wearing?"

"Um, not really. Wait, he'd hung his green jacket on the back of the chair. I got a flash of some unfamiliar logo as he put it on. He wore a cap with the same logo."

"Do you think the man who was visiting was the same person you saw in the hallway the night Wolverine was killed?"

"I really couldn't tell. Like I said, I only got a glimpse of the man in the hallway, and only from the back."

"You said the man who apologized had a logo on the back of his jacket. Did you notice that logo on the jacket of the man you saw in the hallway?"

"I don't recall a logo on that man's jacket. But the hallway lights were dim, and I only saw a flash of him. I really can't say if his jacket had a logo or not."

"Do you remember if he left through the front door, or did he use a different exit?"

"Now that you mention it, that was strange. He seemed to be in a hurry and he left through the emergency exit at the far end of the hallway."

Tatty thanked the nurse, then hung up the phone, no closer to knowing about the mystery man who'd been seen in the hallway, or the identity of the man who'd visited without signing in. Unable to contain her curiosity about the mystery man in the dark, possibly green jacket that might or might not have had a logo on the back, Tatty called the three Iqaluit hotels. The desk clerks were surprisingly open to discussing their guests, but none remembered a man wearing a green jacket with a logo and matching cap.

After a cup of coffee and a slice of toast, Tatty put on her uniform and walked to her vehicle. With the engine idling, she racked her brain for another way to identify the person in the green jacket. Remembering a sign for a bed and breakfast near the airport, Tatty decided to pay them a visit.

The building was a two-story house that might've been home for a family of five at one time. Now, there was a faded sign in the yard that read Iqaluit B&B. Not sure if she should knock, ring the doorbell, or walk in, she opted for the last option. The front door opened into a large living room that looked comfortable but was filled with slightly worn furniture. An *Inuit* woman walked out of the kitchen wiping her hands on a towel.

Surprised to see a constable's uniform, the woman froze.

"Can I help you?"

"Is one of your guests a middle-aged man who wears a green jacket with a logo?"

"Is there a problem?"

Not wanting to announce that the man might be a murder suspect, Tatty's mind raced. "We're just trying to locate him."

"He hasn't been here for a couple of days, but I expect he'll be back soon."

"Who would that be?"

"Mr. Curtis rents a room from us for the entire summer every year."

"Eric Curtis, the outfitter?"

"Yes. He shuttles customers back and forth to the airport. We sometimes prepare a meal for them if they're here overnight before starting their raft or canoe trips."

Struggling to maintain her composure, Tatty smiled. "Do you expect him back soon?"

"Yes, he's making a quick trip down the Soper to make sure his usual camping spots are still usable and that the river isn't too high."

Taking out a business card and pen, Tatty wrote her home phone number on the back of her card. "Please call me, either at the RCMP office or my home, when Mr. Curtis returns."

The woman accepted the card, then studied the numbers. "I'll have Mr. Curtis call you."

"Please call me yourself. I'll stop by to have a chat with Mr. Curtis when he's here."

Back in her car, Tatty took a breath and processed the information. Eric Curtis was rafting down the Soper with Christopher. The same person may have been talking with Wolverine the night before his murder and may have been seen in the hallway the night of the murder.

Tatty closed her eyes, recalling previous conversations. Wolverine owned a section of land by the Soper and planned to give it to Christopher. Eric Curtis was leasing the land for his outfitting trips. Had Wolverine transferred the land to Christopher or was he just talking about it? Did the land transfer to Christopher upon Wolverine's death if the deed wasn't changed? Would Eric Curtis kill Wolverine over a lease dispute? Why take Christopher on the raft trip? Hanta was worried about Christopher's spirit. Were Hanta's dreams omens or dementia?

Tatty drove to the RCMP office. "I need to call Kimmirut to see if Christopher and Eric Curtis have arrived."

Carole McKittrick was sitting at her desk, with Sergeant Gerri Carson standing next to her looking at her computer screen. They both looked up when Tatty walked in. Carole held up a piece of fax paper. "Eric Curtis just reported that Christopher Pokaik fell out of a raft in the rapids above Soper Lake. The Kimmirut Mountie chartered a boat captain to search for him."

Tatty was speechless. She dropped into Carole's guest chair and hung her head. "Is there any chance Christopher survived?"

"The Mountie said the water is so cold that unless he'd been pulled out of the water immediately and put in front of a warm fire, there's hardly any chance he's alive."

"So, they've undertaken a recovery effort rather than a rescue."

Gerri nodded. "It's been more than a day since he fell out of the raft."

"Where's Eric Curtis?"

"I suppose he's flying back here," Carole replied. "He made the report in Kimmirut and probably left shortly afterward."

"Curtis tried, unsuccessfully, to negotiate a lease with Wolverine Pokaik the days before the murder. A person matching Curtis' description was seen inside The Lodge about the time of the murder. There are too many coincidences lining up."

Gerri Carson straightened up. "Can someone identify Curtis as being near the murder scene at the right time?"

Tatty let out a breath. "No. Two people saw someone who was slender, like Curtis, wearing a jacket similar to his, in The Lodge hallway shortly after the murder. There's something involving Pokaik's land grant as a motive. Curtis was negotiating a lease to use that land as a base for his Soper River trips. I suspect the negotiations fell apart with Wolverine and Curtis killed him hoping he'd be able to negotiate a better deal with

Christopher Pokaik. If Christopher wasn't willing to lease the land, his life could've been at risk, too."

Gerri Carson sat on the edge of the desk. "That's all circumstantial, Tatty. Find something solid we can use in court."

Tatty closed her eyes, deep in thought. "Wolverine's room has been cleaned since his death and there have been dozens of people in and out of the room, all leaving their fingerprints."

Carson nodded. "There's no way to recover the murderer's fingerprints in a room that has so many staff people and visitors this long after the crime."

"Maybe the bedding we removed from Wolverine's room will link Curtis to the murder."

"I think the best we can hope for is definitive evidence that a pillow was used as the murder weapon. We don't have the technology to lift fingerprints from fabric and I doubt the killer left his driver's license or VISA card inside the sheets."

Tatty stood. "I know which B&B Curtis is staying at. I'll get a confession out of him."

Carson stood and put her hand on Tatty's arm. "You will NOT question Eric Curtis. You're too personally involved in this case."

"But..."

"No. You're off the murder. Follow up on the Cape Dorset girl. I'll take over the Pokaik case."

Tatty remembered Christopher's smiling face and tried not to picture him as a body being dragged from Lake Soper. Then she recalled how cold the water was there and that bodies don't bloat with gas and float to the surface in the frigid water as they did in the lakes farther south. No, when *Inuit*s died in the water they were gone. *Sedna*, the spirit of the sea, had them.

Tatty stood. "I'm going to The Lodge. I need to talk to Hanta."

Gerri Carson stared at her. "You're not going to talk about the Pokaiks, right?"

"Hanta had visions about Buniq Tingenek. I'm going to ask him about her."

Gerri Carson nodded toward her office and led Tatty around the corner. Closing the door, she leaned against it while Tatty stood next to the guest chairs. "I know you were close to Christopher, so I can't let you continue on this case. You trust me, right?"

Tatty nodded.

"Then let me pursue the Pokaik cases. I'll do my best and perhaps we'll make an arrest. Look into the Tingenek disappearance." As an afterthought, she added. "Talk to the funeral home, too. Tell them they can proceed with Wolverine Pokaik's burial."

Exhaling, Tatty nodded. "There's no point in waiting around for Christopher's return. O'Keefe can make plans and move ahead."

"Tatty, I don't know if you're Anglican or if you believe in the *Inuit* spirit world. Either way, Christopher is free from his earthly bonds and in a happy place."

Tears formed in Tatty's eyes as she nodded. "He was so young, with so much life ahead of him."

Carson pulled her into a hug. "I'm so sorry."

"We decided that we were cousins. He didn't have anyone else in the world."

"You were like his big sister more than his cousin."

Tatty took a deep breath and stepped back. Taking a tissue from a box on Carson's desk, she wiped her eyes and nose. "I should go to the funeral home first."

* * *

Stopping at home, Tatty dialed Connie Kootoo's number. "Hello."

"Connie, we got word that Christopher fell out of a raft. The Kimmirut Mounties are searching for him." She held back the darker news that there was little chance of surviving a fall into the icy Soper River water.

"Oh, I..." Blindsided by the news, she had nothing to say or ask.

"I'll let you know as soon as I hear any more."

"Tatty."

"Yes."

"Thank you for letting me know."

* * *

233

A battered Chevy truck and two other cars were parked in front of the funeral home when Tatty arrived. One of the cars, a twenty-year-old Dodge, was idling with the driver's door open. Tatty's cop senses told her something was amiss, so she took the radio off her belt and called the dispatcher. "I need three license plates checked." She recited the numbers to the dispatcher as she walked past the vehicles.

"Are you making a traffic stop?" the dispatcher asked. "Do you need backup?"

"No need for backup at this time. I'm at the funeral home." As an afterthought Tatty added, "If you don't hear from me in ten minutes, send someone to check on me."

Inside, she heard arguing coming from the funeral director's office. "I want him buried in seal skin, not a moth-eaten caribou hide!"

Kenneth O'Keefe's response was quiet and measured. The words weren't discernable to Tatty, but she could tell that O'Keefe was trying to defuse a confrontation. She walked to the open office door and knocked. "Is everything okay?"

A group of seven *Inuit* adults and five children spun around to face the new arrival. The oldest woman, apparently the matriarch of the group, took a step toward Tatty. Her eyes were full of fire and her posture suggested she was ready to pounce. "Who the hell are you?"

O'Keefe looked past the extended family, his eyes pleading. "Constable Etok, what a timely visit. I was just discussing Wolverine Pokaik's burial arrangements with his daughter and her family."

Tatty froze. "Wolverine's only child was a son who died a decade ago."

The older woman's eyes narrowed. "Who are you, the genealogy police?"

"I'm a friend of the Pokaik family. Wolverine was my grandfather's roommate."

Tatty looked past the matriarch and nodded to a woman in her thirties who held a toddler on her hip. "Hello, Charlene. It looks like you're doing well."

The woman, Charlene Seagull, who'd attempted suicide during an episode of post-partum depression, blushed and looked away without answering.

A hard looking man who appeared to be in his thirties gestured toward the door. "I suggest that you leave, Constable. Mr. O'Keefe needs to alter some of the burial arrangements."

"Who are you?" Tatty asked.

"I don't see how that is any of your business."

"You're having a verbal confrontation with Mr. O'Keefe. I'm here to make sure it doesn't get out of hand. Who are you?"

Another young man stepped forward, standing between Tatty and the older woman. "I'm Charlie Thinman, and this is my mother Sos Seagull. We're here making burial arrangements for my grandfather."

Tatty nodded to the son, who sneered at her, then retreated behind his mother without response.

The funeral director stood, looking past Sos Seagull's family toward Tatty. "They want to change the plans made by Christopher Pokaik."

Tatty nodded and looked at the matriarch. "I was here with Wolverine's grandson when he made the burial plans. You don't need to change them."

The woman spread her arms. "Do you see anyone other than me, Wolverine's daughter, and my children who are Wolverine's grandchildren?" Turning, she addressed the funeral director. "I want my father to have the same funeral you did for my son, Alex. You wrapped him in seal skin."

O'Keefe shook his head. "I don't think I can find seal skin this time of year. Alex died last spring, when seals were available."

"Wait a moment," Tatty said. "If you're Wolverine's family, where have you been for the last twenty years?"

Sos Seagull stiffened. "Not that it's any of your business, but I've been taking care of my mother, Wolverine's first wife. My family lives in Apex."

"Whoa! I didn't know that Wolverine had two wives."

The woman smiled. "He was quite a hunter and a good provider. He spent a winter with my mother's family when he was a young man, and he married her. I was born the next summer."

Memories of *Inuit* history flashed through Tatty's mind. The *Inuit* were nomadic people, many had only settled in villages during the past two generations. There were rumors about polygamy, although her teachers said the term was inappropriate for the informal marital situations of the ancient nomadic *Inuit* people. Many families were monogamous, led by the most skilled hunter. But *Inuit* history included young men from other families being welcomed into the family units, especially if there was a daughter interested in an attractive young man who was a good provider. Fathering a child was often viewed as a marriage. Some of those liaisons resulted in long-term relationships. Others ended when the hunter moved on the following spring, especially if he had a difference of opinion with the girl's father.

"Was Wolverine's first marriage recorded? Is Wolverine listed as the father on your birth certificate?"

The woman took a step towards Tatty. "You're *Inuit*. You understand that *Inuit* marriages aren't church affairs like the ones Catholics and Anglicans have. In years past, there were understandings as binding as any marriage certificate. As for my birth certificate, I was born many miles from Iqaluit, or any other city. My grandfather didn't hitch up the dogsled and race here to register my birth. However, that doesn't make me any less Wolverine's child. As his first child, all that he owned is now my birthright."

"This is not the time or place to argue Wolverine's estate."

O'Keefe watched the conversation and chose that moment to interrupt. "Excuse me. I have to respect the wishes of Mr. Pokaik's grandson. I understand that you may be his family, but Christopher Pokaik is the person who came forward as the decision maker."

A chunky younger woman sneered at O'Keefe. "You know nothing about who Wolverine's family is. Bury him the same way you buried my brother."

O'Keefe struggled to maintain control of the situation. "I have to talk to Christopher Pokaik before I'll change the burial plans."

The young woman shrugged. "Perfect. Get his butt in here and we'll have a family reunion. Hi, Chris, I'm your cousin, Cheri."

The youngest child started crying, apparently rattled by her mother's tone of voice.

"Cheri, get your brat out of here," the older woman said. She turned to O'Keefe. "I want Wolverine wrapped in seal skin."

"I don't have any seal skins," O"Keefe replied. Seeing that answer was unacceptable he looked to Tatty for support. "I have to notify Christopher Pokaik that you've requested a change in the burial plans."

"Fine. Have your burial with my father wrapped in that ratty caribou skin. It's on you if Wolverine's spirit can't find its way." The woman stormed out with her extended family in tow, slamming the door as they left.

O'Keefe let out a breath. "Thank you, Constable. The discussion was getting rather heated, and I was running out of ways to placate the woman. I think she might be mentally unstable."

"What's the older woman's name?" Tatty asked as she took out a notebook.

"Her name is Sos Seagull. She lives in Apex."

"Did she show you anything to substantiate her claim that she's Wolverine Pokaik's daughter?"

"She offered to draw a family tree. I said that wouldn't be a legal document. I doubt she has any documentation showing her relationship to the deceased."

Tatty drew a deep breath while she considered the situation. "You're free to proceed with Wolverine's burial. The pathologist and coroner have released his body."

"Great. I'll arrange it as soon as I hear back from his grandson."

Tatty fingered her notebook nervously. "I'm afraid his grandson may not be available."

"He returned to Toronto?"

"He fell out of a raft on the Soper River. He's missing and presumed drowned."

O'Keefe stiffened. "Oh, no."

"Go ahead with the burial. I'll bring my grandfather, Hanta. He will make sure Wolverine's spirit is freed."

"What do you want me to do about the woman who claims to be his daughter?"

"Ignore her. Anyone can walk in and claim to be a relative. Without a birth certificate or someone who can attest to her parentage, we're going to ignore her."

Tatty stood in the funeral home lobby, considering the revelation that Wolverine may have had a daughter and an extended family. *I doubt that Wolverine had a will, which means he died intestate. Without a living spouse, his estate will be split among his children and grandchildren. I need to look for a will in Wolverine's belongings. I wonder if he actually transferred ownership of his land and house to Christopher before his death. That would certainly clean up the question of inheritance.*

Tatty answered her radio as she walked out of the funeral home. "I've got the owners of those vehicles," the dispatcher announced.

Tatty wrote the names in her notebook. "Are all the surnames Seagull or Thinman?"

"That's correct," Carole replied. "Sos Seagull, Cheri Seagull, and Charlie Thinman.

The vehicles are all registered to the same address in Apex."

* * *

Hanta was sitting in the lobby, talking to the cute receptionist at the front desk. He looked up when Tatty entered, but kept flirting with the girl, who seemed to be accepting of his attention. Tatty leaned on the counter next to him and smiled at the girl, "Be careful. He's a dirty old man with twenty children and a hundred grandchildren."

Hanta's eyes sparkled, and his smile broadened. "My third wife died a few years ago and now I have nowhere to spend my million-dollar fortune. I don't suppose you're in the market for a rich husband?"

The girl laughed and shook her head. "I'm only nineteen."

"My first wife was only fourteen," Hanta replied.

"Isn't that illegal?" the girl asked.

Hanta snorted. "What happens in the igloo, stays in the igloo."

Tatty tapped Hanta's shoulder and pointed down the hallway. "I think you've harassed this young woman enough for one day."

Hanta nodded at the girl. "I'll see you tomorrow." Then he walked alongside Tatty down the hall. "I think she was impressed with my virility."

"I suspect the mention of a million dollars interested her more than your many offspring. Young people are less impressed with a man's ability to sire many children than they are with money."

Hanta glanced over his shoulder to make sure they were out of the girl's hearing. "She's a skinny little thing. I don't think her hips are wide enough for bearing many children." Hanta glanced at Tatty's hips. "Your body is better suited for bearing children. When are you going to find a man?"

"My marital situation is none of your business, Grandfather."

"I worry that you're past your prime. All the good providers your age are already married."

Ending the marriage discussion, Tatty said, "I have sad news. Wolverine's grandson fell out of a raft on the Soper River and hasn't been located."

"*Agloolik* overturned his canoe?"

"I don't know any details. The outfitter paddled their raft into Kimmirut and reported him missing to the RCMP."

Hanta stared into the distance. "The Soper water is unforgiving. Unless he was wearing seal skin and got to shore quickly, he probably froze to death."

Tatty steered Hanta into his room and they sat in chairs by the window. "What do you know of Christopher's spirit?"

"I haven't been listening."

Tatty cocked her head. "You're a shaman. I thought you heard spirits and demons all the time."

"Don't you turn off the radio when you're tired of listening to music?" Hanta asked.

"My radio has a button. I didn't think you could choose to not hear the voices."

"To hear the spirits, I stop listening to the world around me. The sounds of people and The Lodge noises drown out the voices of the spirits. I sit quietly or lie in bed to hear them. They speak the loudest when I try to sleep."

"Flirting with the receptionist drowns out the voices of the spirits?"

Hanta smiled. "The voice of a young woman has always drowned out many sounds, including my own voice of good sense."

"There was a woman at the funeral home today. She claimed to be Wolverine's daughter from his first marriage."

When Hanta didn't immediately respond, Tatty thought he hadn't heard her. He eventually said, "Did you understand what I said to that young girl?"

Thinking Hanta's dementia had moved his mind to a new topic, Tatty said, "I'm not sure what you're talking about."

"What happens in the igloo, stays in the igloo."

"I thought you were teasing her."

"Times were different when Wolverine and I were young men. We sometimes visited igloos and stayed with a pretty woman for a time. Some of those visits were considered marriages."

"Did Wolverine ever tell you that he'd been married?"

Hanta shrugged. "We spoke of many things from the past."

"Were there *Inuit* wedding ceremonies when you were a young man?"

"It depends. Sometimes our bond with a woman was no more than a *kunik* and an invitation under her seal skin."

"Was that considered a marriage?"

Hanta continued to stare into the distance. "If the visit resulted in a child, I suppose you could call it a marriage."

"If marriages were that informal, was polygamy common in the old days?"

"I didn't know that word until I came to Iqaluit. We didn't know about polygamy or monogamy. We lived in families and the best hunter made the rules. We all understood that children should have fathers from other families, but we also knew that the strongest hunter sometimes didn't tolerate a challenge from his daughter's lover. Children were born into families. The mother cared for the child and the strongest hunter provided for them. Who is a father? The one who feeds her children, or the man who gave her a *kunik* and warmed her seal skin one winter?"

"So, you think that the woman at the mortuary might be Wolverine's biological daughter?"

"Have you not been listening? What's a biological father to a hungry woman and her children? The man who fed them is the father of her children."

"Wolverine moved to Iqaluit and married Christopher's grandmother."

Hanta nodded. "There's your answer. Wolverine fed his wife and her child. They were his family. His son fed a wife and his son, then Christopher. They were his family."

"But there are marriage licenses and birth certificates."

"Yes, there are...now. What do they mean? Is the man's name on the birth certificate the father of a child? If he dies and the woman remarries, who is the father of her children? If a man deserts a woman and her children, is he the father or is the kind man who comes to her aid, loves her and feeds the children. Is he not their father?"

"So, the woman at the mortuary isn't Wolverine's daughter?"

Hanta looked out the window. "Wolverine never fed a girl child. She is not his daughter." Hanta turned and frowned. "That woman may have spent her early life in a residential school. What did you say her name was?"

"She called herself Sos Seagull."

"The *Inuit* name for seagull is Nauja. The residential school social workers and teachers probably couldn't pronounce her *Inuit* name, so they changed it to Seagull.

That happened to many children." Hanta grew somber. "So many *Inuit* children died in the schools. They caught diseases like smallpox and tuberculosis from the teachers and were beaten for speaking *Inuktitut*. The dead children were buried in ways that trapped their spirits.

"That was a sad time. Now, our children are being taught to speak and read *Inuktitut* in school. Some villages hardly speak any English or French."

"What did the Seagull woman want?"

"She was arguing with the funeral director about Wolverine's burial arrangements, unhappy that Christopher chose a caribou skin for the burial wrap. The woman thought Wolverine should've been wrapped in seal skin."

Hanta clucked his tongue. "What did she say about his harpoon and fishing gear?"

"She didn't mention those things."

Closing his eyes, Hanta bent his head forward. "That woman didn't care about Wolverine's spirit journey. It makes no difference if the body is wrapped in seal, caribou, or fox. What matters are his tools, the things he needs to hunt when his spirit passes into the cloud world. That woman has a demon spirit. You must deal with her."

Tatty stiffened. "*I* must deal with her?"

"You are prepared to take on demons. You are strong and you know that she's coming. Don't allow her to trick you into believing that lies are the truth, and don't join forces with her when she invites you to be her friend."

"I don't know how to deal with those things. I'm barely able to talk a teenager out of committing suicide once in a while."

"Go home and turn off all the noise. Let your mind focus on the voices of the spirits who speak to you but are drowned out by the sounds of your world. Close your eyes and open your mind to the voices."

"What if I hear bad voices?"

"There are more bad voices than good voices. Listen to them all. Each has a lesson for you. The lessons that cause you pain are the ones you'll remember."

"But I have to deal with the Seagull woman and her children."

"It's not her place to determine the path for Wolverine's spirit. Be strong and you will understand. There are many dark spirits around the Seagull woman. Be careful that one of them doesn't attack you when you're dealing with her."

"You're speaking in riddles."

Hanta shook his head. "No, you must prepare for your demon battles."

"Help me prepare."

Hanta shook his head. "I'm tired. Help me into bed."

Tatty touched Hanta's cheek with her nose. "I have to follow up on Christopher Pokaik's search."

Hanta blinked, then closed his eyes. "Christopher's spirit is well. You don't need to worry."

Tatty froze, knowing that Hanta had said spirits were well when people were safe, or when their spirits had departed after death. "Is Christopher alive?"

"His spirit doesn't need your worry. Now, go."

Walking from Hanta's room, Tatty fumed as she talked to herself. "I'm not supposed to worry? You're driving me crazy with your indirect, incomplete visions. Is Christopher alive or dead? It's an easy question. He's one or the other. Which is it?"

The young receptionist looked up when she heard Tatty's ramblings. "Constable Etok, your grandfather is funny."

Composing herself, Tatty smiled. "Yes, Hanta is very entertaining."

The girl motioned Tatty to the reception desk. "Your grandfather is very proud of you."

Tatty must've looked surprised. "Really?"

"Hanta said you're very brave by being a constable. He said we need leaders like you to make Nunavut a better place, people who care about their elders, and who are willing to step into the problems our community faces."

Smiling, Tatty said, "Thank you. You've made my day."

Chapter 18

On the third day of Christopher's trek with Bud and Larry, the trail became distinct due to the greater volume of day-trippers who ventured only far enough to get a taste of Nunavut without spending the night in a tent. Walking up a rocky rise, they were treated to a view of Lake Soper and the distant town of Kimmirut. Bud slapped Christopher on the shoulder. "By golly, I think we're actually looking at civilization."

Larry snorted as he walked past, continuing on the downslope. "Anyone who thinks of Kimmirut as civilization has never been to civilization."

Christopher felt the pace quicken as they followed well packed dirt trails marked with the footprints of previous hikers. Coming over a rise ahead of them, a pair of hikers dressed in vivid colors waved to them as they approached. It took nearly ten minutes for the two groups to actually come face to face.

The other pair were a young man and woman wearing head nets to protect them from the mosquitoes and carried daypacks intended to carry supplies for a one-day round-trip hike. Unlike Christopher and his companions, the man and woman looked clean and freshly groomed. The woman, with her blonde hair protruding from under a stocking cap, spoke first. "The Mounties told us to be on the lookout for the body of a man who fell out of a raft a couple of days ago."

Bud put his meaty hand on Christopher's shoulder. "The reports of my young friend's demise are premature."

The male hiker pulled off his gloves. "If you're the guy they're looking for, you're a miracle. They told us there was no way anyone could fall out of a raft in the rapids and survive. If the river rocks didn't kill you, they were sure hypothermia would."

Christopher nodded toward Bud. "If not for Bud's first aid training, and Larry's cooking, I'm sure I'd be an icicle laying on the shore."

The man checked his watch, then looked at the woman. "We were going to hike another half hour before turning around, but I'd like to see the Mountie's face when the missing person walks into their office." The man gestured toward the woman. "This is Ann and I'm Drew Skaar."

Offering his hand, Christopher introduced himself and his partners.

Ann's eyes went wide, "You're really the missing man?" She dug into her daypack. "We've got tons of energy bars and chocolate. Would you guys like something?"

Bud laughed and put out his hand. "That'd be great. We've been packing food into Christopher to warm him up. He's burned through pretty much anything we brought along that has carbs and calories."

Christopher accepted a Snickers bar and stripped off the wrapper. Savoring the first bite and smiling he said, "I'll find some *akutaq* to swap for this when we get to Kimmirut."

"*Akutaq*?" Drew asked.

"It's the *Inuit* equivalent of an energy bar."

Ann shook her head. "Nope. No way. I'm sure it includes some disgusting internal cod organ."

Christopher smiled as he took another bite of the candy bar. "There's no cod in *akutaq*. It's high-quality seal blubber and berries. It's tasty and has a lot of calories."

Ann gagged. "Oh God, that sounds worse than the veal liver my grandmother used to cook with bacon and onions."

Drew, reveling in his wife's discomfort, smiled. "I'll give it a try."

Bud grimaced. "I think any variety of blubber is off my menu."

After finishing a candy and an energy bar each, Bud, Drew, and Christopher were ready to go. Ann and Drew set a quicker pace than Christopher was prepared for, but the prospect of getting to Kimmirut and the candy energized him.

* * *

With a population of slightly over 400 people, Kimmirut wasn't a large town and the walk to the Mountie station took less than ten minutes from the time they passed the first building. Jack Kacinski was leaning over his desk studying a map when Bud walked through the door, followed by Christopher, Larry, Ann, and Drew. He straightened up and glanced among them. "I've already heard about the polar bear up by the airport."

Bud wrapped his arm around Christopher's shoulders. "This is the dead guy you're looking for, the one who fell out of the raft."

"You're kidding."

"I'm Christopher Pokaik. I was rafting down the Soper River until Eric Curtis shoved me out of the raft as we went through the rapids." Gesturing toward Bud and Larry he added, "If not for these two men, I'd be dead."

"There are a whole bunch of people looking for you, Chris."

"Christopher, please."

The Mountie waved off the correction. "I've got to let some folks know that you're here and alive."

Bud's eyes narrowed. "Where's Eric Curtis? I'd like to give him a piece of my mind."

252

Larry snorted. "If I get to him first, I'll kick his butt so hard he'll be using Chapstick on his hemorrhoids."

"Easy fellows," the Mountie said. "Curtis has a different version of that story, and we'll need to sort it out before anyone kicks anyone's butt. Eric Curtis flew out of here this morning. I'll call the RCMP sergeant in Iqaluit and have him held until this assault allegation gets sorted out."

"Can you get me on a flight to Iqaluit today?" Christopher asked.

The Mountie chuckled. "There's no regular air service between Kimmirut and Iqaluit, or anywhere else for that matter. Let me talk to Sergeant Carson. We'll see what arrangements she can make."

Kacinski lifted the phone while everyone watched. As he dialed, Christopher said, "If Special Constable Etok is there, I'd like to talk to her."

Kacinski raised a finger when he got an answer. "Carole, is the sergeant around? Our missing rafter just walked into my office." The Mountie, apparently on hold while they contacted the sergeant, stared at the floor and held the phone silently while he waited. He looked up when someone spoke to him. "Yes, Sergeant. Christopher Pokaik is standing in front of me."

Christopher took the phone when it was offered. "Hello?"

The female voice was cheerful. "Mr. Pokaik, this is RCMP Sergeant Carson. We've been very concerned about you."

"It's been a crazy few days, Ma'am."

"Are you okay now? I mean, do you need a hospital or doctor?"

"Thanks to a pair of hikers, I'm warm now. I don't feel like I need a hospital."

"My clerk is calling the airport now. We'll arrange to have a pilot pick you up in Kimmirut. A car will meet you at the Iqaluit airport and the driver will take you to the hospital for a check-up. Okay?"

"Um, sure. Can you do something special for the guys from Thunder Bay who found me half frozen and nursed me back to health?"

"Absolutely! Give the Kimmirut Mountie their names and addresses, and I'll write up a commendation for them. I'll have it presented by their local RCMP detachment."

"Ma'am, is my cousin, Special Constable Tatty Etok around? I'd like to speak with her."

"She's not in the office, but if I can reach her, I'll have her meet your plane when it arrives." Sergeant Carson paused, "Mountie Kacinski said you were pushed out of the raft. Is that correct?"

"We were in the rapids and the raft kind of spun around. I was trying to hold on, then I felt a pain in my ribs. Eric Curtis pushed me out of the raft with his paddle."

"I'll need you to make a formal statement about the incident when you get out of the hospital. I'll review the incident with Mr. Curtis after our call."

"Sergeant, he didn't expect me to live through the cold-water immersion. He'd told me earlier in the trip that falling into the icy water was a death sentence unless you got immediate medical attention. He tried to kill me."

"Curtis reported you missing when he arrived in Kimmirut. We'll review his statement with him and ask if he'd like to amend it."

"Is he under arrest?"

"Not at this moment." The sergeant paused as someone spoke to her. "My clerk found a pilot in Kimmirut who's making a trip to Iqaluit this afternoon. He's waiting for you at the airport."

Chapter 19

After hugs and thanks at the Kimmirut airfield (calling it an airport would be grossly overstating the size of the unpaved landing strip and facilities), Christopher walked to the pilot, who was inspecting the plane. Wes Sharp took a step back and looked Christopher over from head to foot. "Aside from mosquito bites, a layer of dirt, and a couple of scratches, you look none the worse for the wear." He gestured for Christopher to sit in the right-hand co-pilot's seat.

Christopher stepped up and into the seat as Wes held the door. "What do you mean by that?"

"After Eric Curtis' report to the RCMP, everyone assumed you were dead."

"How well do you know Curtis?"

Wes closed the right-hand door and walked to the other side of the plane. Once inside, he put on headphones and buckled in. "I fly a few charters a year for Eric, but he's not a buddy I'd invite over to my house."

"He knocked me out of the raft and left me for dead."

The plane's engine turned over, sputtered, then caught. After checking gauges, Wes checked the area around the plane, then started taxiing to the downwind end of the gravel landing strip. As the engine roared and they started to roll, Wes glanced at Christopher. "I haven't spoken with Eric, but the story around town is that he tried to save you, but you fell over the side in the rapids. There was nothing he could do without endangering his own life."

"I'm surprised he's not telling people that *Agloolik* came out of the rapids and shook the raft like a wolf shaking a caribou calf."

The plane rose slowly, making a loop over Soper Lake, giving Christopher a look at Kimmirut and North Bay beyond. "Listen, kid. I'm not a big fan of Eric Curtis. He's a client who pays on time and follows my safety rules. If he's in trouble with the Mounties, that's on him, not me. Personally, I think he's an arrogant rich jerk who feels he can manipulate people with his money and influence. I treat him well because I want his business."

They flew in silence, crossing over the tundra below with the Soper River snaking through it. Wes spoke into the microphone, in a conversation with the Iqaluit airport. Ignoring him, Christopher tensed as they turned on the final airport approach. *I wonder what my parents thought in those final seconds before their plane crashed.*

Were they focused on the horror that their lives were about to end? Did my mother cry out, thinking about me, who would soon be alone in the world?

Christopher was snapped from his thoughts when the pilot touched his elbow. "Hey kid, make sure your seatbelt is tight."

The plane taxied to the small private aviation terminal where an RCMP vehicle was idling. Christopher waited until the pilot turned off the engine and removed his headset. "Can I get out?"

"Keep your head on a swivel. Look out for other aviation traffic."

Nodding, Christopher stepped down from the plane. He checked the area around them, then darted across the concrete to Tatty, who stood next to an RCMP vehicle. In an uncharacteristic move, Tatty hugged him. When he gasped, she released her hug. "What's the matter?"

Christopher pulled up his shirt, exposing three dark bruises that were fading from blue to purple, green, and yellow.

"What happened?" she asked.

"Those are where Eric Curtis jabbed me with his canoe paddle."

Tatty opened the passenger door for Christopher. "We'll take some pictures of those marks at the hospital."

"I don't need a doctor."

Tatty slid into the idling vehicle and buckled her seatbelt. "Sergeant Carson told me to deliver you to the ER where you'll be evaluated."

"I'd rather find Eric Curtis and..."

She reached out and touched Christopher's arm. "Sergeant Carson is interviewing Mr. Curtis. You won't confront him."

"But he tried to kill me!"

"That's not the story he told us when he reported you missing."

Christopher clenched his teeth as they drove into Iqaluit. The town hadn't changed, but his perspective had. Iqaluit was his home, and he'd accepted it as the only place he'd ever known. Now, it appeared different. Less grand, but...comfortable. He knew the buildings and stores. The faces, *Inuit* and white, were familiar as they walked along the street.

"I'd like to see my grandfather."

Tatty glanced at him. "You remember that he's in the funeral home, right?"

Images flashed through Christopher's mind: *His grandfather taking him to the store. Standing over his first caribou kill where his grandfather explained that the animal possessed spirits that needed to be acknowledged and would forgive him if he shared the meat with the elderly and their other neighbors. His grandfather's face inside the body bag.*

"Is he wrapped in a caribou skin with a harpoon and fishing gear?"

"Yes, I think he's prepared for burial."

Christopher tried to count back the days since his grandfather's death. "we're past the fifth day since he died. Is this the proper day for his burial?"

"Um, no. His burial was delayed because...of questions. It's okay. His spirit wasn't ready to depart until his body told us how he'd died."

"Wasn't a stroke the cause of his death?"

As they turned into the hospital parking lot, Tatty said, "The pathologist ruled his death murder by asphyxiation."

Christopher turned to her. "What does that mean?"

"He was smothered, possibly with a pillow."

"Who would do that?"

"We don't know yet. His pillow is being tested, and we're interviewing people who were in The Lodge that night."

Thinking of his grandfather's room, Christopher asked, "What did Hanta see or hear?"

"Hanta was asleep, but another resident saw a man sneaking out of The Lodge. The night nurse also saw someone."

"Have you arrested him?"

Tatty unbuckled her seatbelt and opened the door. "Not yet."

At the hospital's front desk, Tatty explained who Christopher was, and that the RCMP wanted a doctor to examine him and to document his injuries."

Under his breath, Christopher repeated his earlier statement. "I'm fine."

Tatty took him aside while they waited for a nurse to escort him to an exam room. "You are NOT fine. You're bruised, hypothermic, dirty, and mosquito bitten. You're a mess. Let the doctor check you over, then we'll get some pictures of your bruises. After we eat, I'll drive you to the RCMP office and we'll take your statement."

Christopher glowered at her. "I don't need…" He stopped, then studied her face. "You're worried about me."

"I've been worried about you since you arrived here. I've been sick with worry since you left on the stupid raft trip. The last two days, I've been grieving because I thought you were dead."

The nurse appeared and called his name. Turning to Tatty, he touched her cheek with his nose, giving her a *kunik*. "Thank you. A week ago, I hardly remembered you. Now, you're my best friend."

"I've been updating Connie every day. She's been worried, too."

Christopher looked surprised. "You've been calling Connie?"

"Actually, she called me at the station. She was worried because she hadn't heard from you."

"I was going to call, but we kind of rushed off the morning we flew to the river."

"She knows that you're okay, but she'd really like to hear your voice."

Christopher turned to follow the nurse to an exam room, then paused to look back at Tatty. "I'll call her as soon as the doctor releases me."

"I think you should eat something first."

"I'm really looking forward to a restaurant meal, cousin."

Shaking her head, Tatty smiled. "What would you like on your pizza?"

"Pepperoni!"

* * *

A young man wearing a white smock with a stethoscope hanging around his neck walked into the waiting area and nodded to Tatty. "Please come back, Constable."

Following the doctor into an exam room, Tatty was surprised to see Christopher bare-chested, sitting on the exam table. Feeling blood rushing to her face, she tried to act nonchalant at seeing so much of Christopher's bare skin.

The doctor, who introduced himself as Ray Simpson M.D., walked to Christopher's side and leaned down. "I took pictures of these bruises, but I thought it would be helpful if I explained what I'm seeing."

Looking where the doctor's finger pointed, Tatty saw a nearly purple diagonal bruise on Christopher's left side, a cascade of green and yellow showing below the darkest part. "In my professional opinion, this contusion was caused by a severe blow, probably from a canoe paddle blade. It didn't break the skin only because Mr. Pokaik was wearing multiple layers of clothing. The insultation in his jacket probably protected his ribs as well."

"The attacker contends that he extended the paddle to aid Mr. Pokaik when he fell from the raft."

The doctor composed his thoughts before responding. "That bruise wasn't the result of someone *pushing* a canoe paddle into Mr. Pokaik's hand." Pointing to the bruise, he continued, "This is the result of a vicious blow, not an accidental push." Moving to the side and pointing at Christopher's back he added, "The two additional bruises on his back reinforce that opinion."

"Has the patient recovered from the hypothermia?" asked Tatty.

Smiling, the doctor nodded. "The hypothermia probably made the bruises less painful and minimized the bruising. We always tell people to ice their bruises. I'd say Mr. Pokaik took that advice to the extreme. As for the hypothermia, the firemen who rescued Mr. Pokaik undoubtedly saved his life. They did all the right things to raise his body temperature and probably needed to deal with his mental and physical limitations. Getting back to Kimmirut in three days of hiking was quite a feat."

Tatty nodded toward the door. "Can I ask a few more questions while Christopher gets dressed?" In the hallway, Tatty asked, "Would you say that the attack was an attempt on the patient's life?"

"Hell yes! Knocking that kid into the icy water was attempted murder. In Nunavut, we lose more fishermen and hunters to hypothermia than to drowning. It's supposedly a less unpleasant way to die, with your brain shutting down before your heart stops, but immersion in ice water is deadly." The doctor paused and smiled at Tatty. "Mr. Pokaik said you are his cousin."

"Perhaps. We're both *Inuit* and the branches of the family trees here are tangled. I'm certainly his voluntary cousin."

"Constable, Mr. Pokaik is a mess. I mean mentally, he's struggling. I suggest you get him to a counselor. He's an orphan, an attempt was made on his life, and he's preparing for his grandfather's funeral. You know the Nunavut suicide statistics as well as I do. Your cousin needs support very badly right now or he could slip into a dark place."

The exam room door opened, and Christopher stepped into the hallway. "I'm ready for pizza if the doctor is through with me."

The doctor offered his hand. "You're a lucky man. I hope you listen to your cousin. She's smart and very concerned about you."

Christopher waited until they were outside of the hospital before he spoke. "What did the doctor mean about listening to you?"

Tatty smiled. "Didn't you hear him? The doctor said I was smarter than you, and that you should listen to what I say."

"I got that part. But there was something unsaid, too."

"You were very lucky. Many demons were chasing you, but you survived. That's a sign that you are meant to do greater things."

"I didn't fight off the demons very well. I almost died, and I didn't recognize the demon who was closest to me until he shoved me into the water."

"Do you still have Hanta's knife?"

Christopher patted his side. "It's right here."

"You used it very effectively."

"What are you talking about? I never removed it from the sheath."

"Sometimes our best weapons offer the most protection without removing them from the sheath."

Christopher got into the RCMP vehicle and turned to Tatty. "You're talking in riddles like Hanta and my grandfather."

"Hanta never took that knife out of the sheath to defend himself, yet he's been fighting off demons for himself, and others, his entire lifetime. Your inner strength is in the knowledge that it's there, not in using it to stab or slash someone."

Christopher chuckled.

"What's funny?"

"I doubt a polar bear would be impressed by the inner strength I got from Hanta's knife."

"Perhaps the value of the knife is knowing that it's not effective against a polar bear, and not putting yourself into a position where you'd need to defend yourself."

"Ah, the Crocodile Dundee thing. 'Never bring a knife to a gunfight.' The corollary being, 'Don't bring a knife to a bear fight.'"

"You're catching on."

Christopher suddenly patted his pockets. "I'm sorry. I lost my wallet; I can't pay for pizza."

Tatty laughed. "Let's get real. You're a college student and even if you'd brought your wallet, there probably isn't any money in it."

"I could pay for my half of a pizza."

Tatty parked across the street from the pizza café. "I'll make you a deal; you pay for the next pizza we share."

"I already owe you for the groceries you brought to Wolverine's house."

"He paid me to stock the refrigerator."

Christopher held the door for Tatty. "I sincerely doubt that. He was a cheapskate."

Tatty chose a table near the kitchen and sat facing the door. "It doesn't matter who paid for the groceries. You need to be here, and the people who care about you made that possible."

"I owe a lot of people an awful lot."

Tatty nodded. "Pay us back by becoming an upstanding citizen who cares about other people."

"I don't know what that means."

"Like I said before, don't waste your life. Do something meaningful."

They ordered soda pop and a large pizza. Christopher waited until the waitress stepped away before speaking. "When you say, 'do something meaningful', do you mean move back here and become a teacher?"

"That would be meaningful, but there are thousands of other ways to make a difference in people's lives."

"Give me some examples."

"I like to think that being a constable is important. Being a doctor or nurse impacts people's lives, but so does painting or writing stories. As I said, there are a thousand ways you can make a difference in the world."

"I'm majoring in education with an emphasis in Indigenous Studies. I thought I'd probably teach on a reservation."

"What you've experienced this week will change you forever. Let the events settle and then reassess what you want your life to be."

"I might own a section of land between here and Kimmirut. I'm not sure what that will mean to me."

Tatty laughed. "I don't think that will anchor you in Nunavut. It's not like you'll build a house and plant a garden there."

Christopher became somber. "Eric Curtis said Wolverine had a daughter. Do you think I have an aunt?"

Their pizza arrived before Tatty could answer. Once she'd set out plates, napkins, and forks, the waitress left. Sliding two slices of pizza on her plate to cool, Tatty unfolded her paper napkin and leaned on the table. "I met a woman at the funeral home who claimed to be your aunt. She said her mother was Wolverine's first wife, but when I asked about marriage documents and birth certificates, she avoided the question. If Wolverine was her father, there's no proof of it, and he wasn't a part of her life while she was growing up."

Puffing after taking a bite of too hot pizza, Christopher struggled to get a word out. "Is she my aunt, or not?"

Tatty looked directly at Christopher and said, "I don't think we'll ever be sure of that one way or another. Wolverine isn't here to confirm or dispute her claim, and there's no documentation that he's the woman's father."

"What does that mean?"

"That's up to you. If you want to meet her and embrace her as your aunt, you're welcome to do that. If you choose to ignore her claim, you can forget her and move on with your life."

"That's not helpful."

Tatty shrugged as she bit off a piece of pizza. "I'm just telling you like it is. Do you want to have a bossy aunt with poor manners?”

“Eric Curtis said that she has a better claim on my grandfather’s land than I do. He also said my aunt was going to protest my *Inuit* membership and have me dropped from the membership rolls because I’m only a quarter *Inuit*.”

“Do you want to disavow your *Inuit* heritage?”

“No! Eric said I didn’t qualify as an *Inuit* because my blood quantum isn’t high enough.”

“Your parents registered you as an *Inuit*. You’ve lived as an *Inuit*. Nothing is going to change that. Your aunt can file to have you removed from the rolls, but I’m sure the council would uphold your membership if you protest her move.”

Christopher nodded and continued to eat. He was sliding a third slice onto his plate when he froze. “When is my grandfather’s burial? Has it already happened?”

“The funeral director has been waiting for your return. I think he could arrange for it tomorrow, if you’d like.”

Christopher grimaced. “We already missed doing his burial on the fifth day. Will that make it hard for his spirit to go into *Adlivun?*”

“I’m not a shaman. We’ll have to ask Hanta, the expert on *Inuit* demons and spirits. I suspect he’ll have a way to make sure Wolverine's spirit goes wherever it should."

* * *

Once at home, Christopher was ready to collapse into bed. Then he saw the slip of paper with Connie's number next to the phone. He dialed, intending to leave a message, but was surprised when she answered.

"Um, hi. I thought you'd be at work."

"It's my night off. I've been so worried. Are you okay?"

"I've got a few bruises and a ton of mosquito bites. Other than that, I'm okay."

"You didn't call, then Tatty said you'd fallen out of a raft. It's been..."

"Connie, I'm fine."

"I'd like to see you. I want to touch your face and make sure you're really okay."

"I don't know when that could happen. I've got to bury my grandfather and then the Mounties have more questions about what happened on the river. It's going to be crazy for a few days, then I have to fly back to Toronto."

"Did you think about me while you were on the river trip?"

"You were in one of my dreams."

"I hope that's a sign."

Embarrassed by a sudden wave of emotion, but unsure of how to express himself, Christopher drew a breath. "I guess."

"Christopher, I want to see you before you go back to Toronto."

Between being very tired and unaccustomed to verbalizing his feelings, Christopher said, "I'd like to see you, but I don't know how to make that happen."

* * *

Sergeant Gerri Carson was waiting for Eric Curtis at the Iqaluit B&B when he returned from supper. Eric blanched when he saw the POLICE logo on her bulletproof vest. Recovering his composure, he smiled. "I'm surprised to see the RCMP sitting in my living room. Is something wrong?"

Carson gestured toward a couch near the overstuffed chair she was sitting on. "I need to clarify part of your earlier statement about the incident on the river."

Curtis sat on the couch and crossed his legs. "I thought my statement was complete. We went over it two or three times before you typed, and I signed it."

"That was before Christopher Pokaik walked into Kimmirut."

Curtis' eyes widened. "He walked into Kimmirut?"

Carson nodded. "Two hikers found him and treated his hypothermia. They arrived at the Kimmirut RCMP office this afternoon.

His version of events leading to his fall from the raft is slightly different from yours.”

“In what way?”

Carson removed a notebook from her pocket and flipped through the pages. The move with the notebook was totally for show. She knew exactly what she was going to say and ask without consulting her notes. “Christopher said the raft spun around, causing him to be pressed against the side. He grabbed the tube to hold on, but was struck in the ribs by your paddle, which pushed him over the side. While in the water, you shoved him away from the raft.” She looked up from the notebook and asked, “Is there anything you’d like to amend in your statement?”

“As I said, I held out my canoe paddle to Christopher, so I could pull him into the raft. I might’ve been a little overly aggressive in my move with the paddle, but I was pumped up with adrenaline. It was purely an attempt to give him something to grab so he could pull himself into the raft.”

“Christopher was examined by a doctor who said,” Carson looked down into her notebook, as if consulting the doctor’s statement, “Mr. Pokaik was struck forcefully by the blade of a paddle in the ribs and his back. If not for the heavy clothing he was wearing, the paddle would probably have broken his ribs and possibly punctured his lung. The injuries are consistent with a vicious assault.”

"My adrenaline was pumping. I may have overreacted."

"Two of the bruises are on his back, as if he was being pushed from behind."

"I was trying to turn him around."

"The doctor also noted that the victim's exposure to the icy water resulted in hypothermia that would probably have been fatal if he hadn't been found by two firemen who knew how to treat him and who probably saved his life. In the doctor's view, the blow that knocked Mr. Pokaik into the water was attempted murder."

Curtis sat up. "Whoa! I was trying to save the kid, not murder him."

"In Mr. Pokaik's statement, he mentioned your threat to..." Carson flipped ahead in the notebook and read, "have him out of the way so you could negotiate a lease agreement with his auntie?"

"I mentioned the kid's aunt, but I didn't say anything about getting him out of the way. His aunt is the old man's only living child, so she should have legal standing to inherit the land I lease. I was trying to explain that to the kid."

"Prior to revealing your negotiations with the aunt, you attempted to negotiate a lease with Mr. Pokaik, who'd refused your offer. Correct?"

"Christopher and I had some general discussions about his grandfather's lease."

"Have you also discussed the lease with the woman who claims to be Wolverine's daughter, Sos Seagull?"

"I've met Ms. Seagull."

"Have you had discussions with her about the Pokaik lease?"

Curtis leaned forward and straightened a magazine on the coffee table while he formulated his answer. "Ms. Seagull approached me. She apparently feels that she's going to inherit the land grant with the leased airstrip."

"How many times have you met with Ms. Seagull?"

"Um, I believe we've met twice."

Carson took out a pen and made a note. "Was one of the meetings here, in the B&B?"

Curtis Appeared surprised by the question. After a moment of consideration he replied, "Yes, it was."

Carson nodded. "Did you meet in your room and did Ms. Seagull spend the night?"

"Listen, she approached me about the lease. We hit it off, and she came back here. We're two consenting adults. Okay?"

"Did you offer to pay her legal expenses if Ms. Seagull was willing to contest Christopher Pokaik's *Inuit* membership and his right to inherit the land you're leasing?"

"She may have suggested that, but we haven't..."

Carson closed her notebook and stood. "Mr. Curtis, are you a United States citizen?"

"I am."

"Please bring me your passport. You aren't allowed to leave Iqaluit until my investigation is complete."

"Wait a minute."

"I'll follow you to your room so you can get your passport." Carson turned toward the kitchen. "Mrs. Polartak, will you join us upstairs? Bring the key to Mr. Curtis' room in case he's lost his."

Curtis jumped up. "You can't..."

Carson smiled. "I can't what? You're a guest in a private home. Mrs. Polartak can access your room at any time, and she can grant me search rights. Either you produce your passport, or I'll search the room for it while Mrs. Polartak witnesses the search."

Curtis glared at the RCMP sergeant. "You're trampling on my rights."

"Mr. Curtis, you're one step away from being arrested for attempted murder and conspiracy to commit fraud. I suggest you hire a lawyer. I'm speaking with Mrs. Seagull next. If she decides to make a statement about your joint actions, I might be back with an arrest warrant. For now, consider yourself under house arrest."

Chapter 20

Christopher was eating a granola bar and drinking the bad coffee he'd brewed for himself when Tatty knocked on the door and walked in. "Good morning." Without waiting for an invitation, she poured herself a cup of coffee from the 1960s percolator and sat across from her cousin at the tiny kitchen table. Smiling, she sipped the coffee. Her smile turned into a grimace. "This coffee is terrible."

"I didn't know how much coffee to use, so I filled the basket with ground coffee. It's kind of strong and a lot of the grounds spilled over into the bottom."

Tatty carried her mug to the sink and poured the coffee out. Wiping the excess grounds from the cup with a paper towel she said, "If you can get yourself prepared, the funeral director can do Wolverine's burial at ten o'clock."

Stunned, Christopher stared at her. "This morning?"

Tatty rinsed the mug and set it on the drying rack. "Yes, in less than two hours."

"I don't..." He was unable to verbalize the questions swirling in his head. "Who officiates at the ceremony?"

Tatty walked to the table and picked up Christopher's mug. "You requested a traditional Inuit burial. There's no minister, per se, no viewing, no church funeral ceremony. A group of family and friends go to the burial ground outside of town and we place his wrapped body in a grave dug down to the permafrost, then we cover him with rocks."

"Who's attending?"

"Hanta asked to come along. Aside from him, there are you and I, the funeral director, and the four men and women who've dug the grave and will place rocks on the caribou skin wrap."

Leaving Tatty in the living room, Christopher showered and looked through the clothes he'd brought from Toronto. They were casual t-shirts and jeans or had been worn once since his arrival. Hoping to find something appropriate for a burial, he checked Wolverine's wardrobe and found a western-cut shirt with mother of pearl snaps. It was too large, but it seemed appropriate. Christopher felt a wave of emotion as he pulled the shirt over his arms. The last time he'd seen Wolverine in this shirt, they'd been at the Inuit land claims agreement celebration in 1993. The shirt looked like it hadn't been worn since then, with hanger marks on the shoulders from the years in the wardrobe. He chose the dark pants he'd worn on the flight to Iqaluit, then stared at his white athletic shoes and the hiking boots he'd worn on the Soper River trip. They were scarred and dirty. He tried on a pair of Wolverine's shoes, which were too small, then opted for the boots. *Wolverine would understand.*

Tatty looked up when Christopher walked out of the bedroom. "Fancy shirt."

"Wolverine saved it for special occasions. Are we ready to go?"

Checking her watch, Tatty stood. "It's still a little early."

"I'd like to see where he's going to be buried."

They drove the RCMP SUV to The Lodge where Hanta was waiting for them on an outside bench. Christopher moved from his seat in the front to allow Hanta to have the best view as they drove. Tatty helped Hanta to his feet. "Why are you sitting outside already? We might not have arrived for another hour."

Hanta sat on the seat's edge and swung his legs inside. "I knew you'd be here now."

Tatty frowned. "How did you know that?"

"I was the one who taught you it was better to be an hour early than a minute late. It's a lesson that's served you well."

They drove across town, then took a road that led out of Iqaluit over the tundra. To most people living in southern Canada, the land would look desolate. To Christopher, Tatty, and Hanta, it looked lush and green. Wildflowers were blooming, and the last of the snow had melted into puddles in the soft soil above the permafrost. A kilometer ahead, a pickup and car were parked where several men were gathered near piles of dirt and stones.

Tatty parked behind the pickup. After helping Hanta out of the SUV, Tatty held his arm as they walked across the uneven ground. Separately, Christopher walked to the four men who were standing around a rock pile. On the other side of the shallow grave was a pile of mucky dirt. Tatty nodded to the men and Hanta introduced them to Christopher. All had calloused hands and faces lined from years of outdoor work and exposure to the tough Nunavut weather.

The oldest man gestured toward a white rock set aside from the pile. "We will place that rock last. It sits over Wolverine's face, so his spirit knows where to escape and go to the east."

"I thought his spirit was already gone," Christopher replied.

Hanta nodded. "His *iñuusiq*, life spirit, went to the underworld the night his heart stopped. His *iḷitqusiq*, personal spirit, will leave for the east after his burial. His *atiq*, name spirit, will find another body."

Tearing up, Christopher looked toward town as a black van approached. "Is that the funeral director?"

Tatty nodded. "I think so."

"Is the woman who claims to be my aunt coming? You said she was at the funeral home."

Hanta shook his head. "That woman and her family don't feel the restlessness of Wolverine's spirit. She doesn't know it's departing today."

"Do you mean no one told her about the burial?"

"Her family's spirits aren't connected with Wolverine and you. She doesn't know that Wolverine's spirit is about to depart."

Christopher frowned as the funeral director's van stopped. "Does that mean she's not really Wolverine's daughter?"

Hanta shrugged as the four men walked to the rear of the van to remove the caribou-wrapped remains. "Spirits don't care about family trees drawn on paper. They are bonded to the important people in our lives. What people say, and what the spirits know, are often two very different things."

The men carried the caribou skin wrapped body to the shallow hole and lowered it gently. The hole, dug down to the permafrost, was barely deeper than the thickness of Wolverine's wrapped body. With Wolverine's remains in the hole, the men knelt down and placed the rocks on top of the body until they were layered over a foot thick atop the caribou skin. The oldest man picked up the fist-sized white rock and handed it to Hanta. With Tatty holding his left arm for balance, Hanta walked to the head of the grave and placed the rock on top of the pile.

Christopher watched in silent reverence, expecting a ceremony or prayer of some type. *Now what?* Christopher's mind searched for the right words, the right prayer. His parents were married in the Anglican Church where he'd been taught about Jesus, his miracles, and a loving God who answered prayers. Asking Jesus for forgiveness of sins assured that your *anirniq*, breath spirit, would go to heaven. Wolverine adhered to the traditional Inuit beliefs, that there was no greater being, no heaven, and no hell.

Everyone stood silently for a moment, then Hanta turned to Tatty. "I'm chilled. Take me back to The Lodge."

* * *

Sergeant Carson parked her RCMP SUV at the government building and walked to the Nunavut land titles office. A smiling clerk looked up. "Can I help you, Sergeant?"

"I understand that Wolverine Pokaik owned a land grant near the Soper River. I'd like to know if anyone has made any claims on it and if there are any liens."

"I just handled the transfer of that property last week. Hang on one moment." The clerk walked to a file cabinet and leafed through folders until she found what she was

281

seeking. Bringing two file folders back to the counter, she laid them open in front of Sergeant Carson. "Mr. Wolverine Pokaik transferred his Soper River land and his Iqaluit house to Mr. Christopher Pokaik on June 26, 1999."

Carson scanned the deeds. "Christopher Pokaik wasn't in Iqaluit until June 30th."

The smiling clerk nodded. "Only the owner needs to sign the deed change."

"What if there's a family dispute about who gets the land after the owner's death?"

"The deed was transferred before the owner's death. Mr. Wolverine Pokaik signed the deed here. I witnessed and notarized the transfers. As far as the Nunavut Territory is concerned, the transaction is over. Christopher Pokaik owns a section of land and a house. I can show you where the land grant is on a map if you'd like."

Carson closed the folders and handed them back to the clerk. "There's no need. Thanks for your help."

She stopped outside the building, smiling. *Well, Eric Curtis and Sos Seagull, whatever plans you had for leasing the land are out of your hands. The remaining questions are: Is Eric guilty of attempted murder? Is Sos an accomplice before the fact? Did Sos really think that Wolverine hadn't transferred the land to Christopher? Who murdered Wolverine?*

Chapter 21

After a silent drive, Tatty and Christopher dropped Hanta at The Lodge. As they drove away, Christopher sighed. "That was nice. I think it's what Wolverine wanted."

"I agree. He was traditional, and the burial was as our ancestors have buried people for centuries."

The RCMP radio dispatcher called Tatty as she drove Christopher home. "Sergeant Carson requests your assistance, Constable Etok."

Tatty acknowledged the call and agreed to meet Carson at the headquarters building. Christopher cocked his head. "Do you get called for assistance often?"

"Anytime there's a uniquely Inuit problem, or a problem understanding our *Inuktitut* language, the Mounties request a special constable to assist."

"Isn't that like every call?"

Tatty chuckled. "Not every call has Inuit connections or language issues. A lot of issues are straightforward, and there are a lot of whites up here who break the law, too."

"Um, I talked to Connie."

"And..."

"I think she's...serious. She asked if she's been in my dreams. When I said, yes, she said she's been dreaming about me, too."

"I'm not supposed to tell you this, but she felt butterflies when she saw you on Canada Day." Tatty paused. "Connie is a special person. She didn't get married and have children the day after graduation. She's got a career, and she's very smart...and pretty."

"She and I had this discussion. I live in Toronto and she's in *Pangnirtung*. I don't know what I'm going to do, or where I'll be, after graduation."

"In nine months, you graduate from college, and you'll move somewhere. Connie is talking about moving to a job at a bigger radio station. Who knows where you'll end up." Seeing Christopher's skepticism, Tatty added. "Don't walk away from Connie because of what may happen. If you're meant to be together, you'll figure it out."

* * *

After dropping Christopher off at home, Tatty returned to downtown Iqaluit and parked outside the RCMP headquarters. Carole nodded toward the sergeant's office as Tatty walked through the door. "She's waiting."

Carson looked up from her computer when Tatty knocked on the open door. "Let's take a drive to Apex," Carson said as she stood and grabbed her jacket."

"What's going on in Apex?"

"We're going to the address registered to the license plates you called in from the funeral home. I think Sos Seagull might be able to put some pieces of the puzzle together for us."

"Puzzle?"

"You're the one turning over the pieces. First, there's Wolverine Pokaik's murder, followed by an attempt on his grandson's life. There are questions about familial ties and land ownership. Sos Seagull seems to be connected to everything that's going on."

Tatty followed Carson out of the door and they walked to her SUV. "Do you think she's going to offer us anything? I think she's a snotty...:"

Carson pulled into traffic and finished Tatty's thought, "bitch."

"Yeah. She was yelling at the funeral director about Wolverine Pokaik's funeral arrangements, then she didn't even show up for the burial."

"I wonder if O'Keefe notified her of the burial plans?"

"That would be an interesting twist. I can see him not calling her just to keep the ceremony civil. She might've made a scene." As they passed the south edge of Iqaluit, Tatty looked at Carson. "Are you going to tell me about this plan to get Sos Seagull to share information, or are you planning to surprise me?"

"I'm going to tell her that Eric Curtis implicated her in a plot to steal Wolverine Pokaik's land grant."

"He said that?"

Carson smiled. "Let's see if she'll offer a different version of the plan. I do know that she spent the night with Curtis after their discussion of the land grant and lease agreements."

"That leaves open the question of who was taking advantage of whom."

"I did a background check on Curtis. Arrested for fraud in Gillette, Wyoming, Curtis apparently offered himself up as a prosecution witness in return for the charges against him being dropped. The scam was a land deal to get an old rancher to sell off his land to one of Curtis' buddies who worked for a mining company. The ranch wasn't worth much as grazing land, but Curtis' geologist buddy had mapped out a vein of coal that looked like it ran under the ranch. The old guy's kids got wind of the sale and started asking questions. When they discovered the nearby discoveries of coal deposits, the rancher's family talked to the county sheriff, and he dug a little deeper into the plan. When they discovered maps of the coal veins in Curtis' pickup, the plan went to pieces and the fraud was exposed. In the end, Curtis' buddies went to prison for a few years, and the old man's family got rich off the mining rights."

"And we're back to him playing games with property and leases." Tatty paused. "Do you think he's interested in anything more than an inexpensive lease for landing plane loads of people going on river trips?"

"I don't know. But I intend to find out."

"Just to warn you, I don't think the woman claiming to be Wolverine's daughter is the sharpest knife in the drawer."

"She wouldn't be the first woman screwed by a man trying to take advantage of her."

Tatty laughed. "Nice play on words, Sarge."

Carson smiled. "That may be the leverage we have over Ms. Seagull. We know that Curtis bedded her to strengthen his hold on her. If she thought he cared for her, she might've been more amenable to his lease offer."

Shaking her head, Tatty said, "Sadly, there are a too many local women who'd be happy to climb into bed with a rich American who promised take them away from here."

* * *

Sos Seagull's house was typical of the utilitarian construction found in Apex. The structure appeared to have been slapped together from studs and plywood, then left without any siding. The roof was minimally sloped, and the yard consisted of a few weeds rooted in thin soil on top of the permafrost. A pickup was parked in the yard and a car was parked on the edge of the gravel street.

Unbuckling her seatbelt, Carson asked, "How many people do you think live here?"

"At the funeral home, Ms. Seagull was accompanied by her four adult children, their significant others, and five or six grandchildren. It was difficult to count them because they were chasing each other around their parents' legs. I'm betting that there are at least three families living in this house."

"But only two vehicles," Carson said as they walked across the dirt yard.

"Maybe one of the adult children has a job."

The knock on the door was answered by a child still in diapers. The young boy stared at them without speaking. "Is your grandma home?" Carson asked.

"*Aanaa*. People!" The boy yelled as he retreated into a hallway.

Carson and Tatty stepped into a living room cluttered with dated furniture, clothing, and toys. The walls were painted plywood and devoid of pictures or decorations other than crayon scribbles on the walls.

Dressed in a loose-fitting shift that covered her considerable girth and carrying a crescent shaped *ulu* knife, Sos Seagull froze when she saw the visitors. Reacting to

Carson's uniform, Sos sneered, "Mounties." Then she looked at Tatty and shook her head. "And, Special Constable Etok, who speaks for the missing Pokaik boy."

"Do you even know his name?" Tatty asked. "You claim to be his aunt."

Ignoring the question, Seagull stared at Carson. "What's up? Do I have an unpaid speeding ticket?"

"I spoke with Eric Curtis, and I'd like to get your side of the story before making an arrest."

A slender young *Inuit* man walked out of the kitchen. "What's the problem?"

Carson glanced at him, then back at Sos. "We have some questions for your mother."

The young man stood tall. "Don't say anything, Mom."

Carson shrugged. "That's your right. But things might get sorted to your advantage if you answer just a couple of questions."

"What do you want to know?" Seagull asked.

"Were you part of Curtis' plan to kill Christopher Pokaik, or did he come up with that all by himself?"

"I don't know anything about someone getting killed. What are you talking about?"

"Eric and Christopher both said that you were colluding on a plan to take over Wolverine's lease and lease payments. Have you filed the papers to cancel Christopher's *Inuit* membership, or were you waiting to see if he lived through the raft trip?"

The young man stepped in front of his mother. "We don't know what the hell you're talking about. I think you should leave."

Sos grabbed the young man's shoulder and pulled him aside. "I had nothing to do with that kid getting pushed out of the raft. Nothing."

"Who told you he'd been pushed out of the raft?" Carson asked.

"You just said..."

"I said you were part of the plan to kill him. I didn't say when or how it happened."

The slender man approached Seagull. "Mom, shut up."

The woman's face turned crimson, and she clenched her jaw as she pushed him aside. "You're putting words in my mouth."

"Eric said you suggested that plan the night you stayed over in his room."

The son spun out of her grip and faced his mother. "You screwed the outfitter?"

The woman lifted the *ulu* knife and pointed the blade at the sergeant and Tatty. "That's enough from you two. You can't come into my house and accuse me of things like this without evidence."

Carson nodded. "You're absolutely right. On the other hand, I've got statements from both Eric Curtis and Christopher Pokaik pointing to you as the person who suggested the plan to take over Wolverine's lease."

"I need the money more than that college kid. I'm Wolverine's daughter, and the money is rightfully mine! I'll go to court and get the will changed so the land goes to me.”

“Ms. Seagull, set down the knife. We’re arresting you for being an accessory before the fact of a murder attempt.”

The son grabbed his mother’s arm. “She didn’t know anything about the old man’s murder before it happened.”

Tatty glanced at Carson, while trying to hide her surprise at what the man said.

Holding the knife out toward her son, Sos hissed, “You shut up. They don’t know anything about the old man’s murder. They’re talking about the kid getting pushed out of the raft.”

The young man raised his hands and backed away from the knife. “Fine, Mom. Whatever. If you want to take the fall for the old man’s murder, it’s okay. They don’t know anything. No one saw me at the old folk’s home that night.”

“What’s your name?” Carson asked the young man.

“Charlie. Charlie Thinman.”

“SHUT UP, Charlie. They don’t know anything. They don’t know when I knew about the kid being pushed out of the raft, and they don’t know about you being at The Lodge the night the old man was killed. Just shut up.”

Tatty cocked her head to see past Sos. “Charlie. Why were you at The Lodge?”

“Mom needs the lease money. Look at this place. There’s eight of us living here and we can't afford to heat it in the winter. That lease money would make a difference to us. That college kid doesn't need it. The old man said he's got a scholarship."

"But he told you Christopher was getting the land and the lease, right?" Tatty asked.

Charlie's fists clenched. "The old man said the kid was getting it all and there was nothing we could do about it."

Tatty nodded. "So, you helped his spirit cross over to *Adlivun.*"

Thinman wrinkled his nose. "I don't believe in that spirit shit."

Tatty glared at the man. "Help me understand what happened. Wolverine was having a stroke, so you helped him along."

"He was sputtering and tipped over. All I did was…"

"Shut up, Charlie," Sos Seagull sputtered.

"No, mom. It was wrong. There's no way that college kid should've got the land. Now you'll inherit and we'll get the lease money."

Carson removed a set of handcuffs from her duty belt and held them loosely. "Charlie Thinman, I'm arresting you for the murder of Wolverine Pokaik."

Charlie spun around and dashed out of the room. Carson took a step, but her path was blocked by Sos, who held out the *ulu* knife. "No."

Tatty turned around and ran out the front door as children wailed and Carson continued to argue with Sos.

Tatty guessed that the house had a back door. Taking a left outside the front door, she ran around the house. Rounding the rear corner, she found a gully containing a network of shiny pipes connecting the nearby houses to the sewer system. Charlie burst through the back door while looking over his shoulder. He jumped off the steps before realizing Tatty was waiting for him there.

Without time to stop and turn, Charlie dropped his shoulder and drove it into Tatty's chest.

Adrenaline pulsed through her system as Tatty grabbed Charlie's shirt, dragging him along as she fell backwards to the ground. Feeling Charlie trying to pull away, she grabbed his ponytail and yanked as hard as she could.

Charlie clawed at Tatty's hands as she jerked him backwards to the ground. "Yeow! Damn you, bitch. Let go of my hair."

Tatty threw herself on top of the squirming man, continuing the pressure on his ponytail while pulling his left arm behind his back. "Stop fighting! You're under arrest." With his left arm secured behind his back, Tatty pulled it upward, causing another howl of pain, which ended his resistance.

"You're breaking my shoulder," he gasped. "Get off."

"Take it easy, Charlie. If you stop struggling and let me handcuff you, I'll take the pressure off your shoulder."

"Let me go, bitch!"

Tatty put more pressure on Charlie's arm, pushing it further up his back. "Calling me names isn't going to make this go any better."

Charlie relaxed and stopped squirming. "Okay. Okay."

"Now put your other hand behind your back."

"I can't. You're laying on top of me."

"Pull it free and hold it alongside your body."

"You're killing me. I can't breathe."

Tatty drew a breath and lifted herself up, into a sitting position on his lower back, and took out her handcuffs. With her adrenaline fading, the spot where Charlie's shoulder struck her bulletproof vest started to throb. Putting that pain aside, she said, "Okay, now pull your other arm out and put it behind your back."

Slowly, Charlie freed his other hand and held his arm alongside his body. Tatty let go of his ponytail and cuffed Charlie's hands behind his back. Once cuffed, she helped him to his feet.

Shouting and cursing could be heard through the back door as the standoff between Sergeant Carson and Sos Seagull continued. Tatty reached for her radio. "Dispatch. Officer needs assistance." She gave their Apex location and pushed Charlie toward the RCMP vehicle.

With Charlie locked in the backseat, Tatty circled around the house, entering through the back door and winding through a back hallway and into the kitchen. Sos, facing away from the kitchen, was holding the *ulu* out toward Carson. Two children were howling in the living room, adding to the insanity of the situation. Trying not to acknowledge Tatty, Carson held her hands out in front of her. "Put down the knife."

"Not until my kid is safe. Where's that constable? Is she chasing Charlie?"

A woman rushed into the living room from a hallway and scooped up the smallest of the crying children. Seeing the confrontation between the two women, she pulled the child to her chest and backed away. Her gaze went from Sos to Carson, then to Tatty. "There's one behind you, Mom."

Sos spun around, extending the knife toward Tatty. "Where's my kid?"

"Charlie is safe in my car. Put the knife down."

Seagull appraised Tatty's soiled uniform. "What happened? You're covered with dirt."

Tatty glanced down and realized that her uniform was covered with muck from her wrestling match with Charlie. "Your son put up a fight. We wrestled a bit before he gave up and let me arrest him."

"Did you hurt him?"

With Sos focused on Tatty, Carson signaled the woman holding the child, putting a finger to her lips. The woman nodded, and Carson edged up behind Sos. As the discussion of Charlie's condition continued, Sos relaxed, lowering the knife.

Speaking *Inuktitut*, Tatty said, "Charlie's safely in our cruiser. We'll take him to the RCMP office in Iqaluit, then you'll be able to visit him. Set the knife down before you do something that can't be undone."

Hearing Tatty's reassurance in her native language, Sos nodded and set the *ulu* on the back of a tattered couch. Carson snatched the knife away and stepped back.

"Am I being arrested?" Sos asked.

"You threatened a Mountie with a knife, and we also need to interview you about your involvement in the assault on Christopher Pokaik and Wolverine Pokaik's murder."

"You don't understand. The old man's land and the lease payments should be mine."

Carson put her hand on Sos' shoulder, then gently lifted her wrist behind her back. "Sos Seagull, you're under arrest for assaulting a Mountie."

* * *

With Sos and Charlie in Iqaluit cells and the crown prosecutor notified, Gerri Carson guided Tatty into her office. Closing the door, Carson asked, "Are you okay?"

"Charlie tackled me. I think my left boob will be purple tomorrow."

"Ouch. Other than that, are you okay?"

"I'm fine."

"I don't know what you said to the woman, but it calmed her down. Speaking to her in *Inuktitut* was the perfect way to diffuse the standoff."

"Thank you."

"We've solved Mr. Pokaik's murder. We'll have the prosecutor interview Charlie, but he confessed to us. Submit a report summarizing the events at the Apex house so we document Sos' and Charlie's admissions. I'll do the same, but I think the prosecutor will agree that we can close the case."

"That's it? This ending seems so…"

"Hollow?"

"I guess that's it. There's no closure."

Carson stood. "There'll be a trial. Hopefully that will give us closure."

Tatty stepped out of Carson's office and turned around. "Thanks."

"For what?" Carson asked.

"For believing in me. For following up on the funeral home incident."

"You were the key to closing the Pokaik murder." Carson snapped her fingers. "Will you tell Mr. Pokaik's grandson that the murder has been solved and the murderer arrested?"

"I'm not sure he'll be excited to hear that a cousin he's never known killed their grandfather."

Carson raised her eyebrows. "Is Charlie really a cousin, or is Sos a gold digger who was out to take advantage of an old man?"

Tatty sighed. "Will we ever know? Do we need to know?"

"The court doesn't care. The relationships aren't key to the case. I don't care."

Chapter 22

Tatty was drafting her report when Gerri Carson looked over her shoulder at the computer screen. "Are you nearly done with the arrest report?"

"I was just rereading it and correcting typos."

Carson slid a chair over and leaned her elbow on the desk. "How would you like to take a flight to Cape Dorset?"

Frowning, Tatty asked, "What's going on there?"

"The resident Cape Dorset Mountie has hit a dead end in the Buniq Tingenek disappearance. After thinking about Sos Seagull's response to you speaking in *Inuktitut*, it occurred to me that an *Inuit* special constable speaking *Inuktitut* might get different responses than a Mountie asking questions in English."

After a moment of consideration, Tatty nodded. "A lot of people see a Mountie and...feel uneasy. If the Mountie can direct me to a few key people, like Buniq's friends, I'll talk to them and see if they'll open up to me."

Carson smiled and stood. "There's a plane taking a load of groceries to Cape Dorset from the main Iqaluit airport. The pilot is leaving in half an hour."

"What's the airline and pilot's name?"

"It's a PolarAir plane and the pilot is Glenn Flynn."

Tatty lifted her coat from the back of her chair. "Please let him know I'm on the way."

Carson nodded. "I'll have the Cape Dorset Mountie meet you at the airport."

After rushing to the airport, Tatty parked at the commercial terminal and was directed to an outside area where a middle-aged man was walking the perimeter of a mid-sized twin-engine plane with a polar bear logo. He noticed Tatty as she approached and walked over, offering his hand. "I assume you are Special Constable Etok."

"Please call me Tatty."

"I'm Glenn Flynn, your pilot. I assume you've flown, so you know to keep your seatbelt buckled at all times. Don't pull any handles, flip any switches, or push any buttons while we're in flight."

"I'm trustworthy and not suicidal."

Flynn laughed. "You have your choice of sitting with the cargo or in the co-pilot's seat."

"I have a bit of claustrophobia, so I'd prefer to sit up front where I can see out of the windshield."

With a flourish, Flynn gestured to an open door with built-in steps. "Your wish is my command. Climb in, sit in the right seat, and I'll close the hatch."

Walking up a narrow aisle between piled boxes of groceries secured with heavy netting, Tatty was pleased that she'd chosen to sit up front. She climbed past a bulkhead and eased into the right-hand, co-pilot's seat. Being careful not to touch knobs or switches, she buckled herself in as Flynn climbed in and put on a headset. Sitting back with her arms crossed, Tatty watched silently as the pilot flipped switches, spoke with the control tower over the radio, checked the area around them, and watched as workers removed wheel chocks.

A man with red-coned flashlights signaled the pilot, and he started one, then the second engine. They taxied to the runway, the plane lumbering along under its load. At the end of the runway, the pilot revved the engines, released the brakes, and they rolled along the runway, slowly gathering speed. To Tatty, it seemed like they were going to run out of runway, but the pilot pulled back on the yoke and the plane lifted off the ground. Immediately, the pilot raised the landing gear, and started a turn as they gained altitude.

Once airborne, Flynn glanced at Tatty. "Are you okay?"

"You could've left the landing gear down for a couple more minutes. You know, in case our engine went out."

Flynn laughed. "If we'd lost power after leaving the runway, the landing gear wouldn't do us any good. The plane has better aerodynamics with the gear up. We're better off flying as best we can, than hoping the wheels will save us if we crash."

"That's a happy thought."

"It's the reality of flying."

"Do you fly a lot of freight?"

"That's my primary business. I haul the necessities of life to all the little Nunavut communities. Some get boatloads of supplies in the summer, but a lot of them are too small to accommodate a barge, so I fly in perishable food, medicine, spare parts for generators and snowmobiles, you name it."

"How long will you be in Cape Dorset?"

"I'm spending the night there. It'll take a couple hours to unload, then another hour to do the paperwork so everyone gets paid. By then, I'll have been on the job for twelve hours, so I can't fly anymore today."

"Where do you stay?"

"There's a little inn downtown. It's nothing fancy, but the beds are clean and comfortable. If the RCMP doesn't have a place set up for you, I'd give the inn a try. I don't think they're ever overbooked."

"Too bad my sergeant didn't suggest I pack a bag with a change of clothes."

Flynn laughed. "Well, you can rinse out your underwear in the sink, I suppose. The inn probably has a spare toothbrush and toothpaste."

"Great," Tatty replied with an eye roll.

An RCMP SUV was idling at the airport when they landed. The Mountie who stepped out was tall, blonde, and fair skinned. Tatty's first thought was, *I thought we were trying to find people who fit the community. This guy is about as far from being an Inuit as you can get.*

The Mountie smiled and offered his hand as Tatty approached. "Constable Etok, I'm Frank Porter. Welcome to Cape Dorset." He looked around. "Do you have a bag?"

"I didn't realize I'd be staying overnight when I got on the plane."

"Oh, sorry. I guess I didn't tell Sergeant Carson that the PolarAir flight spent the night here."

"We'll sort it out. Tell me about your investigation into Buniq Tingenek's disappearance."

Porter nodded toward his idling SUV. "I've spoken to her family, her friends, the school, and poked around the airport and boatyard. I know that she was unhappy, but no one seems to know exactly when she left, how she left, or where she's gone."

Inside the SUV, Tatty asked, "Is there anyone who seemed less than forthcoming when you asked about her?"

"Her friend Chu seemed like she might've known something more, but she wasn't willing to share it with me. I interviewed Chu in front of her parents. The girl kept looking at her mother before she answered."

"You couldn't catch Chu away from her family?"

"No, her mother was very adamant that she be present during my interview."

"Let's go to their house."

"Sure. Do you think you can pry the girl loose from her mother?"

"I won't have to. You'll be questioning the mother in English while I speak to the girl in *Inuktitut*."

The Mountie shrugged, "Let's give that a try."

Chu's family house was small, possibly just two rooms. The girl was at the kitchen table chopping onions while her mother was frying something on the stove. The mother's reaction was very blunt when she saw Porter. "We've already told you all that we know about Buniq."

Tatty edged past Porter and slipped in the door before the mother could stop her. "I'm Tanaraq Etok, a special constable from Iqaluit. Can I have a moment with Chu?"

"We're preparing supper."

"I just flew in from Iqaluit, and I need to ask Chu a few questions."

Porter gestured for the mother to continue her cooking and he stood next to her, asking questions as the woman browned meat and poured sauce over it. Tatty sat on a chair next to the girl.

Speaking in *Inuktitut*, Tatty introduced herself and said she needed more information about Buniq's disappearance. Chu looked at her mother, expecting some support or an admonition not to reply.

With the mother busy talking to Porter, Chu drew a breath and looked into the distance. "I don't know where she went," Chu replied in *Inuktitut*.

"Was she running away from something?"

Chu shook her head, still looking past Tatty into a corner.

Reaching out and touching Chu's arm, Tatty got the girl's attention. "We need to tell Buniq's family what happened to her. They deserve to know."

Chu's look darkened. "They are the reason she's gone."

"Her family drove her off?"

"Her father beat her for...things she didn't do. Her mother let him."

"Was there something specific that was the problem?"

"She went to a boy's house after school. She wouldn't tell them who he was or what happened."

"Something happened?"

"No." Then she paused. "I don't think Buniq would..."

"Who did she see?"

Chu looked past Tatty again. "I promised not to tell anyone."

"She's missing."

Chu shrugged.

"Twelve *Inuit* girls and women are missing right now. We assume bad things have happened to them, but we don't know. Buniq is missing and we need to know if she's safe and alive."

Chu looked into Tatty's eyes but didn't reply.

An argument broke out between Porter and the mother. The frying pan was banged and the mother rushed to the table. "What have you been asking her?" she asked in *Inuktitut*.

"Buniq Tingenek is one of a dozen missing *Inuit* girls and women. We're trying to find her."

"The Mountie already asked about Buniq. You can leave us so we can eat supper."

Tatty turned to Chu. "I need a name."

The mother grabbed Chu's arm and pulled her up. "Buniq is not our problem. Talk to her parents...her father." The woman shuffled Chu into the other room and closed the door.

In *Inuktitut* Tatty asked, "What does the father know about his daughter's disappearance?"

The mother's eyes focused on Tatty like lasers. "He dealt with a bad situation. If you believe in *Eeyeekalduk*, the healing spirit, you'll know Buniq looked for healing with a sickness that couldn't be healed. I think she may have stared into his eyes too long." The woman walked to the door and held it open. "Go."

Tatty walked to the RCMP SUV with Porter on her heels. "I didn't get any of that. What did she say?"

In the SUV Tatty summarized the conversation. "Buniq sought healing from an *Inuit* spirit. She sought healing for a sickness that couldn't be healed, and the healing spirit made her ill."

"I don't understand," Porter repeated.

"Buniq has a sickness that couldn't be healed. What illness can't be healed?" Tatty asked.

Porter shook his head. "I don't know. Leukemia? Brain cancer?"

Tatty hung her head. "An illness that couldn't be healed, but the spirit made her ill."

"What does this have to do with her disappearance?" Porter asked.

"Let's talk to her family. You keep Buniq's father busy while I talk to her mother."

Porter started the SUV and pulled onto the street. "You do realize that Chu's mother was ready to clobber me with a frying pan while you and the girl were whispering."

"You must've done a good job of defusing the situation."

"Yeah, that's become my specialty here in Cape Dorset. I'm the Mountie who keeps getting himself in situations where he's got to talk his way out of being killed by someone with a frying pan, skinning knife, seal harpoon, or liquor bottle."

"Booze is illegal," Tatty said.

"So is beating your wife, but that doesn't mean it's not done here."

"Where does the booze come from?"

"I think it came in on a fuel barge from Quebec. The sailors seem to have lots of cheap cigarettes and trinkets they sell to the locals. There's always a crowd on the docks when the barges show up."

"Do you think she might've stowed away on a fuel barge or tugboat?"

"I don't think so. People watch the docks closely when the shipments of fuel and canned food come in. It'd be hard to slip onto one of those shipments."

"Hard, but not impossible. Buniq could be in Quebec."

"I suppose Quebec would sound like heaven compared to life in Port Dorset."

Porter parked in front of a larger house than they'd just left. "Here's Buniq's house."

They got out of the SUV and Tatty reminded Porter, "You keep the father distracted."

"Great. My role in life is providing distractions."

Tatty knocked on the door, then looked at Porter. "Is providing distractions a problem?"

"No, it just seems like a waste of my criminology degree and six-month RCMP training."

Tatty smiled. "Think of it as covering my back."

"That *is* so much better," he replied as the door opened. The man who opened the door was chunky, with a face lined from years of outdoor work.

"Mr. Tingenek, we'd like to talk about Buniq."

Anuun Tingenek glared at Porter. "I've already answered the Mountie's questions."

Tatty nodded, then explained that she was new to the case and needed to hear his answers for herself.

The interior of the house seemed warmer and more welcoming than Chu's home. Mrs. Tingenek sat at a table with a jigsaw puzzle laid out. She'd completed most of the frame and was sifting through the pile of pieces to find the rest of the edges. Porter took Anuun aside.

Tatty quickly took a chair next to Buniq's mother. Introducing herself in *Inuktitut*, "I'm trying to find your daughter."

"The Mountie was here earlier. Anuun told him we didn't know where she went."

"I heard that she'd fought with your husband and that drove her away. I also heard she'd sought help from the healing spirit."

The woman didn't look up but stopped sorting the jigsaw puzzle pieces. "You speak in our language and understand the spirits."

"*Eeyeekalduk* is usually a healing spirit. However, he can be a vengeful spirit if you seek healing from him but aren't really sick, or if you ignore his advice."

Glancing at her husband, the woman nodded. "Pregnancy isn't sickness."

Tatty tried to hide her surprise at getting a straight answer. "Buniq was pregnant? And she left to have the baby?"

The woman shook her head. "She sought *Eeyeekalduk* to end her pregnancy, but he wouldn't help because she wasn't really sick."

"Do you know where Buniq is?"

Again, the woman glanced at her husband. "She and her boyfriend took a boat to *Mallikjuaq* Island to be away from her father."

Searching her memory, Tatty tried to recall where *Mallikjuaq* Island was located. "Is that the bird sanctuary where tourists go?"

Before Tatty got an answer, Porter's attempted distraction went to pieces. Anuun Tingelek exploded and pointed to the door. "I've told you everything. Go!"

With Porter backing toward the door, Tatty stood and inserted herself in the space between the Mountie and the father. "We're through. Thank you for your time."

In the SUV Porter took off his cap and glared at Tatty. "You can make a distraction at the next place."

"There is no next place. I know where Buniq is."

Porter's jaw dropped. "Her mother knew all the time?"

"Apparently, Buniq is pregnant and went to Mallikjuaq Island with her boyfriend."

"There's nothing there! It's a bird sanctuary where tourists go to fill out their life lists of rare birds. Oh, and there are usually a couple of polar bears there, too."

"How do we get there?"

Porter straightened. "Get there? We know the girl is there, isn't that good enough?"

Tatty rolled her eyes. "She's a teenager who's pregnant. She needs emotional support and prenatal care. She's probably living in a tent, eating raw bird eggs they're stealing from nests, and fending off polar bears with rocks."

* * *

The boat captain who specialized in Mallikjuaq Island bird watching trips wasn't pleased to see Tatty and Porter. He looked like he'd spent a lifetime in the boat with a deeply lined face, large, calloused hands, and a worn coat and overalls. He was packing his gear, getting ready to go home.

Tatty trotted toward the captain. "We need you to ferry us to Mallikjuaq Island."

The captain continued his work. "I haven't got a bird-watching charter until next Tuesday."

Porter, who towered over the ship captain, stepped in front of Tatty. "We want to go now."

"My wife's cooking supper and I'm stowing my gear. I'm not going to Mallikjuaq tonight."

Porter ignored the man's protests. "We understand that there is a young couple camping on Mallikjuaq Island. Are they living in a tent, or did they build some kind of shack?"

"They're in a tent. I told them the place wasn't fit for living. Hell, a polar bear could wander up, and they'd be as good a snack as a seal."

"Take us over to them."

The captain looked at Porter and frowned. "I've got some folks coming in next Tuesday. I could probably fit you in with them."

"Now," Porter replied.

"No way! I told you. I'm done for the day, and I'm going home to eat supper."

"If those kids are in danger of being eaten by bears, you're taking us now. The sun doesn't set for another two hours and there will be twilight all night. We're going now."

"And if I say no?"

Tatty pushed past Porter and pointed at a missing child poster featuring Buniq's picture. "There's a poster right there asking for information about the girl who's on the island. If you know where she is, why didn't you call?"

"It's none of my business."

"It's all of our business when an *Inuit* girl disappears. I should issue a citation to you for wasting RCMP resources. Do you have any idea how many hours we've spent searching for her while you knew she was camping on Mallikjuaq Island?"

Porter had enough. "Get your ass on the boat or I'll throw you over the gunwale and shove you behind the wheel."

The captain gave Tatty a pleading look. She shrugged. "I wouldn't cross him. He's been grumpy all day. I think he's about ready to cuff you and lock you in a cell."

"I'm going to send the RCMP a bill for this," the captain said as he threw gear back into the boat and gestured for them to climb in.

"I suppose you'll charge us overtime," Tatty said, watching the captain untie the ropes from the pier.

"Hell yes!"

Tatty glanced around, looking for a life jacket. "Aren't you going to give us a safety talk?"

Shaking his head, the captain pulled an orange life jacket from a locker and handed it to Tatty. "Not that it'll do you any good. You'll die of hypothermia before anyone gets here to rescue you."

* * *

The water was rough, and it pounded the 36-foot boat as it crossed to the island. Halfway across, Tatty asked, "Did you take the kids over here?"

The captain shook his head. "The damned fools took a little dory with an outboard motor. They probably bailed water the whole way across. They're lucky it wasn't swamped or pounded to pieces."

With practiced skill, the captain eased the boat up to the small pier on Mallikjuaq Island. A pink nylon tent was visible less than 100 meters away. Tatty jumped onto the pier and trotted across the rocky landscape to the tent while the captain secured the boat. Stopping outside the zipped opening, Tatty cleared her throat.

"This is the RCMP. We're here to check on your safety."

There were muffled voices inside the tent, then the zipper opened. A young man's face with a week's scraggly beard appeared. "We're okay."

Tatty knelt as Porter walked up behind her. "We're concerned about Buniq. She's pregnant and not getting prenatal care."

The zipper opened fully and Buniq's round face appeared. Tears streaked her

314

cheeks and she sniffled. "I'm not pregnant anymore."

Tatty reached out and touched the girl's cheek. "Then we need to get you back to the clinic to make sure you're healthy and safe. Okay?"

"My father said he will kill us."

Porter knelt beside Tatty. "No one is getting killed. We'll make sure you get medical care, then I will personally make sure that you're physically safe."

Buniq looked at the young man. "What do you think, Mark?"

"You're still spotting blood and we're almost out of food. I don't know what we'd do when the last tuna is gone."

After breaking down the tent and packing what little gear they owned, Mark and Buniq walked to the boat with Tatty and the Mountie. In *Inuktitut*, Tatty asked Buniq, "When did you lose the baby?"

Tears welled in Buniq's eyes and she pointed to a battered dory visible down the beach so far away it was nearly out of sight. "During the crossing. We were getting pounded by the waves and I got thrown around quite a bit. Then I started having terrible cramps."

Tatty put her arm around the girl's shoulders. "It's okay. It wasn't your fault."

"Maybe if I'd gone to the doctor like my mother suggested. But then, my dad went nuts when he heard. He threw me out of the house."

Tatty held the girl close on the trip back to Cape Dorset. The captain radioed ahead announcing to the Coast Guard that he was transporting a person in need of medical attention.

As they neared shore, Buniq whispered to Tatty. "The baby was nothing. I mean, like blood clots. We dropped her into the ocean. Is that okay?"

Tatty thought back to Hanta's words about the girl's life spirit being taken by *Sedna*, the spirit of the sea. It was the baby's spirit, not Buniq's, who'd gone to the sea spirit. She pulled Buniq close and whispered to her in *Inuktitut*, "Many *Inuit* have gone to the sea for their last resting place. Your baby's spirit is in the hands of *Sedna*, the sea spirit with the spirits of many other Intuits."

Buniq turned to Tatty and stared into her eyes. "Are you a shaman?"

Tatty shook her head. "I'm just well schooled in the ways of the *Inuit*."

* * *

Unsure of how to deal with Tatty's information about Connie or his future, Christopher dialed the young woman's number. Prepared to quickly say goodbye and good luck, Christopher was amazed that their conversation went on for over an hour. By the end, he knew goodbye wasn't an option.

"I have to go back to Toronto."

"I've never been there. Is it pretty?"

"It's hard to describe when Iqaluit's the biggest city you've ever seen."

"Christopher, we have television in *Pangnirtung*. I've seen England, Australia, the U.S., and New Zealand."

"Okay. So, Toronto is a big city with lots of things to see and do. It's a melting pot of cultures and you can eat curry on one corner and walk down the street for a pizza."

"Does your world revolve around food? Curry. Pizza."

"Those are just examples. There are movies, museums, plays, orchestras, and more. I'd like to show you Toronto…"

Connie sighed. "Let's see what comes up. If I can't get to Toronto, maybe you can fly back to *Pangnirtung*."

"In the winter? Are you kidding?"

"I'll be here to keep you warm."

Christopher chuckled. "There is that, but still…"

Chapter 23

Eric Curtis was surprised to see Sergeant Gerri Carson and a man he didn't recognize sitting at the table when he came down for the B&B supper. The man stood and extended his hand. "I don't believe we've met. I'm Edward Amaqjuaq, from the Department of Economic Development and Tourism."

The trio sat as the B&B owner appeared from the kitchen with a carafe of white wine and a plate of sliced cheese and crackers. Smiling, she asked, "Would any of you like a glass of wine?"

Carson declined the offer, but the two men said, "yes."

The owner smiled at Carson. "I'll bring you a glass of water. The Irish cheddar is wonderful."

Amaqjuaq waited a moment for the B&B owner to leave, then removed a sheaf of papers from his coat. "We've learned that you've violated the terms of your outfitter's license by trespassing on private land and picking minerals."

Ignoring the papers being offered, Curtis shook his head. "I have a verbal agreement with the landowner. He said I could bring my customers in anytime I wanted."

Spreading the papers on the table between them, Amaqjuaq leaned closer to read the top sheet, which was Curtis' outfitter's license. "It appears that your verbal agreement didn't address the issue of your customers removing pieces of lapis lazuli and pargasite." He flipped over a page. "As a matter of fact, your Nunavut outfitter's license specifically requires that you sign contracts with all private landowners before entering or crossing their property. A verbal agreement is insufficient for fulfilling your licensing obligations. I contacted the landowner, Jack Moon, and he has requested compensation for the gems your customers have removed from his land."

Curtis leaned back, shaking his head. "A couple of people may have picked a couple of worthless rocks. If Jack wants me to pay him a few bucks for that, I'll write him a check."

The tourism officer flipped to a third page. "After Sergeant Carson reviewed your trip permits with him, Jack filed a claim with your insurance company for one million dollars. It's reimbursement for removal of semi-precious and precious gems. His claim also stipulates that you cease and desist from further unsupervised entry onto his property and the removal of minerals or gems."

Curtis stood as his dinner was delivered. "A million dollars? Hell, all we did was pick up some rocks that are just laying on the ground."

"I sent notices to the clients listed on your entry permits for the past ten years asking if they removed any gems, how many gems they removed, and how large the gems were. A few called our office and were quite embarrassed that they'd been misled into believing that picking lapis and pargasite was part of your lease for the gem field. Nearly everyone I spoke with offered to reimburse the landowner or return the stones they'd taken."

Curtis ran his fingers through his hair. "I can't believe it. You've contacted my clients about this?"

Amaqjuaq gathered and folded the papers. "It was the most straightforward way of quantifying the value of the stolen gems."

"Stolen gems?" Curtis sputtered. "They're rocks!"

Carson smiled. "I'm sure you realize that you were picking lapis lazuli at the only place it's found in North America. The Pargasite isn't as pretty, but it's even rarer than the lapis."

Continuing to run his fingers through his hair, Curtis paced as he processed the information. "Fine, I'll work with my insurance company to reimburse Jack Moon, and I'll get a lease from him before we bring any more clients onto the property."

Carson stood. "Bringing more clients onto his land won't be a problem. Your outfitter's license has been revoked. You won't be guiding any tours in Nunavut and your bond has been forfeited. I'll also advise the other territories and provinces of your suspension, too."

"Wait! You can't do that. I have people arriving next week!"

Carson removed a set of handcuffs from her duty belt. "You can talk to your lawyer about contacting those customers."

Curtis put up his hands as if he was going to stop Carson. "You can't arrest me for removing a few rocks."

"You're right, Mr. Curtis. I'm arresting you for attempted murder. Please put your hands behind your back."

"Murder?"

"Shoving Christopher Pokaik out of the raft knowing he would probably die of hypothermia was attempted murder. Put your hands behind your back. You can call your lawyer from the government center after we process your arrest."

* * *

Tatty rode along when the Mountie drove the runaways to the Cape Dorset clinic. He'd called ahead to make sure the physician's assistant received the boat captain's message and would keep the clinic open until they arrived. Megan Morris, R.N.

321

was a matronly woman with a smile that exuded warmth. She stood when they walked in and addressed the teens. "I understand you've been camping."

Both Buniq and Mark stared at their shoes and didn't respond.

The nurse held out her hand to Buniq. "I'd like to check your vital signs. Will you come with me?"

Buniq grabbed the boy's hand before giving him a pleading look. He nodded toward the nurse. "Something's not right. You should go with her."

Buniq leaned close to him, rubbing her nose against his cheek. "I love you."

The nurse followed Buniq into the examination room, leaving Mark with Tatty and the Mountie. "They won't let us stay together, will they?" Mark asked.

"How old are you and Buniq?" Tatty asked.

"She's fifteen. I'm fourteen. But I've been living on my own for two years."

Soft crying sounds came from the exam room, interrupting the interview. Mark looked at the door, then at Tatty. "Is she going to be okay?"

"That's why we brought you here. To make sure that you're both safe and healthy."

The boy stared at his tattered tennis shoes. "Will you let us stay together? I've got a space in the back of Charlie's scrimshaw shop. I'll ask if Buniq can sleep there too."

Porter, the Mountie, remained silent. Tatty looked at him, and he shook his head. "I'm afraid we have to get Family Services involved because you're both underage."

"What will they do?"

Tatty forced a smile. "Well, I hope they'll feed both of you before they do anything else."

"And after that?" Mark asked.

"They'll find a place for you to sleep. If your parents are unable or unwilling to provide shelter for you, they'll try to find a relative or a foster family who has a safe space for you to stay."

Mark shook his head. "But not together."

Porter let out a sigh. "No, not as a couple. You're both underage and should be attending school."

The exam room door opened, and the nurse emerged with her arm over Buniq's shoulder. She looked at Tatty with concern. "Buniq needs to go to the hospital in Iqaluit. She needs to see an OB/GYN specialist."

Mark looked at Megan, then Tatty. "What's that?"

The nurse stroked Buniq's straight black hair. "Buniq appears to have complications from her miscarriage. I'd like a specialist to examine her."

Everyone turned when the clinic door opened, and a stocky *Inuit* woman walked in. She looked stern, but her appearance softened when she saw Buniq with the nurse. The newcomer nodded to the RCMP officer.

"I came as soon as I got your message. Are these the children you mentioned?"

Mark bristled at being called a child. "I'm an adult. I've been living on my own."

The woman clasped her hands in front of herself. "I'm Anigan Qarpik, the Cape Dorset Child and Family Services worker. I'd like to speak with Buniq alone for a moment."

The nurse gestured toward the exam room. "Why don't you go in here. I've examined Buniq and she needs transportation to Iqaluit to see a specialist when you're through."

Mark glared at Porter. "You've planned this all along, didn't you? You're going to split us up."

Porter, who was only ten years older than the boy, shook his head. "My hands are tied. Under Nunavut law, you and Buniq are minors. My only options are to return you to your parents or to involve Child and Family Services. Leaving you two together to find food and shelter isn't an option."

Mark sat in a waiting room chair as if his legs gave out. He buried his face in his hands. "All we want is to be left alone."

Tatty sat beside him and put her hand on his back. "I'm sorry, but we have to make sure that both you and Buniq are safe. As minors, we can't leave you on your own. I'm sure Anigan will find a family you can stay with where you'll be safe, fed, and able to return to school."

"I don't need any more school. I can hunt and fish."

Tatty glanced at Porter and the nurse, then smiled. "I'm afraid being able to hunt and fish are no longer the basic skills an Inuit needs to survive. Talk with Anigan and see what options she can provide. Okay?"

Mark looked up, tears staining his face. "No, it's not okay. Buniq and I are in love. We just want to be left alone."

Tatty sighed. "I'm afraid love isn't enough when you're only fourteen. Nunavut has changed and we're all adapting. Everyone is more prosperous and there are more programs to improve our lives. Not many of our people are living by hunting and fishing alone anymore."

"My grandfather said…"

Tatty cut him off. "We're not living in our grandfathers' time. In our grandfathers' youth, people starved to death every winter. People got sick and died without medical care or medicine. You don't have to live in an igloo, depending on seal oil for light and heat. Our lives are so much better."

Mark glared at Tatty. "If it's so much better, why are people killing themselves?"

The nurse sat next to Tatty. "As always, there are people who become depressed and feel helpless. I help some of them and direct others to resources who get them through rough patches. Cape Dorset life is getting better. Finishing high school will give you skills that will bring more options for a better life."

The exam room door opened, and the social worker emerged with Buniq. "Mark, could we talk?"

Buniq took Mark's chair when he walked to the exam room. Tatty put her arm over the girl's shoulders. "Do you have a plan?"

Buniq nodded. "I'm staying with my aunt tonight, then I'm flying to the Iqaluit clinic to see a doctor."

Tatty rubbed the girl's back. "That sounds like a good plan."

The nurse leaned close. "Keep in mind what I said about safe sex."

Buniq's cheeks colored, and she stared at her clasped hands. "No one ever..."

The clinic door opened, and a woman swept in, her eyes searching until she saw Buniq. She rushed to the girl and knelt in front of her. "I'm so sorry. I didn't know you were in trouble." She reached out and took one of Buniq's hands in both her hands. "Let's go. I warmed some stew and made the couch into a bed."

Buniq stood, then hesitated. "I'd like to say goodbye to Mark."

The Mountie looked at the exam room door, then back to Buniq. "It might be better if you went with your aunt. I'll tell Mark that you're safe."

"Have him come over..."

Porter shook his head. "I'm sorry, but Mark can't know where you're going or what your plans are. All I can tell him is that you're being cared for."

They all watched Buniq leave. The nurse spoke first. "Young love, snuffed out like an oil lamp." She waited a second, then added. "Buniq was clueless. There aren't any sex education books written in *Inuktitut.* Everything she knew about sex she'd learned from hearing her parents grunting and moaning in their bed or from her school friends. She didn't know what a condom was or how one was used."

The Mountie shook his head. "No wonder teen pregnancies are rampant."

The nurse nodded. "And why I treat so many sexually transmitted diseases?"

Tatty looked at Porter, the Mountie. "I'm dead on my feet and there's nothing else we can do here. Can you drive me to the Cape Dorset Inn?"

"Sure," he replied.

Tatty smiled at the nurse. "At least we solved the case of one missing girl."

The nurse held the door as Porter and Tatty passed. "I'm sure there are more who disappear under similar circumstances. There are so many clueless girls and women who are searching for a way to escape to a better life. I'm sure some are lured away by predators, but others get pregnant or think they're in love only to be jilted."

"Suicides and kidnappings?" Tatty asked.

The nurse sighed. "I really wish they'd come to see me before they're so desperate that they can't see an option besides suicide."

As they walked to the RCMP vehicle, Tatty reflected on Hanta's historical stories of old people climbing onto ice floes and drifting away so their families would have one less person to feed, never to be seen again.

Chapter 24

After a night at the Cape Dorset Inn and a flight back to Iqaluit, Tatty drove home, showered, and changed into a fresh uniform. At the RCMP office, she updated Sergeant Carson about Buniq, then completed her reports on discovery of the missing girl and the plans for her continued safety. Carson told Tatty about Eric Curtis' arrest and his outfitter's license suspension.

Tatty drove to the Pokaik house and knocked before walking in. Christopher was watching television and eating popcorn. Tatty joined him on the couch and took a handful of popcorn. Christopher chuckled, "You look tired."

Leaning her elbows on her knees, Tatty looked at Christopher. "It's been a long couple of days. We arrested your grandfather's killer yesterday. Sos Seagull's son admitted to smothering Wolverine with a pillow."

Christopher stopped chewing and sat wide-eyed. "You found the killer?"

"Charlie Thinman admitted to murdering Wolverine."

"Who's Charlie Thinman?"

Tatty sighed. "He's Sos Seagull's son. We've arrested him for burglary and selling drugs a few times. Sos Seagull is the woman who claims to be your aunt. If you're really related to her, and I'm not convinced of that, Charlie is your cousin."

Christopher sat quietly, processing the information. After a minute, he nodded. "He's less of a cousin than you are."

Tatty leaned over and touched Christopher's cheek with her nose, giving him a *kunik*. "Yes, cousin. I'm here for you."

Christopher frowned as Tatty squirmed to adjust her clothing under her bulletproof vest. "Are you okay? You look uncomfortable and tired."

Deciding not to discuss her bruised breast with her male cousin, Tatty nodded. "I'm okay. A couple of bruises, but nothing serious. How about you? What's the next step in your spirit journey?"

"I'm wrestling with my plans. Iqaluit feels like home, but Toronto has so much to offer."

Tatty nodded. "I think you should wait a week or two before you make any life changing decisions. Let the grief and sadness settle, then move ahead."

"I need to return to Toronto to finish my degree regardless of what else happens."

"That's a wise decision."

"I spoke with the Iqaluit school principal. He's not sure what his hiring situation will be a year from now, but he encouraged me to consider applying for a teaching job here or in one of the other Nunavut schools. Like you said, they need *Inuit* role models for the students."

"Keep that option open. Make sure you could be happy coming back here for the rest of your life. Also keep in mind that Iqaluit is Nunavut's largest city. If you taught in any of Nunavut's other towns, you'd be in a very small community."

Christopher looked around the familiar living room. "This is home. But, like I said, Toronto has so much more to offer."

"If Connie isn't part of your plans and you decide to stay here, I'd be proud to introduce you to the women in my book club. Three of them are single. I also have a cute neighbor who is a waitress."

"Whoa! You're a matchmaker?"

Tatty smiled. "I'm just a cousin who likes to see people happy."

"Are we really cousins?"

"I asked Hanta about our family tree. He thinks we might have a common branch somewhere."

"What about my aunt, the Seagull woman?"

Tatty rubbed her face. "Hanta and I have had a couple of discussions about Sos Seagull and her relationship with Wolverine."

She paused, staring at the wall. "And?" Christopher asked.

"Hanta thinks it's about as likely that Sos is *my* aunt, as she is *your* aunt."

"I don't get it."

Tatty drew a breath and let it out. "Hanta and Wolverine lived during a different time. Hanta told me Sos Seagull's grandfather was a difficult man who didn't like the men his daughter chose. Every spring, Grandpa Seagull would chase off his latest common-law son-in-law, leaving his often-pregnant daughter without a husband. Hanta suggested that either he, or Wolverine, might have been the father of one or two of those Seagull children."

Christopher tipped his head back. "Polygamy?"

Tatty shook her head. "There were no formal weddings. At most, there were long-term relationships that might be called common-law marriages. Other times there were short-term relationships like those between Hanta, Wolverine, and Sos Seagull's mother that a dictionary would define as polyamory."

"What's going to happen with Sos Seagull?"

"Sergeant Carson spoke with her. Since Eric Curtis lost his outfitter's license and isn't offering to pay legal fees to have you removed from the *Inuit* membership roles, she's less interested in contesting your ownership of the Soper River property."

"She's not interested in making a claim on Wolverine's tract of land?"

"Apparently not, since it was already transferred to your name. I don't think she sees value in fighting over land in the middle of Nunavut unless it's sitting on top of a gold mine or an oil field."

Christopher looked stunned. "That's it?"

"I think so," Tatty replied. "Well, aside from you returning to school and making a choice about what path your life will take."

Christopher took a swallow of coffee, then sputtered and spit a mouthful of grounds into the wastebasket. "This is crazy! I can't even brew coffee, but I'm supposed to make a decision about what I'm going to do for the rest of my life."

Tatty laughed. "I don't think those two things are related. I can teach you how to make coffee. You're on your own figuring out what to do with your life."

Wiping coffee grounds out of the cup with a paper towel, Christopher said, "Maybe I should ask Hanta what the spirits think I should do."

"Hanta will tell you to follow your life spirit. It's the one that will make you happy."

"My life spirit and I aren't speaking much, so that's not really helpful." Christopher set the coffee cup in the sink and leaned against the counter. "What would you do?"

"I can't make this decision for you."

"Okay, what decision did you make?"

Tatty spread her arms. "My life is here. All of my childhood, I wanted to move away. But once I graduated from college, Nunavut became our *Inuit* homeland. When that happened, I knew my spirit wanted me to be here, where I could help our people."

"That's a huge burden."

"It's what my people need." Tatty paused. "It's also what I need."

* * *

Christopher was packing his backpack when the phone rang. He dashed into the living room and answered on the fifth ring. "Hello?"

"Christopher?" The woman's voice asked.

"Yes."

"Um, hi. This is Connie. I was hoping I'd catch you before you flew back to Toronto."

"I'm packing and I've booked a return flight for tomorrow."

"This seems a little...forward, but the radio station offered me tickets to cover the Toronto Cher concert on July 19. I thought I'd fly down if..."

"Yes! Fly down!"

"I'll talk to the station manager about paying for a hotel and meals, but I was hoping you'd want to show me around."

"I'm sure my calendar is wide open, and I can find a place for you to stay if the station won't pay for a hotel."

"Okay, I'll tell them I'm covering the concert, and we can work out the details when you're back in Toronto."

"Connie, can you stay on in Toronto for a few days? I promise you a longer tour than walking through *Pangnirtung*."

"I'm due a week of vacation. I'll see what I can arrange."

"You could look for a job while you're there."

Connie laughed. "One of the *Pangnirtung* school teachers just took a job in Iqaluit. You could interview here."

"Um..."

"Christopher, graduation in Toronto is a milestone, not an ending. You'll redefine yourself afterwards. I'd like to be part of your redefined life."

"Um..."

"I'm sorry if I'm being forward, but I think we have a chance at something special."

"Fly down for the concert, and we'll see what happens from there. Okay?"

"Okay."

With Connie and Tatty's comments swirling in his head, Christopher finished packing his backpack. After setting it by the door, he stood looking back into the living room, looking at what had been his world for ten years with Wolverine. The living room and kitchen were utilitarian, not filled with the acquisitions of people who marked their success by the things they owned.

Wolverine's teachings focused on life lessons, not who had the newest car and the fanciest house.

Tatty stayed in Nunavut because she felt the need to help our people. She said, "Our school children need *Inuit* role models."

In the silence of the empty living room, Christopher felt the pull of his heritage. *Am I hearing the voices Hanta spoke about? Is my life spirit speaking to me? Have I been deaf to it all these years?*

Dialing Connie's phone number from memory, Christopher listened to the phone ring three times before she answered.

"Did a *Pangnirtung* teacher really resign?" he asked.

"What are you talking about, Christopher?"

"When we were talking about the future, you kidded me about a *Pangnirtung* teacher leaving for a job in Iqaluit. Did that really happen?"

"Yes, I was interviewing the principal about school sports, and he mentioned that a teacher was leaving and how difficult it would be to find a qualified person to move to *Pangnirtung*."

"Do you have his phone number?"

"Why?"

Christopher sighed. "I've been joking about my life becoming Dickens' *A Christmas Carol*. I just had a visit from the ghost of Christopher future, and the spirits whispered that Pangnirtung should be that future.”

“But *Pangnirtung* needs a teacher this coming school year, and you have another year of college.”

“I need a year to finish my second major in Indigenous studies. But I can graduate with a degree in education and my teaching credentials at the end of the summer term.”

“Are you teasing me?”

A feeling of calm swept over Christopher. “Not at all. If you have the principal’s phone number, I’d like to call him. If he’s interested in talking to me, I may take you up on your offer to give me a tour of your hometown.”

There was shuffling, then Connie said, “Here’s the phone number. The principal is Edward O’Hara.”

“I’ll call you back after I speak with Mr. O’Hara.”

Christopher was about to hang up the phone when Connie said his name. “This sounds stupid, but I feel like I’ve known you all of my life.”

“You *have* known me all of our lives. We went to school together for twelve years.”

“It’s more than that.”

“This last week, I’ve learned so much about spirits and *Inuit* traditions. I’ve just learned how to listen to what the spirits are saying to me, and I believe that my spirit belongs here, in Nunavut. My people need me.”

"I've felt our spirits together since I held your hand during the Canada Day celebration."

Christopher chuckled.

"What's funny about that?"

"My cousin Tatty offered to introduce me to the single women in her book club if things between you and I didn't work out."

"You don't need a book club to find the pathway your spirit wants you to follow. Call the principal, then get back to me about your plans." Connie paused, then added, "There aren't many visitor accommodations here. If you fly over for an interview, you can stay with me."

The End

Glossary

Adlivun – An underworld/undersea place where spirits are purified before passing to the happy sky/cloud world

Agloolik – An *Inuit* spirit/demon who overturns boats

Akutaq – A high calorie seal blubber and berry mixture

Angekkok – An *Inuit* shaman

Anirniq – The breath spirit, one of the three "life" spirits. The breath spirit persists after death and departs to find another body (is reincarnated) as either a human or an animal

Anguta – An evil spirit who steals *Inuit* life spirits and brings them to the underworld

Apex – A small town south of Iqaluit

Atiq – A name spirit who departs after death and searches for another body until a child is born and given the name of the deceased

Cape Dorset – A small town on Dorset Island, off the northern tip of Baffin Island. It was renamed Kinngait in 2020 known as the "capital of *Inuit* art"

Eeyeekalduk – A healing spirit found in grains of sand. It becomes a vengeful spirit if its wishes aren't followed

Eskimo – A derogatory/racist term used to describe an *Inuit* person most commonly used in Alaska

Igloo – A temporary/seasonal domed residence constructed of snow or ice blocks

Inuit – pl. The Indigenous residents of Northern Canada, Greenland, and Alaska

Inuk – s. An *Inuit* individual, one *Inuit* person

Inuksuk – A stone cairn or monument built for navigating the barren arctic landscape

Inuktitut – The dialect of *Inuit* language spoken on Baffin Island

Iḷitqusiq and Iñuusiq – The personal and life spirits that leaves the body after burial

Iqaluit – Translated as the place of fish, it's the Capital city of Nunavut Territory, located on the southern end of Baffin Island. Known as Frobisher Bay from 1942 to 1987, the town was built by the US Air Force during WWII as an intermediate airplane stop between Newfoundland and Greenland

Katannilik Territorial Park – The first Territorial Park established in Nunavut, it follows the Soper River from its headwaters to Kimmirut

Kimmirut – The town on the west side of Baffin Island at the end of the Soper River

Kunik – An *Inuit* "kiss", rubbing or touching your nose against the recipient's cheek

Northern Lights – *Aqsarniit* - Aurora Borealis - many *Inuit* believe the northern lights are the spirits of the dead playing ball with a walrus skull. They're interpreted as an omen of death when the spirits use a human skull

Pangnirtung – A small village north of Iqaluit on Baffin Island known for its Turbot fishing industry

Permafrost – A layer of frozen earth/dirt slightly below the surface that never thaws

Qudlivun – The cloud or happy realm (heaven) where spirits pass immediately after a violent death An *Inuit* dying naturally only ascends to *Qudlivun* after purification in *Adlivun*, the underworld

Qiqirn – An *Inuit* hairless dog spirit that sometimes guides people to food or leads them into the spirit world (death)

Sedna – The *Inuit* female spirit of the sea, sometimes known to hide the ocean fish, requiring the begging of a shaman before releasing them to the *Inuit*. *Sedna* is also known to embrace/collect the spirits of *Inuit* who die at sea

Soper River – Across Frobisher Bay from *Iqaluit*, it is the only Baffin Island river suitable for kayak and canoe travel. It's known for its Class I and Class II rapids

Dean Hovey is the award-winning and best-selling author of more than 30 mysteries. He's best known for his Doug Fletcher mystery series. The Hovey family has more than 300 years of heritage in New Brunswick.

John Wisdomkeeper is the Canadian author of 18 books, including "Fly Away Snow Goose" from the Canadian Historical Brides series.